LIVING
UNDERGROUND

LIVING
UNDERGROUND

a novel
by Ruth E. Walker

Seraphim
EDITIONS

The publisher gratefully acknowledges the financial assistance of the Canada
Council for the Arts.

 Canada Council   Conseil des Arts
for the Arts   du Canada

Library and Archives Canada Cataloguing in Publication

Walker, Ruth E.
     Living underground : a novel / Ruth E. Walker.

ISBN 978-1-927079-08-9

     I. Title.

PS8645.A4653L59 2012   C813'.6   C2012-904685-X

Editor: George Down
Author Photo: Stuart Blower
Design and Typography: Julie McNeill, McNeill Design Arts

Published in 2012 by
Seraphim Editions
54 Bay Street
Woodstock, ON
Canada N4S 3K9

Printed and bound in Canada

To the nameless:
A beautiful and perfect baby;
I may never learn your name
but I will hold you
in my heart, always.

And for my mother
who gave me the words.

Frankly, there isn't anyone you couldn't learn to love once you've heard their story.

According to Andrew Stanton, this is a quote that children's TV host Fred (Mr.) Rogers always carried in his pocket, attributed to an anonymous social worker.

OVERTURE

THEY WERE THE ONLY FAMILY on all of Lilac Valley Crescent with a basement apartment: kitchen, living room, bedroom and dinky little bathroom – just a shower.

For Rent:
"fully furnished"

The last tenants bought a few paintings and a second-hand brown rocker recliner. Skipped out one rainy Thursday afternoon – took the paintings but left the chair.

Between tenants, Sheila's job was to give the place a quick wipe up – *got to show nice, Sheila.* After running the mop and dust cloth around, there was time for the hi-fi and the recliner, rocking and rocking to the Top Ten hits. Above, shuffling footsteps or kitchen chair scrapes belonged to another place.

She imagined living there. Playing music, as loud as she wanted: The Beatles or the Beach Boys. Stacks of records – 45s and LPs. And guests – lots of guests. She'd cook for them, wash her own dishes – even better, have a maid. She could read *FaVE* or *Vogue*. All day.

Sometimes, she stood in front of the tiny bathroom mirror. Piled her hair on top of her head, pouted. Tried on sexy: "Oh, Mr. Bond ..."

And sometimes she slow-danced around the small square living room. Eyes half-closed, watching her shadow glide over the walls and the furniture.

Papa danced with her like that. High up in his arms, his face laughing, her little-girl fingers touching his stubble. She almost could hear the music – and then her mother's voice – *Tony Barnes, put Sheila down, you're making her dizzy for Chrissakes . . .*

Between tenants happened a lot.

Her mom said they had to be more quiet – people were downstairs and they all had to close doors, not slam them. They couldn't yell, and the TV sound couldn't go past the mark scratched beside the dial.

But people kept moving out. Mostly, it was when no one was around to ask for the rent.

One day, her mom would see that she was too grown up to share her bedroom.

It was going to happen. Her mother was going to tell Sheila that she should have the apartment instead of strangers who skipped out.

Sheila would just have to wait for the sign and then she'd know.

* * *

Sigmund Maier stepped off the Victoria Park bus just north of Lawrence. He stood for a moment in the shade of a small maple tree then pulled out a notebook from the pocket of his buttoned-up trench coat. Twice, he checked the street name against his notes before he put back the pad and strode down the long curving sidewalk on Lilac Valley Crescent.

He passed dozens of bungalows, their suburban sameness broken only by an occasional one-and-a-half-storey house. They all were red-brick ordinary; bushes planted under front windows, small concrete porches leading to aluminium screen doors – and roller skates, skipping ropes and bicycles scattered on paved driveways and trimmed front lawns. It was mid-morning, and although it was only the Monday of the September long week-end already a few leaves on some of the trees were tinted red and orange. Sigmund Maier kept a steady, sure pace until stopping in front of a compact bungalow just where Lilac Valley Crescent began its bend northward.

He waited for all of thirty seconds, his eyes glancing left and right at the neighbouring homes. It was as if he were listening for something, and he tilted back his head, raising his chin and taking in the breeze that barely riffled through the junipers in front of the house before him. The grey-green Venetian blinds that covered the large picture window were closed tight.

Something must have satisfied him, because he moved up the front walk of the squat little bungalow. Picking his way around two bicycles and a scattering of tiny metal cars and plastic army men, he stepped up the three cement porch stairs and knocked at the front door of number 63.

CHAPTER ONE

SHEILA MARTIN PRESSES A HAND against her diaphragm; keeps her breathing slow, steady. Tries to focus on the intercom panel. Tries to remember the apartment number for Sigmund Maier. She hates the way her throat is all tight and closed; despises the faint musk of nauseating people smells – Eau de Thrift Shop. She glances around the apartment foyer, eyes taking in the attempts at updating what would always be an older apartment with few charms.

Sheila slips her slim leather purse from under her arm and stares again at the endless wall of tiny white buttons and the black plastic strips next to them.

Names.

Initials.

None in alphabetical order.

She sighs, reaches inside the front of her trench coat and shoves a fist into the right-hand pocket of her suit jacket. She pulls out a slip of pink paper. Her hand trembles.

> MESSAGE
> TO: She
> FROM: Robin
> RE: ??

And underneath that, Robin's scrawl: *Sigmund Maier 1740 Lawrence E. Apt 703 2 pm Tues.* And then Robin's looping *HMMM?*

She can't properly see the message without her reading glasses – it's only that she remembers what she's read 15 times in the past 24-plus hours. She squints at the panel again. For just a moment, she wonders if leaving her glasses in the BMW is a sign. Twenty minutes sitting in the parking lot, listening to Mozart. Wonders should she just go home and get ready for tonight's party. Wonders why she's looking for an apartment number next to a name she hasn't thought about since forever.

There. Apartment #703. T & M Willis.

Willis.

She looks again at the pink slip in her hand.

Maier. Sigmund Maier.

Looks back at the name next to #703. She knows Robin can be a pain, but his admin skills are impeccable. She reaches up and is almost there, one manicured fingernail hovering.

The lobby door opens and a grinning man steps into the vestibule. He's followed by a baby stroller and an equally delighted young woman pushing the stroller. Sheila knows this scene and blinks away a long-ago Ken holding the door and her pushing their beautiful Beth in the folding stroller.

The young father continues to hold open the door and nods, letting her into the building. Sheila clicks across the linoleum of the lobby and heads straight for the elevator and the seventh floor.

703 is almost at the end of the dim hall. Her hand hovers at the door, knuckles ready. She practises her apology should a Willis answer.

Sheila cannot hold in her head what Sigmund Maier used to look like. So tall – she remembers that much. What if he answers and she doesn't know him? She feels her front teeth biting her lower lip – all that money on injections and she's wearing down her perfect lips.

Shaking off her hesitation, she straightens. Readies to find out why he called – what he wants – and then she can get back to important things. Like twenty-odd people expecting drinks and some cool jazz tonight while she and Costair do the investment dance.

She taps at the door before she can draw back her hand, and then shoves her traitor fist down into her pocket. Holding everything else still, she tilts her head and listens for something on the other side, a shuffle or creak. Silence. She narrows her eyes and stares at the peephole. Maybe he's been there all along.

She takes a deep breath.

All those years – she's here to get an answer – an apology – and she is not going to leave now without it. Sheila raises her hand to knock again.

The sound of the sliding chain stops her. The door opens. A whiff of liniment drifts into the hall and Sigmund Maier smiles from the other side of the threshold.

She can't think for a moment, wonders why she has such an odd sensation – like falling. Wonders if this is what she had been expecting. Was this old man the same person who moved into her mother's basement apartment all those years ago?

The same and not the same at all. She remembers now. This man is older, yes older and thin. That Sigmund Maier had been substantial – solid. Because she's an adult he is shorter, diminished. The thick glasses are thinner, his frames not a heavy black plastic but now wire. That one difference changes him the most until she hears his voice, hears his old-man quavery-whisper voice.

He clears his throat, his German accent as pronounced as in 1967. "Sheila. So. It is so, ah, good of you to come." There is none of the old firmness, the confidence. "Please, please, come in, yes?" He opens the door wide, shuffles back inside and gestures for her to follow.

She hurries in to just past where he stands. "Hello, it's – it's good to see you too." Then she adds as she turns back, "And you look well, Mr. Maier. You hardly look your age at all."

He pivots slowly in the hall, still smiling. The manoeuvre takes him so long, but he now faces her again. He gestures with one hand out. "Your coat. I will take your coat, yes?" Behind him, the door closes with a *click*.

One sleeve at a time, she tugs it off and holds it out. "Thank you." His hand brushes hers, his skin cool and papery.

He carries her coat to the hall closet, pauses and gestures again. "Please, go in, sit and I will make you some tea."

She moves into his living room, and waits for him. There are two choices: a high-backed leather sofa and the large matching chair. She can see that it is a quality hide – maybe even custom. Can feel her eyes widen – custom furniture in Scarborough. She glances into the dining nook. CD player, CD tower, and compact speakers tucked discreetly into opposite corners. Very nice quality there too. She looks down at the end tables. Not a trace of dust. She cranes a bit and peeks further into the dining room. No clutter.

Behind the couch there are floor-to-ceiling windows and the curtains are open. The clean, clear windows overlook the balcony and the neighbourhood. Out there, beyond the parking lot, more apartment buildings and the afternoon sunlight cutting across the roofs of row upon row of suburban houses. Cookie-cutter bungalows. Just a few streets to the east, and she'd be back at the old homestead. Christ.

The sound of the closet door shutting travels into the living room.

She turns her back to the window and spies a bookcase.

And books. Hardbacks. She glances away to take in the beige walls and a couple of large prints – landscapes – suitably bland. But there are no photos, no signs of anything beyond the bare bones. She squints back at the bookcase. It's in shadow and she can't make out any of the titles.

As he shuffles into the room she inhales and straightens. Must be in his mid-eighties – maybe even older. His expression is the same as at the door: a vague, pleasant smile. She's barely breathing. She releases her lungs and control settles back into her stomach.

"Fräulein – excuse me, Sheila, you are no longer Fräulein." He stands still and appraises her. "A grown woman – a mother, yes? – and so changed from the young girl of years ago. And yet," he nods and something moves through her chest, threatening to set off her nerves again, "and yet, still that same girl, no?"

She shakes her head. "Hardly that same girl. Hardly." With a faint smile she repeats her words offered in the hallway. "And you hardly look your age." He laughs; a full deep chortle that she remembers, and she wills herself to keep her face impassive.

"I was not speaking of the physical, yes? I was speaking of the inside, the self we carry." He shrugs, a slow lift of two narrow shoulders. "You understand that now, Sheila? That you and I, we have changed, yes, but we are still the same two people we were when you were young." His eyes narrow. "You were sixteen, I think."

She hates trying to remember all that mess. But she has come to hear him apologize for skipping out. And it is time to get to the point, to remind him of what he cost her and her family. "I was fourteen when you moved in. I was fifteen when you left. You rented our basement apartment for a few months in '67 and '68. You were, ah, kind to me, but you left." She raises her chin and purses her lips. "You left – owing the last month's rent. In fact, you skipped, Mr. Maier. Skipped – remember? After, we rented the place to a Dutch couple. Thank God my mother didn't have to wait too long." It feels good to remind him of his obligation. She does not smile, but holds still and waits for him to speak, waits for the apology.

"Good. I am not surprised your mother found new tenants. Your home was well located in Scarborough. Close to the bus routes." He rubs his hands together. "Now. Tea? Or would you like coffee?"

Without thinking she answers, "Oh. Tea, please," and sits down before realizing what she's doing. Maybe he's confused. Or perhaps he'll take a bit of time to come to it, to realize he should say he's sorry. She smoothes her skirt, running her fingertips over the natural fabric and then leans forward to check her shoes. She hears the voice of the sales clerk from the boutique. "It's so easy to scuff footwear in the spring."

He's in the kitchen, filling the kettle and setting it on the stove. He shuffles back into the room, and lowers himself into the chair. They sit across from each other, separated by a low narrow coffee table. There is nothing on it, not a magazine or a newspaper.

"Now, Sheila. Tell me how it is with you."

"How it is?"

"Your mother?"

Sheila shakes her head with a quick, tight motion. "No. More than ten years ago now."

"Ah, just so. She worked hard, your mother."

"Yeah. Yes, she did." For a moment, Sheila has a clear image of her mother sleeping on the couch in the living room.

"And your brothers?"

"Paul's on the west coast – he has a travel business. Alan doesn't stay in touch, so I don't really know what's happening with him." She glances down and brushes some lint from her skirt.

"You are still married, yes?" He nods at her ring finger.

"Yes. Twenty-two years. Ken and I have one child. Beth. She's still in high school."

"Ah, a girl. Good, good. She is musical?"

Sheila doesn't miss a beat before answering. "Yes. Yes she is. Beth plays the piano and sings in the school choir. She's a great kid. Talented." She sits back, keeping her eyes wide and happy.

She cannot read his eyes.

"Good, Sheila, good. A daughter with music. And you? Your music business is growing. Musicians' Clearinghouse. Five stores now? I see the advertisements on the buses, Sheila, and I have read about you in the magazines. Sheila Martin: CEO of Musicians' Clearinghouse, Board of Trade award in 1999. And you are on the board of the opera company, Sheila, and the Mayor's Youth in the Arts committee. Impressive."

She looks away. She thinks that maybe she could just sit here and tell him all about the store, could go on about starting with the little place down on Queen East and then building it up from there. The whistle of the kettle cuts through the quiet. She glances back at him. "Shall I get that, Mr. Maier?"

"No, no. I will make the tea." He rises from his chair, both hands clutching the armrests as he pushes up. The kettle is going full tilt, water sputtering onto the stovetop.

"Are you sure? Really, I could just –"

"*Nein!* I will get it, Fräulein." He no longer shuffles but walks in slow and purposeful steps into his kitchen.

He carries it all in on a tray: teapot, mugs, sugar, milk and two colourful coasters. She waits – resists helping – while he sets out the coasters and then pours the tea. On a small china plate are six plain cookies sprinkled with a little sugar. He catches her eyeing them.

"Yes, I still like those digestives. And you can see that I have lived a long life." He speaks in a deep and serious voice. That thin quality she heard at the door now all but vanished. "I think it was these biscuits, no?"

"Sure. Those biscuits." She really doesn't know what he means, but nods and smiles anyway. "So, why did you call me? No. Wait a moment; first tell me how you found me. I had no idea you were still, still …"

"Still alive? Oh, please, please, I know you meant nothing. After all, I am surprised that I am still here. Why should you not be surprised also?"

"Well, in any event, I don't understand how you managed to find me."

"I searched for your marriage registration. Then I had your married name. I started with Martin in Toronto."

"But how many Martins must be—"

"Many. But not so many Kenneth Philip Martins. And his information on his company website mentions his wife Sheila and a child. I had hoped his Sheila was my Sheila. And you were."

She keeps her voice steady. "You went to the Laurentian website?"

"Yes. Incredible tool, this Internet. I visit the library often, and they have been so helpful to me. So helpful. I found Kenneth P. Martin, C.A., Chief Financial Officer for Laurentian Publications. And on his web page I find his curriculum vitae. Impressive."

"Yes. He's impressive." She leans forward, shaking her head. "So, I am back to my first question, Mr. Maier. Why did you track me down?"

He slurps his tea then holds his mug with both hands; one finger threads through the handle. "It is nothing, really. There has been a, a small mistake, that is all. A misunderstanding."

"Misunderstanding about what?"

He takes one hand from his mug and waves it in the air as if shooing a fly. "There is some confusion. Something about my papers when I immigrated."

"Surely you're a Canadian citizen by now?"

"I am a landed immigrant, but not a citizen." He shrugs. "This country is my home, yes? I admire Canada, but I was too old to take on the responsibility."

"Responsibility?"

"Of being a citizen." Both hands now back on his mug. "It was, I think, a mistake. But now I am too old."

Her grandmother's whispers rise up in the back of her head. *Is he German, Eleanor?*

She wipes the corners of her mouth with a napkin. "I don't think I have the whole picture, Mr. Maier. What's this confusion all about?"

Again he shrugs. "I am not sure. I have nothing to hide. But I must give them papers – information about me. Documents. And that is why I need your help."

"Me? What can I do?"

"Just so. You knew me in 1967 and in 1968. You can sign the papers. You can let them know that I was a good immigrant, a good tenant, that I paid my rent. Went to work every day, yes?"

His blue eyes give nothing away. She wonders for just a moment whether he might be afraid – that she won't sign. That she will tell them – tell them that yes, he paid his rent every month ... until he skipped out.

"Why do they need this information?" She sits back, one hand resting in her lap.

"There are people who think I am someone I am not. They have been looking for this man for a long time, and they think they have found him. But they are mistaken." He reaches into his pocket. "And so, here is a lawyer's card. If you call him, he will receive the papers from you."

She takes the card. *Kris Douglass, LLB ~ Immigration Law.* She might have met this Douglass, perhaps at some fundraiser or another. "Oh. I just call him and ..."

"Yes, you call him and he will tell you."

"Tell me what, exactly?"

"He will tell you what he needs you to write."

She stares back at the card. "He'll dictate it to me? He'll just, you know, tell me what to write?" She looks up and crosses her arms over her chest.

"*Nein* – no, Sheila, no. You write what you want to write, but Mr. Douglass, he will explain what the government people need to know." He gives a small shrug. "I am an old man and am sometimes confused. It is best that you speak with him. Now, Sheila," he rubs his hands together, "you have pictures of your daughter?"

She takes another look at the business card then slides it into the outside pocket of her purse. He doesn't seem to be asking too much, she supposes. She writes letters and memos every day.

Reaching inside, she pulls out her wallet, fumbling a bit to find the clasp. She glances up, apologetic. "It's new." She flips over the wallet and snaps open the clasp. "These pictures – they're kind of dated. Once they get older, children don't want pictures for their parents. Beth is like most kids, I guess." She eases out her daughter's Grade 8 graduation shot and hands that over. Then she grabs the edge of a family picture from two years before and gives him that one too. He nods, smiling as he looks at them, and Sheila feels her throat constrict. She holds out her hand.

"One moment, Sheila, one moment. Old eyes need time." He looks back at the photos. "Your Beth, she does not look like her father. She is like you." He glances up at Sheila again. "No wonder she likes music."

She almost laughs. What would he say if she told him Beth quit the choir last year in Grade 10? And if daily nagging equalled playing piano then what she said earlier wasn't a lie. There are all sorts of truths.

It might even become easy enough to stay here in this warm, sunlit afternoon chatting about family with a man she once knew for a few months or so – when she was a child. She may even get him to tell her why he left all those years ago, why he skipped out. But really, what is the point? She was just the landlady's daughter, someone he was nice to for a while.

She glances at her watch.

"Mr. Maier, I'm sorry to cut this short, but I must be getting home. Ken and I have some people coming over tonight. I've had a long day and I really must run." She stands. "Look, I'll call your lawyer in the morning. It won't take me long to write up the letter. Okay?"

"Just so, Sheila. That is good." He also stands, walks with her to the hall closet. "And it has been good to see you again. I hope that we will have another visit soon, yes? You will bring your daughter, Beth, and your Ken may come also, yes?"

She tries to look positive. "I will tell them you'd like to meet them. Kids are always so busy these days, and Ken, well, he's up to his ears in year-end, but you never know. I'll do my best."

"And you, Sheila? You will come back soon, yes?" He holds out her coat.

She puts her arms in the sleeves as he moves it onto her shoulders. His old-man breath brushes against the back of her head; she feels it move through her hair. "Oh sure, but it may be a while. It's an intense time at the Clearinghouse, with the expansion and all, but when summer comes, things should slow down a bit. We could have a visit then." She puts her hand on the door handle.

"Wait, Sheila. I want you to see something. Before you leave."

She takes a deep breath as he turns and strides back down the corridor. He barely shuffles. And there's no hesitation. He passes by the entrance to the living room and opens the door at the far end of the hall. Sheila can see the foot of a bed and part of a dresser. It is to the dresser that Sigmund Maier walks, and then he turns around and comes back toward her. Clutches a small picture frame but she can't make out the photo. He smiles as he comes closer and holds it up for her.

Her Grade 8 graduation picture. The colour has faded. Or maybe she was always that pale and washed-out looking. No, even as ghostly as she must have been, Sheila can see the photograph is dulled by the years. And that stupid haircut. A Beatles' cut, it was. Took her all summer to get her hair even close to her shoulders again.

She's wearing a turtleneck. Her graduation picture and she's wearing an old mock turtleneck sweater that day. Arriving at school and everyone else in her class is dressed up. The mod look everywhere. But not on ungroovy Sheila Barnes. Mom had one of her mega-spells the night before; who could remember it was picture day?

She swallows. "I don't know what to say. This old photo ..."

He looks almost embarrassed. "I – I just want you to know that I have thought of you. Often. Thank you for coming today. You are a good girl, Sheila. You were always good to me, yes?"

Forty minutes later, as she sits in the dim and quiet light of her three-car garage in Thornhill, sits in the clean almost-new leather smell of her BMW, sits within the sweet lift of Mozart's *Eine kleine Nachtmusik*, she quells the desire to hit something, anything: the steering wheel, the dashboard, the empty bucket seat beside her. Son of a bitch. She wipes at the ridiculous tears on her cheeks. Son of a goddamned bitch. That was the time to ask him. Right then, with his old man smell in the air and his hand shaking, holding her stupid kid picture. Why, Mr. Maier? Why on earth did you leave?

CHAPTER TWO

ON SUNDAY OF THE LABOUR DAY weekend, 1967, it was a really good night at Sheila's house. Even Alan and Paul were leaving her alone. It had to be a sign, an omen.

Wayne and Shuster were on Ed Sullivan, and for once she was getting some of the jokes. She sat on the floor, her back resting against the base of the couch, with her legs stretched out under the coffee table. Granny Underhill reached forward and tapped Sheila on the head.

"You're growing up, Sheila." Leaning over to Sheila's mother, Granny repeated, "Sheila's growing up, isn't she, Eleanor?"

Sheila snuck a sideways look. It was a trick she'd learned, to flick her eyes to the corner for just a blink and then back. Her mom was looking at her, not the TV. And then she spoke, still looking in her direction; Sheila could tell that from how her voice sounded. "Yeah, Mother, I guess she is."

Granny and Mom almost never agreed. That had to be another good omen. Just like her horoscope in today's paper: *A long-held wish comes true.* During the ads, she decided to risk it. She'd ask about the basement apartment, and then hold her breath. Sometimes if she held her breath it worked.

Her mother looked blank at first, and then took a slow deep swallow from her bottle. Sheila chewed her lower lip and watched those lines on her mother's forehead start – underneath the frown, the blue eyes were getting small and sharp.

"Don't be so foolish, Sheila. You know we need the money the apartment brings in. What would you do with all that space? A thirteen-year-old girl?" The room was moving into dark. Sheila shifted to fix it. "Okay, Mom – it was just an idea. Just if we can't rent it, that's all."

"Oh for Christ's sake; of course we'll rent it."

"Yeah, you're right. We'll rent it for sure."

"Damn right."

That night, Sheila stayed awake long after the house had gone quiet. She was mad. She should've said she was fourteen – fourteen since last May. It probably wouldn't make a difference about the apartment, but a mother should know how old her kid is. She really should.

Her mom was on midnights this week, so Sheila had the bedroom to herself. Usually, she'd be reading. If she had batteries, she could also spin the dial of her red transistor radio, plug in the earphone and fall asleep to the hit parade. *Two in a row on Ten-Five-Oh*. Not tonight. In two days, she'd be starting at Ashbrook. And high school was even scarier than taking the subway downtown by herself.

Three floors, a cafeteria – and an auditorium. Everyone else could hardly wait to get there.

In the schoolyard of East Hill Public School, Sheila stood close enough to the popular girls to catch most of it, but not close enough to be noticed. They all giggled and yakked, nobody saying what they were really thinking: high school guys. No pimple-faced Grade 8 shrimps.

From behind the chain-link fence of East Hill, Sheila watched the Ashbrook guys pass by: tall, slender boys strutting in flaring pants, football jackets or long woven vests catching the wind. Some of them even had sideburns and goatees. And the girls! Walking with the guys, laughing and swinging their purses, dressed in really short skirts and wearing boots. Boots. Not one in baggy cotton stockings and brown shoes.

All of them just like Twiggy.

It wasn't just her clothes that made her different. She was one of the fringe girls, the stand-arounds, hanging out with Brenda Babcock and Julia Newton, the only Negro in Intermediate.

There were two good things about Brenda. She was so fat that she made Sheila look thin. And Brenda's mother would drive them to places: the movies, the bowling alley and, once, on a picnic in the country. The Babcocks had a light blue Volkswagen

Beetle. Sheila loved to sit in the back seat and watch how the two leather straps hung down on the inside, just at the back of each door. The straps waved every time they turned a corner. They made her think of old suitcases and steamer trunks and big ocean ships.

Her papa travelled with a steamer trunk, a big blue one with metal corners and studs all along the edges. He played in a band on cruise ships and big hotels, and he'd been gone for a long time. But one day he was coming back to take her with him. It was their secret. He snuck into her room when she was little and whispered it into her ear.

Papa has to go but I'll come back for you soon and we'll sail away.

I love you, Papa.

Julia Newton was way more fun than Brenda. She taught Sheila to dance, or tried to. On Saturday afternoons in Julia's rec-reation room they played record after record, doing the Boogaloo and learning all the Supremes' moves. The Newtons' music was really different from the stuff her brother Alan put on his record player. One night at dinner, she told Granny that Julia's music was great and she was teaching her to dance. Alan looked up from his plate and snorted, "Monkey music."

Granny Underhill and Mom gave each other a funny look. Sheila frowned at her brother, who didn't know everything. "It's called arenbee music." She didn't really know what arenbee meant, but it's what Julia and Mrs. Newton called it, and she wasn't going to look stupid and ask.

Alan hooted and Sheila wanted to smack him. It was like that a lot; people making jokes or saying things that she didn't get. And then, sometimes she understood more than she wanted. She stopped bringing Julia around after school when Granny asked why she didn't play with anyone else besides the little darkie girl.

She just wanted to be going into Grade 8 again. But maybe if she had the basement apartment, if her mom said "Yes," Brenda and Julia would be impressed; even the popular girls might want to see it.

And as she lay on the bed, listening to the crickets outside her window, Sheila imagined that maybe this time ... It had been more than three weeks. The ad was still tacked up on the A & P bulletin board. Her mom typed it up and then wrote out their phone number on the dozen cut strips that fringed the ad's bottom.

It always just took a few days posted at the variety store and the A & P to bring the tenants. This time – not a single call.

She fell asleep just thinking how it was three weeks already and nobody called.

On Labour Day morning, Sheila stood in front of the closed grocery, hands cupped around her eyes. She peered in through the storefront glass at the peg board with all the announcements and flyers and such. Her mom's typed sheet with the untouched fringe of telephone numbers was still there. "No one's going to call," she whispered. "For sure, no one's going to call."

Later that morning, Mr. Sigmund Maier came to see the apartment.

Sheila was just starting up the stairs to hang out the wash. He was coming down the stairs, a gigantic square block of a man made even larger by his long, black overcoat. For a moment, Sheila found herself facing his black shoes and thought that she could see her reflection. His coat fell open a bit, and she caught a glimpse of his white shirt. Backing down the two bottom steps, she stood aside as he passed, her mother practically tripping over herself as she followed him.

The man glanced back at Sheila over his shoulder and spoke with a heavy accent. "Fräulein." His blue eyes were huge and watchful behind his black-framed glasses; he had thin white hair combed straight back and kept in place with some kind of grease. Brylcreem, for sure. He inclined his head, his shoulders and back straight; did he click his heels? That accent. She thought of Goldfinger from James Bond.

Sheila's mother looked at her, the furrows just beginning and then disappearing as she turned back to the man. "Of course, you'll have full use of the laundry, Mr. Maier. I'll show you after you've seen the apartment." As Sheila slipped out the side door, she could hear her mother pointing out the apartment's features. "Now, the bedroom is just off the living room ..."

After pinning the corners of the last sheet to the clothesline, Sheila pulled forward the top wire to feed the wash out into the yard beyond the house shadow. The sun was warm, but the air that tugged at the wash was cool. It was going to be another long winter of taking off frozen wash. She wondered if they were the only family in the suburbs that didn't have a dryer. Maybe the entire country.

She knew one thing for certain; they were the only house on Lilac Valley Crescent with a basement apartment. And she wasn't going to get it for herself.

* * *

On the same day he came to see the apartment, Mr. Maier moved in. He brought a small suitcase and a beat-up steamer trunk.

During dinner, Eleanor Barnes was almost glowing. "He offered to pay two months in advance," she announced.

"Did he pay you in cash?" Granny asked.

Sheila watched her mother pause and lift her chin before answering. "Listen here, Mother. I told him I didn't need two months in advance – I'm no charity case. I took one month. But I told him I expect him to knock at the door here," she pointed at the door to the side entrance and basement stairs, "at the end of every month with the exact cash. Or out he goes." She gestured with her thumb, like a hitchhiker.

"Does he work? You should have taken his two months, Eleanor. What were you thinking?" Granny asked, and then, raising a teacup to her lips, added in a soft dark voice, "His name, Eleanor. Is he German?"

Sheila's mother banged the flat of her hand on the table. "He's a tool and die maker, Mother. Almost an engineer. A professional, for God's sake. Maybe he's German; maybe he's Czechoslovakian. As long as he pays his rent, that's all I care about."

Her brothers looked at each other across the table, grinning.

Alan ran his hand over his brush cut and started in. "Gee, Mom, I don't like being down there with some German guy." Alan's small bedroom was wedged between the furnace room and the laundry. Her mother said it gave him some space of his own. Sometimes, Sheila wondered if it was meant to give her mom some space away from Alan.

Ten-year-old Paul took a quick glance at Alan then up at his mother. "I bet he sounds like Colonel Klink in *Hogan's Heroes*."

"Listen here, Boys, that's enough. Just eat your supper." Her tone was final. Even Alan knew to keep quiet.

Sheila lowered her eyes to her plate, moving her peas from potatoes to meatloaf and back again. No way was she going to get dragged into her brothers' nasty games. She shifted a bit in her chair and strained to hear the sounds of the hi-fi, the squeak of old springs. She tried to imagine him in her apartment, sitting in her chair. From the basement, there was only silence.

Her mother started to speak again; her voice almost happy-sounding. "Mr. Maier is going to pay an extra $5.00 a month for laundry and light housekeeping." Sheila stopped pushing her peas around and glanced up; her mother was actually smiling. "So, Sheila, I'm going to need your help down there."

Sheila bit her lower lip. Down there – with his things all over her apartment.

"Sheila Barnes, don't you give me that look. My shifts don't always work out for me to do this."

Her mother's happy expression was now completely gone, replaced with hard eyes. Sheila hesitated before answering. "What about my newspaper route?"

"Look, it's just a few minutes on Friday after school to wipe the woodwork and damp-mop the place – just once a week for Chrissakes! And just some underwear and shirts."

Sheila lowered her head and went back to moving her peas. She cleared her mind of dirty underpants. But no basement apartment meant no chance to be something special at school. So. What else was new? She nodded and answered her mother. "Okay."

The next day, being special at school was the last thing she worried about. Just like she thought, Sheila got lost three times in the morning. She didn't have a single class with Brenda or Julia. And nobody looked as bad as she did in the ugly blue bloomers gym suit. Worse still, Julia's lunch period was before hers and Brenda's after, so they only met up after school in the washroom.

But it wasn't all hell at Ashbrook. By the end of the first week, she found that music class with Mr. Bernstein and Miss Clarke was better than she'd expected – even though the rest of her Grade 9 classmates thought the electric guitar was the one true instrument.

Mr. Bernstein actually talked like he wanted them to like playing band music. But Miss Clarke used sarcasm to keep everyone in line. The sheer terror of being her target was enough to keep them trying to hit the right notes.

Mr. Bernstein handled the woodwinds. Sheila thanked God every day because she picked clarinet. Even so, the thought of squeaking and squawking while others listened was terrifying. Piano lessons way back in Grade 2 ended after she caught her hand in the car door. Sheila heard the piano lady tell her mother about the year-end recital. "We've booked the hall at Eaton's College Street," said the lady, and then Sheila could hardly breathe – it would be on a stage. She'd already been in a play at school, knocked over the Baby Jesus' cradle and listened to all the parents laugh and laugh at her. And when the Baby Jesus' head fell off, Susie Campbell cried and they had to stop the whole play until Mrs. Dolenz got her calmed down. Sheila couldn't do that again. Wouldn't. It wasn't hard just to hang onto the door for those few seconds.

Soon after, her father went away and there wasn't any money for piano lessons.

CHAPTER THREE

IT TURNED OUT THAT MR. Maier's housekeeping was pretty easy, and that was good because her mother was too busy to help. Sheila wondered if he'd actually moved in. He left almost nothing around – just a small pouch with a chrome lighter sitting on the arm of the recliner and a pipe in the ashtray stand. And his smell – tobacco and a kind of spice – but there wasn't much else. No books, no magazines or papers on the coffee table. No knick-knacks. Sheila figured that men probably didn't have knick-knacks.

Her brothers had stuff on shelves over their beds, but they weren't men. Alan acted like he was all grown-up, but Sheila knew he sometimes still wet the bed. She could smell it on his sheets when she washed them.

Mr. Maier's bedroom was almost as empty as the rest of the apartment. He had a polished wood-handled hairbrush and a rectangular box on top of the dresser. His initials – SM – were carved on top of the wooden box and the clasp and hinges were polished brass. There was no closet. A few shirts, sweaters, slacks and two plastic garment bags hung from a metal clothes rack. A couple of hats and small cardboard boxes balanced on the top rack, while the bottom was all lined up with his shoes. He had two extra pairs of shoes, all polished and shiny and in a straight row like he'd used a ruler. Even his leather slippers were polished and lined up with the others.

In the month and a half since he'd moved in, Sheila cleaned the apartment every Friday. Every week it was the same. Not even a salt or pepper shaker on the kitchen table. On the Friday of Thanksgiving weekend, she dumped the mop bucket into the sink, looked around at the empty counter and the small table, and wondered if he was human.

"Maybe he doesn't eat." She didn't realize she'd spoken out loud until her words echoed back at her from the empty basin. Maybe not Goldfinger. Maybe Count Dracula. What did a Transylvanian accent sound like?

Sheila put down the bucket, rinsed out the sink and then hurried into the living room. She turned on the hi-fi. Instead of The Beatles on "Two in a row on Ten-Five-Oh" the room filled with orchestral strings. Sheila had heard music like it – at the movies and on some TV shows – but that TV music had been different, far off and mostly boring, something she pretended to listen to so she'd look grown-up.

This time, Sheila felt the music. Mop in hand, she stood still and paid attention. She started to recognize the melody, the way all the instruments were playing back and forth with each other – almost teasing, rising up and sliding back in on each other. It was so strange, like something she knew. The sounds held her steady while moving all around and through her. Closing her eyes, she swayed to the rhythms, rising up on the balls of her feet, one hand keeping time like Mr. Bernstein did. She wondered how to dance to this stuff. She imagined twirling in her papa's arms, holding his face in hers, spinning faster and faster.

Mr. Maier. She smelled him before she knew he was there. Tobacco and spice. She spun around, and he was standing just inside the kitchen, the door closed behind. She sucked in her breath, let out a kind of strangled squeak and steadied herself with the mop.

"I am sorry, Fräulein, I did not mean to frighten you." Mr. Maier kept his hands at his sides as he spoke.

Her face burned and she tightened her grip on the handle. He looked like he'd just arrived – his coat was still on.

He spoke again, "There was a problem with the boilers. The plant, ah, we closed early today." He shrugged, as if still apologizing.

Her throat almost closed up and when she spoke, the words came out all tight and harsh. "You changed my station."

He blinked. "Your station?"

She shook her head. "On the radio. I always listen to 1050 CHUM."

Tilting his head, he smiled. "Ah. I see. But," he took a couple of steps towards her, "you seem to be liking my station, yes?"

"You were watching me. Spying."

"This is now my apartment, yes? My radio?"

Sheila opened her mouth then closed it. She turned around and shut off the hi-fi. In the quiet, she heard the sound of her own hard breathing. "Excuse me." She grabbed up the furniture polish and cloth from the coffee table and dropped them into the bucket just inside the kitchen. Mop and bucket in hand, she marched around him to the door.

"Fräulein, please."

She stopped, the fingers of one hand clutching the knob.

"Teenagers, I understand, you like the rock and roll. That is so, yes?"

After a moment she nodded, her back still to him.

"If you desire to listen to your music, please do so. You will remember to put back to my station?"

Turning the knob, she nodded once more.

"But ..."

She was still and held her breath.

"You like my music, no?"

Sheila half-turned and offered over her shoulder, "I don't know. Yeah, I guess it was kinda pretty."

"Yes, just so." She thought she heard him sigh. Opening the door, she escaped without another word. She held onto the banister at the bottom of the stairs and tried to calm down. If she told her mom, it would be her fault. It was always her fault.

* * *

Sigmund Maier listened to the sound of her footsteps racing up the stairs. He shook his head. A strange child. Her radio? Her station? He shrugged and then moved over to the big chair and his pipe and tobacco. After tamping some shreds into the bowl, he aimed the lighter's flame and drew deep, releasing long rich streams of smoke as the tobacco caught. The aroma flavoured the room around his head. Ah well. It did not matter. She did not matter. This day had been strange. First the boilers at work, then this little mouse of a girl who does not know what is music. He shook his head and drew in another puff of smoke. No matter. Now, he would smoke and think about what he would prepare for his evening meal.

* * *

She waited all week for the storm. She knew she wasn't supposed to touch anything down there. *Go in, do a good job and for God's sake don't touch anything unless it's to clean it.* If Mr. Maier said something to her mother, Sheila never heard. To be safe, she knocked two times before letting herself in the following Friday. As usual, there was nothing much to do in the kitchen. The small square table and the counter were both clean and empty.

When she moved into the living room, Sheila sensed the change. Then saw it. The hi-fi lid was up; an album cover lay flat just to one side of the opening. Paper-clipped to the right hand corner of the cover was a small white note.

> *Fräulein,*
> *You may think also this is pretty.*
> S. Maier

The picture on the cover was a battlefield; smoke and flames from cannon fire filled the background. In the centre, a soldier in a red waistcoat gripped a rearing horse between his legs, his sabre raised overhead. *Tchaikovsky's 1812 Overture* in large fancy letters shouted across the top of the cover, *The Berlin Philharmonic Orchestra* was printed in smaller type underneath. In even smaller type below that was *Romeo and Juliet.*

The record was already on the turntable set up to play Side Two. She had only to flick the switch once to the right and place the needle on the edge. After a second or two of crackles and clicks came the music. Soft and sweet. This was not some battle music; it was quiet. Nice. After a moment, she started to clean, all the while drifting through the sounds, listening.

She moved so quickly that she was done before the music finished. So she sat in the recliner, rocking. There was so much to listen to – the music kept changing, like the person who wrote it couldn't make up his mind. But it wasn't like it switched – the changes swam into each other, from soft and sweet to rushing and tumbling to sad and, well, sweet again. And it surprised her that she wanted to listen to it – to imagine Romeo and Juliet running away together, rushing and stumbling to find that priest to marry them. And when he drank that poison and then she stabs herself in the heart ...

When it was over, she lifted up the record and slipped it back inside the cover. She was careful to touch only the edge. That's what Julia's mom always said about records, to touch only the edge and there'll be no smudges. Sheila put the album on the closed lid, gathered up her cleaning equipment and left.

Upstairs, Granny had supper ready. Since she came to live with them, supper was always on the table at the same time. It was beef stew, and one of Sheila's favourites. Her grandmother made the gravy so thick that she could spread it on a slice of bread and eat it like a sandwich, the carrots and peas squishing off the edges and onto her plate.

Granny was at the sink and called over her shoulder, "Can you set the table, Sheila? I just got your mother up and she'll be out any minute. At least, she better be."

Sheila looked at the clock over the kitchen table. It would be a fast supper to get her mom out the door and off to work in time.

The TV was on and she listened to snatches of fake laughter mingle with Paul's snorts and chortles. She reached into the drawer and pulled out the cutlery. "I guess he's too busy to do anything, Granny."

"Don't be like that. He's a boy, Sheila. It's only natural." She ran the tap and rinsed off her hands. "Besides, I've no time to worry if he's done it proper."

Sheila went to set each place at the table, knife and spoon on the right, fork on the left. "Granny, why do some people use extra knives and forks?"

"Hmm?"

"On TV and in some magazines, they do up the tables with all sorts of knives and forks and stuff."

Granny shook her head. "Stuff – what do you mean?"

"Oh, you know, wineglasses and standing-up napkins and candles and stuff. I'm just thinking if I ever got invited some-place with all those knives and forks, how would I know how to help set the table?"

Her grandmother snorted. "You are a funny girl, Sheila. If you ever got invited to such a place, what makes you think you'd be setting the table?"

Sheila didn't say anything, but she turned her back and moved over to the fridge and opened the door. She stared inside; there was only one milk bottle and it was three-quarters empty.

"Now, Child, don't get all quiet on me. I only meant if you were invited to a fancy dinner, they wouldn't be asking you to set the table. Most likely, they'd have it all done."

Sheila turned back from the fridge, clutching the milk bottle at the neck. "Or maybe they'd have a maid."

"What's this about a maid? Who has a maid?" Eleanor Barnes strode into the kitchen from the back hall. She'd just had a perm and her hair looked really nice. Sheila put a hand to her own short hair, willing it to grow further out of that terrible cut Brenda had talked her into. Her mom was struggling with a but-ton on the cuff of her blouse. "Damn it!" she muttered just before they all heard the clicking of her button bouncing and rolling on the linoleum. "Now I've got to either fix that or iron another blouse. Either way, I'm gonna be late."

Granny rushed to follow her. "Now, Eleanor, you sit and have your supper. I'll sew that button on."

"I don't have time."

"But you have to—"

"Look, Mother, I don't have to anything, except get to work. Somebody has to work around here." The bedroom door

slammed shut and, after a moment, Sheila listened to her grandmother shuffle back up the hall to the kitchen.

Sheila held her hand out in front, the button in the centre of
her palm. "I could sew it on tonight, Granny."

Her grandmother said nothing. She took the button and
slipped it into the pocket of her apron. Several minutes later,
Sheila's mother rushed down the back hall into the kitchen and
yanked on her coat. "My purse. Where's my purse?"

Sheila slipped into the living room, stepped over her younger brother's sprawled-out legs and picked up her mother's purse
from the coffee table. "It's here, Mom. Where it always is." She
stepped back over Paul's legs and walked back to the front hall
and held it out.

Her mother grabbed the purse from Sheila, her eyes narrow
slits. "Are you being smart with me?"

Sheila blinked and shook her head. "No."

"Good. Because I don't have time for smart mouths." She
pulled open the front door, and paused for a moment. "Did you
finish downstairs?"

Sheila glanced down, and then looked up and nodded.

"What? Did you break something?"

"No! What do you mean?"

"Just now. You looked guilty."

"No. I'm not. I mean I didn't do anything."

Her mother stared at her and Sheila held her breath. Then
Granny called from the kitchen.

"It's ten after five, Eleanor."

For an instant, her mother looked like she was going to say
something to Sheila. And then she turned and left. Moments
later, the car backed down the drive and roared up the street.

CHAPTER FOUR

WHEN SHEILA WENT DOWN TO the basement the following week, there was another record. And something else. A small gold wire rack squatted on the floor beside the hi-fi. In it were two album covers: Tchaikovsky's *1812* and a royal blue double album. She bent over to read the front. It was Beethoven. Lots of sonatas and Symphony Number this-n-that. Like the last time, the hi-fi lid was raised and there was another note just sitting to one side of the open lid.

Fräulein,
Perhaps von Beethoven will interest
you – Sonata in C Sharp

S. Maier

Once again, the album was set up for her. And as before, she finished the cleaning and had time to listen. She was pretty sure she'd heard this Sonata in C Sharp some other time. It made her think of snow falling, the way it always swirls and dances. And like he said, it was interesting – for most of it.

Before she left, Sheila returned to his note. There was a pen on the coffee table and she used it to add to the bottom:

They were nice. Thank you.

She read her note. She wanted to write down how the C Sharp one was nice until Beethoven made it all sour in a couple of places and spooky at the end. But maybe she didn't get the music and then he'd know she didn't have a clue and that would be that. She left without adding anything else.

Later that night, Sheila stretched out in the bathtub, humming the sad little piano melody. Not Dracula, she decided, stopping the drip from the tap with her big toe. The whole thing was a little freaky, but maybe he knew about how her papa was a great musician and he just figured she'd like it too. At least she didn't have to talk about the music, because then he'd see that she didn't know too much at all. She only had to listen to his music when he wasn't there.

* * *

The first time Sigmund's bus passed by the Golden Mile Plaza he noticed the record store. Above the wide plate glass window was a sign: Bennett's Records. And in the storefront were posters and hand-lettered announcements and notices. He was on his way to work and stared at the red and white pole bolted to the brick in front of the barber's next door.

A few days later, when it had been almost three weeks since his last haircut, he reached up from his seat, pulled the bus cord, stepped off at the corner stop and strode directly to the barbershop.

The small Italian at the first chair was efficient; despite the man's constant chatter and frenzied hand gestures, Sigmund found himself standing outside the shop much sooner than he expected.

He glanced at his wristwatch, raised his head to take in the traffic on the roads beyond, then turned and went inside the record store next door. Soon enough, he was stopping here even when he did not need a haircut.

* * *

It got so that Sheila could hardly wait for Fridays. She started watching the clock during last period, barely listening to Miss Norris go on and on in English. Not even Julia's best bathroom gossip could keep her after the bell rang. Racing home, she wondered what piece he had picked out that week.

The third Friday in December, her mother met her at the side door. She carried polish and a cloth in one hand, the mop in the other. "I figured I'd take a turn down there."

Sheila blinked a couple of times and smiled. She took hold of the mop and eased it from her mother's grip. "It's okay, Mom. You go have a coffee and I'll do it."

Her mother just stared at her, so Sheila kept talking, "I don't mind. Really. You work hard. Let's just make this my regular job." She didn't relax her grip until her mother agreed.

She was almost at Mr. Maier's door when she remembered the stuff for the toilet. She'd left all that in the upstairs bathroom. When she made it back to the top of the stairs, she saw the door wasn't closed all the way. She could hear her mother and Granny talking in the living room. She heard her name. She stopped and leaned forward to listen.

" ... ask too much of that girl, Eleanor."

"It's good for her."

"She has a paper route, she's always doing things around here and she has school. She's a smart little girl."

"Listen here. A genius doesn't repeat Grade 3."

"Now, that was a bad year, Eleanor. A bad year for all of you."

There was silence for a moment. Then her mother spoke again. "She gives me the creeps. Two months, she doesn't say a word. Not to me, not to nobody."

Her granny made a *tsk* noise. "It was a bad year. Tony–"

"Don't you say that name! Don't you ever."

Sheila held her breath. She heard her mother slap a hand down on the couch.

"Okay. So she's not been so – so strange lately." Her mother moved from the couch and stomped to the kitchen. Her voice pitched higher. "And I think, Mother, I think she's better 'cause I keep her busy. Busy, busy, busy. Now just drop it."

Under the cover of her mother opening and slamming shut cupboards and drawers, smashing lids on pots, rummaging through the cutlery drawers, Sheila hurried down the stairs and into Mr. Maier's apartment.

Mozart, Chopin, Bach, Strauss, Debussy.

Sheila started to keep a list of Mr. Maier's records in the back of her music notebook. She wondered if there were as many classical composers as rock 'n' roll stars. Mr. Maier's little notes were getting longer. He was using lined paper now, with comments like *Listen for the repetition of theme at the finish* and *Pay close attention to the pastoral in the second movement. It is underscored by strings.*

And she was answering him on the bottom of each note with a few sentences. *The part with all the trumpets and horns blasting and big drums made me think of a huge battle, and then the single trumpet was like our Remembrance Day stuff* and *The flute sounds so much like a bird singing, and when it goes higher and higher I thought of the lark flying up into the clouds.* What did she know, really? She was cheating by reading the notes on the albums and sometimes just using the cover pictures for ideas. But it was good to be polite. She knew that much.

By the new year, he was leaving library books on the coffee table. Sometimes, they were poetry books – and she didn't actually get too much of it – but mostly, they were big picture books of sculptures and paintings. Always, there was a note to look at certain pages while listening to the music. But she liked to thumb through and see the other stuff. She skipped the pictures of the van Gogh paintings and other crazy paintings like them. She wanted to see pictures of real people in beautiful clothes and jewels. Rich ladies with dogs on their laps and fur on their collars, and their kids, all dressed like fancy little grown-ups.

Some of the pictures showed naked men and women, but they were all in museums so it was okay. Mr. Maier never wrote her to look at those pages and Sheila thought she would die if anyone caught her looking at them. She knew she didn't look like any of these people when she was naked. Every so often, she would peek inside the top of her blouse and try to will her boobs to get bigger. There were enlarging creams she could buy – she knew that from the ads in the back of *True Confessions.* But there was nothing for short dumpy legs and fat hips. All the popular girls had big boobs and tiny waists and their legs looked fab in miniskirts. None of the boys ever looked at Sheila, except for Myron Gozowski, who she did her best to avoid at all times. He played the accordion and had more acne on his face than skin. Not one of Mr. Maier's records had an accordion playing anything.

Once, when she was downstairs listening to the fast part of an opera, she touched herself in the private place. The woman was singing with such a lovely voice what Mr. Maier told her was an aria. Sheila was looking at a painting of a soldier who was wearing nothing but a helmet and scabbard, and he was grabbing a half-naked woman. It made Sheila all tingly in her stomach and between her legs. The music was so sweet and fast, and then she felt warm in her chest too. She rubbed her hand against her panties – slowly at first and then pressing harder and faster, feeling excited and warm and nice until the sound of her grandmother moving overhead made her stop. She ran to the bathroom to wash. She washed her hands two more times before leaving the apartment.

One Saturday in early February, Sheila met Mr. Maier on the stairs. She was heading up with the laundry and he was coming down with his big heavy footsteps. She thought what Miss Moneypenny would say to James Bond and started, "Oh, Mr. Maier, how good to see ..." She winced as she tried to think what Miss Moneypenny might really say. Her cheeks started to burn as she stepped back down to let him pass. He gripped his overshoes in one hand, and with the other hand he was returning his wallet to his pants pocket. Sheila heard the door at the top of the stairs close; he must have just paid the rent.

"Excuse me, Fräulein." He smiled as he passed and bowed slightly. He did not click his heels.

She smiled in return and started up the stairs.

"Fräulein?" Sheila turned and stood still on the step, eye to eye with him now. "You have been liking the music, yes?"

"Oh, yes!" She stopped and swallowed the excitement, afraid of wrecking things, of shifting the rhythm or changing the tone.

"Next week, I was thinking of another opera – Wagner – *Die Walküre*."

Valcure – she saw it in her mind. The word meant nothing, but she was curious. After a moment, she realized that he was expecting her to say something. She glanced over at the closed door to Alan's room; The Stones' *Satisfaction* throbbed from inside.

"Ah," Mr. Maier pursed his lips. "I do not think he would like our music, yes?"

Trying to hold back a grin, Sheila shook her head and said, "No." She turned to leave, but then stopped.

Sigmund Maier was just opening the door to his apartment as she spoke again and said "Excuse me?" but she didn't think he heard her. His keys were rattling and the door was sticky so it was noisy when he opened it.

She tried again. "Mr. Maier?"

He stopped and glanced up. "Fräulein?"

"Thank you for the books, too."

"It is good that you read them."

She smiled. "And Mr. Maier?"

"Yes?"

"My name is Sheila."

Sigmund Maier stood for a long moment just looking at her, this little mouse. *Mäuschen.* She was uncertain, he could see that. But determined too, and, underneath it all, perhaps a little bit brave. *You changed my station.* He felt the corners of his lips twitch. She shifted the laundry basket, her front teeth biting onto her lower lip.

"Ah, yes, Sheila. Just so." He nodded. "Next week, it is Wagner then?"

"Yes," she added, "please."

CHAPTER FIVE

HE CLOSED THE DOOR OF his apartment and waited until he heard the girl's footsteps rush up the stairs. After hanging up his coat on the back of his door and removing his shoes, he ran his palm across the top of his head, smoothing his hair. He left his over-shoes on the mat just inside his apartment and carried his shoes into his bedroom.

The child had left a dust cloth on the dresser, crumpled into a mass next to the wooden box. He walked back into his kitchen, took out a brown paper bag and returned to his bedroom. With two fingers, he dropped the cloth into the bag and closed the top, fold by fold, before he placed it in the bottom of the wicker wastebasket.

He straightened and ran a finger over the top of his box, lingering for just a moment on the initials: S. M.

He remembered how his grandfather Mann with his dim and clouded eyes had to touch almost everything, had to run his filthy twisted fingers over the food on the table, the walls as he shuffled to his bed, crumbs and tobacco ash trailing off from his wool jacket. "That half-blind son of a bitch!"

He spat out the words, savouring the hollowness of the sound in the narrow bedroom. Except for his mother, his grandfather had been the one constant in his childhood – a wretched constant he could have done well to miss.

Sigmund had never known his own father.

Helmut Maier's picture always stood on the mantel. Brown-washed and set in an ornate frame, his photograph father was eternally erect and impassive, well outfitted in the Kaiser's uniform. His mother rarely spoke about him but sometimes Sigmund spied her whispering while she dusted the glass front. Though it was the only thing that sat on the mantel, his grandfather never even looked at it.

Passchendaele.

As a child, Sigmund used to imagine his father's death in the trenches. A brave soldier, his father killed many – perhaps hundreds, thousands – then was cut down while holding the line, pressing back the enemy through smoke, fumes, mud. Blood mixing with the mire, determined to stay in position: This was his father.

The few times his grandfather spoke of Helmut Maier, it was always 'that idiot son of a farmer'. His mother would *tsk* softly under her breath, but she never spoke up, never said a word about her soldier husband. Sigmund didn't understand this. Whenever he tried to speak with his mother privately, to ask her to tell him about his father, about why Grandfather Mann hated him so, Hilda would shush him. "Go to sleep now, Siggy. That was long ago. There is nothing to be done."

It was left to Sigmund to imagine his father, to lie in his bed at night and think how different things would be if his brave father had lived.

One rainy day, when he was nine, his grandfather called him a terrible name. Sigmund was playing jacks and tipped over his grandfather's humidor. "Frau Maier," the old man said, "the little bastard has knocked down my humidor. Ach – look at my tobacco – everywhere. Ruined!"

His grandfather called him "the little bastard" as if he were describing a set of stairs or the price of tobacco. Even at nine years of age, the flavour of the term was understood by Sigmund. At his school the other children called skinny Friedrich Grunner a bastard; Friedrich's mother Marlene was a whore and a drunk and all of the school knew it.

She does it Sunday nights with the Schuldirektor – it is the only way Friedrich can stay here.

Friedrich was routinely beaten by the other students. Sigmund could not ask his mother if he was like Friedrich. So later that day, when his grandfather was napping and his mother was humming that tune she always hummed as she prepared supper, he asked about his father, about what he was like.

She stopped humming, put down the ladle and just stared at him.

"*Mutter*, I want to know about my father. I am nearly ten years old. You never say anything. Tell me."

After a moment, she answered. "Your father was a very intelligent man, Sigmund. He read Goethe and Schiller, and was a top student at the Academy. You have, I think, his brain." She cupped his chin. "You have his eyes."

He thought for a moment, and then pulled away and slipped into the parlour. He stared hard at the picture, squinting to make his eyes smaller. After a moment, he took down his father's photograph and came back to stand in the kitchen doorway.

"Is there a picture of you with my father?" He held the photograph face out and against his knit vest.

"Sigmund. Return that immediately." Wiping her hands on her apron, his mother peered through the kitchen door into the parlour. The old man was snoring beside the fireplace, his pince-nez askew and his slippered feet on the ottoman.

Stubbornly, Sigmund continued to grip the picture frame, the filigree pressing into the soft flesh of his palms. "Where is my father's family? Where is their farm?"

"They do not want to see us, Sigmund. I will speak no more of this."

He held the frame tight, his lips pressed together, staring at his mother, willing her to tell him more.

Hilda ran a hand over the top of her head, stopping at the neat twist at the nape of her neck. Her fingers gathered up a few stray blonde hairs, working the escaped tendrils back into place. "Sigmund, those days, they were so different. It was all so strange; there was no time, and no money." She peered closely at him, her eyes reflecting the kitchen lamp. "Put back the picture, Sigmund. It is all that I have left."

Hilda spun on her heel and returned to her turnip soup. In silence, Sigmund walked into the parlour, placing the picture back in its spot on the mantel. Grandfather Mann continued to snore.

Sigmund reached up to his sleeping face and straightened the pince-nez. He watched his grandfather's chest rise and fall, and wondered – if he had said something to the old man, if he had challenged the terrible name he called him, would his grandfather see him differently? His mother was like a mouse, scurrying here and there to appease her father. What if Grandfather was just jabbing at her to make her stronger?

He glanced into the kitchen. Hilda was silhouetted in front of the small window, her arms wrapped tight against her waist, her back to him as she looked out at the rooftops and alleys below.

His mother's few words about his father did not make Sigmund feel better. She was never a person who inspired confidence; later, as an adult, he understood it was not in her nature. The old man's small pension may have paid the rent, but the child wanted her to shame his grandfather, to demand respect – if not for her soldier husband, then for her and for her son.

* * *

The Monday after Mr. Maier learned her name, Sheila ran all the way home from school. There had been a lunchtime assembly for all the music students. In May, the junior band and the senior band were going to a festival in London, England. Music students were coming from all over the place – from other provinces, from the States and from Europe. It would be a wonderful chance to travel and there were tours of the Queen's castle, the Tower of London and a couple of museums.

Sheila pulled out the pages of mimeographed blue paper from her book bag and looked again at the itinerary. It was not going to be too expensive because Miss Clarke said they'd made arrangements for accommodation at one of the universities, and they would charter a plane. Sheila had no idea what that meant, except that it wouldn't cost as much to fly.

She spent part of the evening making a budget, writing out columns of figures, crossing some out, changing others. She tried to calculate how many more papers she could handle, and if she maybe sold Regal cards door to door could it help her with some spending money. She wouldn't need to eat much – maybe even skip some meals.

At the top of the page, she wrote her goal and drew stars all around it.

London, England.

Her mother just stared at her when Sheila brought it up at breakfast the next day. Granny put down her teacup, her eyes confused and blinking. "Sheila, how can you even ask to—"

Sheila held up the registration form. "Wait – they only need a little bit – a down payment of fifty dollars. I can pay that back before May. I can get a job, make some extra money. Take an extra paper route, maybe?"

Her mother reached across the table and took the papers. "Two hundred and eighty-five dollars, Sheila." Her mother put a hand to her head. "My God. Do you live here?"

Sheila looked down at her cereal.

"I said, Do – You – Live – Here?"

She looked up at her mother and nodded, holding her bottom lip in her teeth to keep it from trembling.

The expression on her mother's face was like nothing she had seen before – not angry or frustrated. Her mother's eyes were wide and frightened. "I can't pay the milkman. I can't pay for new tires on the car. I can't get you a new coat. Your brothers are growing out of their boots. And you – you want me to pay for half of this? My God! What is the matter with you? Are you completely stupid?" Her mother's voice cracked, and Sheila could see tears in her eyes before she turned and pushed herself away from the table. All the music trip papers were jammed down into the garbage under the sink and her mother strode off to the living room.

The TV came on. It was too loud.

Sheila, her grandmother and brothers finished eating in silence. Granny stood up and announced, "Boys, get your things ready for school," then she went to her room. Alan stood up and shook his head at her, "You're a real moron," and Paul chirped up, "Yeah, a moron." Then her brothers left her to clear the table.

She was just hanging up the dishcloth when the doorbell rang.

The milkman was on Sheila's front porch, and he was not happy. Huge clouds of vapour steamed out of his nostrils and mouth and into the cold February air. He lowered his head and fixed her with a look. "You tell your mother I'm not deliverin' another bottle of milk to this house 'til she pays her bill. You can go to the variety store for all I care."

Sheila eyed the wire basket with the three slim bottles inside. "But we need the milk."

He put down the wire basket and reached into his breast pocket. "Five weeks overdue." He thrust the bill in her direction. "An' outta my pocket, Miss. My pocket."

"Just a minute. I'll get my mom." She turned her head and called into the living room around the corner. "Mom. The milkman's here."

"Close the door, Sheila. It's winter."

Sheila took a quick look at the man on the porch. He was really frowning now. "Mom," she called over her shoulder. "He needs to talk with you."

"Sheila! Get in the house and shut the door."

Sheila felt her throat get all tight, thinking how to make the milkman go away. But he was not going to leave. She called back, "Mom, he's got a bill. He—"

Her mother was off the couch now. Sheila could hear her moving, gaining momentum, each foot landing harder and harder on the floor, bringing her closer. Casting one last desperate look at the tall thin man on her front porch, she begged, "You should go. Try later – next week."

He shook his head. "Not this time."

Sheila's mother rounded the corner and started towards the door. "I told you to shut the goddamned door, and I meant shut it!" Sheila was shoved aside, and her mother pushed the door with both hands but the milkman was too fast. His foot jammed the bottom, and his right hand and forearm pressed against the upper part. His left hand gripped the doorframe for support.

Eleanor Barnes was no match for him, but it didn't stop her from hollering curses and threats as the door opened wider.

The man on the porch was determined. He just kept pushing and, soon enough, he was standing in the front hall. "Lady," he started, "I'm not leavin' here without my money. Five weeks owin'."

Sheila watched as her mother drew back her arm, her hand clenched in a fist. He was too fast; he ducked and she ended up whacking the edge of the open door. She fell to the floor, wailing and carrying on. Sheila's stomach flipped. She turned to the man, "Look what you've done to my mother! Just get out. Get out now!"

Her mother crawled along the floor toward the kitchen. She was still crying. Paul came out of the rear of the house, took one look at his mother then barrelled through the kitchen and down into the front hall, arms flailing as he punched at the lower half of the milkman.

By now, Granny had come out of her room and was alternating between trying to get Sheila's mother to get back up and screaming at the man standing in the front hall. "You terrible man – what have you done to Eleanor? Oh sweet Jesus! Help us."

Sheila grabbed Paul around the waist and backed him away from the milkman, who was now trying to turn around and escape.

The door at the top of the basement stairs flung wide open, and Alan raced past his grandmother and mother tangled up at the end of the hall and straight at the milkman. Sheila lost her balance and, with a struggling Paul in her arms, fell against Alan. His socks slipped on the hardwood and the three of them fell to the floor.

This was just the break the milkman needed. He turned tail and scrambled back to his waiting truck. Alan struggled to his feet, ran through the door and kept going down the snow-packed driveway. He reached the curb just as the milk truck got to the top of the street and turned the corner.

Sheila watched as her brother hit the tops of his legs with two closed fists. He stood there for a moment, then turned around and came back into the house. They all now looked at their mother, who was sitting in the middle of the kitchen floor, her back against the cupboard under the sink. She had stopped crying and was just staring at the kitchen clock. Granny stood near by, her arms folded across her chest. She clucked and spoke to Sheila's mother in a soft voice. "Come now, come to bed, Eleanor. Come have a lay down. Come on."

Sheila's mother shuddered then bent one leg, and then the other. She moved over onto her knees and Granny held out a hand and helped her to get up. Together they moved off toward the back hall. Sheila listened to the sound of the bedroom door closing. No reading in bed tonight. No transistor radio. No sleep.

Without being asked, Sheila moved to the phone in the hall and dialled. She told her mother's supervisor that Eleanor Barnes would not be in for the afternoon shift, that she was having car trouble. The woman on the other end of the phone paused, and then replied by asking if Mrs. Barnes would please call the manager in the morning. "First thing," she added in a curt voice, and Sheila's stomach flipped again.

Sheila hung up the phone. She watched as Alan peeled off his dirty, wet socks and tossed them down the basement stairs. Then he put three bottles of milk into the refrigerator before he carried the wire basket downstairs with him as he headed to his room.

She glanced at the clock. Just past 8:30. Thank God Mr. Maier hadn't been home. The last time Mom had one of her big upsets, the people in the basement apartment moved out. *Too noisy* they said. Too noisy.

* * *

For as long as Sigmund could remember, a well-used wooden table and two chairs sat in the large foyer just beyond the main door of their apartment house in Dresden. And every morning as he left for school and every afternoon when he returned, those chairs were filled by two men.

Lukas Grimmel sat with his broad back to the door, his shoulders hunched over the chessboard that sat on the table between him and his opponent. Across from Grimmel and peering over the top of his wire-rimmed glasses, Dietrich Schneider looked up each time the door opened. Every arrival and departure was announced in a thin, nasal tone; Herr Schneider gave a summary of events.

"Ah, Lukas, Frau Maier has returned from the market. *Guten Tag*, Frau Maier, I trust the butcher kept his hand off the scale today. Did you hear that Frau Bergen's cat had kittens, but Lukas and I told her they must be gone by Saturday. Sunday at the latest."

His strange voice would always echo past the cracked plaster of the foyer and follow Sigmund and his mother up all three flights of the marble staircase to the top-floor flat where they lived with his grandfather.

Sigmund used to wonder why neither Herr Schneider nor Herr Grimmel worked. Money, the lack of money, ways to get money, ways to keep money – it was a constant in his home; he couldn't imagine anyone living without that. His mother told him Herr Schneider was contracted to maintain the building and was given an apartment at the rear. Herr Grimmel was his boarder.

As a very young boy, Sigmund thought they were the guardians of the apartment house, like palace sentries in the old building. He'd turn right from Pragerstrasse down their little side street, up the stone steps, through the arched entranceway and, pushing open the large wooden door with the brass lion knocker, he'd step inside the foyer. To his young eyes, it was like a fairy-tale castle. The tiles were cracked and the crown moulding was grey-tinged and crumbling, but the marble stairs and ornate railing were in good condition. Rumours, likely circulated by Herr Schneider, suggested that Mozart had spent a summer on the second floor, under the brief patronage of the Archbishop's cousin.

"Fabrication," muttered Grandfather Mann when Sigmund ventured the tale one evening. "Little boy stories for the simple-minded." When he was older, he credited the old man with developing his discerning and careful eye for the truth.

His mother was out one evening, and Sigmund escaped to Herr Grimmel's and Herr Schneider's apartment to learn chess. The next morning, his grandfather asked him what "the pigshit farmers" had showed him.

"Chess, Grandfather, they showed me chess."

His grandfather laughed so hard he coughed. "A game for half-men with soft, white palms and a love for pigshit. Did they show you their white palms?" He leaned forward and licked his fat lips. "Did they show you where they keep their pigshit?"

His mother came back in their apartment from the lavatory. "Father. You must not speak like that, he is only a boy."

"If you are not careful, he will soon ask you to make him a dress. If those two—"

"Father – *nein!*"

Hilda's tone shocked her father and, for once, he stopped talking. Gunther Mann sulked all day before Hilda apologized. And long after, Sigmund tried to understand what his grandfather meant about pigshit and white palms before he put it all from his mind. When he finally understood, he learned how important it was to pay attention to everything. Everything.

Much more than a cynic, Sigmund learned to ferret out what others wished to hide. As a secondary benefit of his grandfather's constant criticism and his mother's inability to articulate, Sigmund learned to do what was necessary to keep a smooth surface. Pay attention, watch for signals from those around you but give nothing away. Reveal nothing. Eventually, he travelled this plane quite well, all the while watching for any undercurrents, listening for the unexpressed.

He recognized Sheila's navigation skills on sight.

CHAPTER SIX

SHEILA OFTEN LISTENED FOR THE sound of music from the basement, but either Mr. Maier played the hi-fi very quietly in the evenings, or he never listened to any of his albums. She thought that was strange, but then, what music did they ever listen to in her family? Either they had to keep things quiet because her mother was sleeping, or they had to keep things quiet because her mother was tired. Or watching television. Or thinking. "I can't think with that noise on," she would say. So, while everyone else in the world listened to the hit parade, Sheila had to wait until she went to Julia's house.

The day after Valentine's she was over at the Newtons' and asked Julia if she ever listened to classical music. Her friend frowned a bit, and then smiled. "Sure. Mom's got some Billie Holiday albums. She says Billie's a real classic. Wanna listen?"

Because Mr. Maier hadn't brought home any Billy Holiday yet, Sheila thought maybe he was an American composer. She nodded. "Sure."

After the first couple of notes, Sheila realized this wasn't somebody who composed symphonies, but still, she liked what she heard. The record was pretty old, and there were lots of crackles and a couple of skips, but that lady sang like she knew what it was like to be last-pick in gym. Like today, for instance.

In Grade 11, she would be able to drop gym. She could hardly wait.

Snuggled into huge cushions tossed around the rec room floor, they listened to the whole album. Just before the last song finished, Julia's mom came down and leaned against the doorway. Mrs. Newton was one of the most beautiful women Sheila had ever seen. She had long, lovely legs and arms; she always dressed in flowing kaftans or capri pants and shirtwaist cotton tops. Her black frizzy hair was smoothed back into a tight bun and held in place with large clips, often with huge colourful bows. She had freckles across the cocoa skin of her nose and cheeks. Sheila thought the freckles made her look even younger.

And her name was Carlotta. Carlotta Marlena Newton. Sheila used to practise writing Julia's mother's name in her diary with a fountain pen. She'd add curlicues on the ends of the letters. She thought that when she was old enough, she'd change her own name from Sheila Helen Barnes to Sheilagh Helena Barnetta and wear capris all the time.

"Billie Holiday, eh?" Mrs. Newton grinned. "You girls are just too hip to be believed."

Sheila felt colour rise to her cheeks. *Hip.* Nobody ever called her hip before. She giggled.

Julia moved as if to rise and then stopped. "Mom, I hope you don't mind – we're playing your special albums."

Mrs. Newton kept smiling. She gestured with an elegant hand for Julia to sit back down. "Honey Girl, you just let Sheila listen to Lady Day and learn." She turned to Sheila. "One day, I swear, you are going to get The Beat."

It was the Newton family joke. Sheila, trying to learn to dance to Wilson Pickett and always missing The Beat – she'd nab the downbeat on the up, or miss it altogether. Mashed Potato became Mushed Potato; her feet tangled when she focused on her body and her body froze while she concentrated on the footwork. But Mrs. Newton and Julia persevered. "You're our little project, Sheila Barnes. And you're gonna get this if I have to send you home with half of my record collection."

Sheila managed to avoid bringing home any of the records by saying she was afraid that she'd wreck them. If she'd ever brought one home, she could just imagine what Alan would say. And do.

Billie Holiday stopped singing and the arm of the record player returned to its cradle. The three of them looked at one another, and then Julia said, "Mom, can you change the record?"

"Just get on up and change it yourself, Lazy Bones."

"Aw, Mom."

Mrs. Newton raised a single eyebrow and smiled.

Julia leaned back into her pillow and turned toward Sheila. "You do it, Sheila."

Mrs. Newton turned and looked at Sheila. The single eyebrow rose again.

This was the way some families played with each other, and they were making her part of it. Sheila remained seated and grinned at her friend. "I changed it the last time; you do it, Julia."

Julia turned back to her mother. "Mom, change the record. Puhleeze."

Mrs. Newton crossed her arms; her face now held a mock expression of sternness. "I don't think so."

Julia rolled her eyes. "Mom. C'mon."

Sheila sat straight up. "I know how we can settle this, everybody." Her tummy felt all tingly, and she pointed at Mrs. Newton before Julia could say another word. "Eeny."

She pointed at Julia. "Meeny."

She pointed at herself, then hit the centre of her chest with a ramrod finger. "Miney."

Back to Mrs. Newton. "Moe."

Julia. "Catch."

Herself. "A."

Mrs. Newton. "Nig—"

She stopped there. The beginning of the word hung in the room, large and ugly, and Sheila's finger still pointed at Mrs. Newton. She tried to catch the piece of the word, catch it and pull it back, back to her lips, inside her mouth and down her throat.

"I – I …"

All the possible things to say flashed through her brain, unsaid.

Mrs. Newton straightened from leaning against the doorway. "That's okay, Sheila." Her voice was bright and up high; her eyes, all smiling. "Hard to break down all that schoolyard stuff." She moved to the stereo. She removed the album, slid it back inside the jacket and returned it to the cupboard under the stereo cabinet.

Julia wouldn't look at her.

Sheila stood up and went to the doorway. "I better get home. Granny will have dinner ready." She looked down at her socks. They were purple, the same colour they were when she put them on this morning. Julia said they looked really Mod. Sheila turned and went upstairs, put on her coat and boots and ran past all fourteen houses that separated her house from Julia's. She was inside her own house, breathless, when she realized that nobody had said goodbye. Not her. Not Julia. And not Carlotta Marlena Newton.

* * *

"Frau Maier, where are my spectacles? Where is my *Kaffeetasse?* And my pipe, Frau Maier?"

Early on, Sigmund understood that his grandfather lost things on purpose. Even though he complained of poor eyesight, the old man always noticed when his grandson's ears needed a wash, or when he had a collar unbuttoned. Sigmund later understood that losing things gave his grandfather a reason to call for his mother. But he never heard his grandfather say "Hilda". Not once *"Tochter"*. Nothing but "Frau Maier". And he almost never spoke directly to Sigmund.

He wondered what he could do that would please his grandfather. High marks on his examinations were met with soft words of praise from his mother; Grandfather said nothing. Even the occasional carrots and potatoes Sigmund earned running errands for the greengrocer were met with silence. Sigmund smiled to himself when he spied the old man fondling and sniffing a wilted cabbage; if not his heart, then he knew he could at least please his stomach.

Hilda added to her father's pension with tailoring and dressmaking assignments. Sigmund and his grandfather shared the single small bedroom; they were moved to the sitting room while the women were being fitted. His mother called them clients.

They were mostly middle-class women who coveted a more exclusive look than provided by the local shops.

Whenever his grandfather started to shift in his chair and mutter about "Pretentious pigs – nothing but farmers' daughters," Sigmund switched on the wireless. He had long given up trying to read newspapers aloud; he stumbled over far too many words to suit his grandfather. The broadcasts let the old man shift his attention elsewhere. Ranting about the Republic and the humiliation of grovelling before foreign kings was usually enough.

Even so, he once chased Hilda and one of her clients from the bedroom. Dressed only in a slip and stockings, the shocked woman clutched a grey satin evening gown to her chest as the old man shook his fist in Hilda's face.

"Get out, Frau Maier, get out. You and this *Weibstück* have had my room long enough."

The woman left with the evening dress, refusing to pay.

"*Jüdin!*" He spat into his handkerchief.

Hilda did not have a bedroom of her own; she slept on a fold-up cot tucked into an alcove beside the kitchen. Each night, she wheeled the cot into the sitting room after Sigmund and his grandfather went to bed.

Many nights Sigmund fell asleep to the waxing and waning *whirr* of her mechanical sewing needle, and the soft *thump, thump, thump* of the foot treadle. Sometimes, he would wake to the same sounds in the morning.

Sigmund scarcely remembered the time far from the cramped flats and the sounds of sewing machines. But he could recall a long-ago Christmas: the scent of pine and the flicker of tiny candles; the delicious odours of citrus, cinnamon and ginger. Even then his grandfather never looked at him – always, his grandfather turning away, turning away. Strange that he could not remember his mother in that great big house with the dozens and dozens of doors, always closed. But he did remember his grandmother, his busy, flustered grandmother. She wore big wide hats with jewelled hatpins, and fur stoles and collars. He recalled how she fussed with his nurse that he would catch a cold or be overheated. Always calling on the maid to see to this or see to that – *schnell!*

When he was barely four it all changed and they moved here. No dozens of doors. No servants. He remembered that his grandmother hated their new way of living, complained constantly about not enough to eat. He had a clear memory of her at the small table in the kitchen, her blue eyes wide and staring at her plate and the single grey potato there. She pushed the plate into the centre of the table and rose, her voice quivering and high-pitched. "I will not eat again unless there is white bread and lean, unspoiled meat. Nothing to pass my lips until then."

The influenza epidemic helped keep her oath.

So then there were just the three of them in the small flat. Meals were mostly potatoes, or turnips and hard dry bread. Margarine, when it could be found, replaced butter. When a postage stamp cost over a million Marks, turnips were all that were served. Turnip soup. Turnip bread. Turnip coffee. When there were not even turnips, Hilda would take one of their few hidden heirlooms to sell on street corners and at pawnshops. Sometimes, she was away long into the evening hours. "I had to wait in line," she would say. Once, she brought home a wedge of cheese wrapped in paper and a small loaf of white bread.

Sigmund's grandfather stood with one hand on the mantel and sniffed. "Who gave you this?" Narrowing his eyes, he asked, "Who is a happy man tonight?"

Hilda moved into the kitchen, placing the food on the table. She cut three thin slices from each, careful not to tear the bread. The old man took his portion, consuming it rapidly. When Sigmund asked for more, his grandfather reached across the table and landed a hard blow on the side of his head.

"Idiot." The old man sat back, rubbing his hand. "A slut and an idiot."

His mother rose from the table as if nothing had happened. "I waited in line, Father. Nothing more." She began to rewrap the food. First, the bread in brown paper and a linen towel, and then the cheese.

His grandfather left the table, and Sigmund gingerly pressed his palm to his ear. He lowered his hand into his lap. There was a small drop of bright red on the centre of his palm. It was the only time he could remember his grandfather ever touching him.

He shifted in his chair to watch his mother, busy at tidying the kitchen. She turned to look at him, her expression unreadable.

"Go to bed, Sigmund."

* * *

In early March, Sheila's Granny fell and broke her hip. Sheila came home from delivering newspapers in time to watch them load her into the ambulance. As the flashing lights disappeared around the corner, she realized she had no idea where they were taking her grandmother. Paul just shook his head and shrugged when she asked him, and Alan was nowhere to be found. She called three hospitals before finding the right one. Then she called her mother at work to tell her.

"Sheila, for God's sake, why didn't you go too? Those idiot doctors will probably make it worse – cut off her leg or something. Why the hell didn't you go with her?"

Before she could answer, her mother hung up. Sheila held the phone for a moment, looked at the handset gripped in her fingers, and finally hung up before heading into the kitchen to keep supper from burning.

Because her mother was at the hospital a lot, Sheila had less time on Fridays to stay in the apartment and listen to the music. There was too much to be done elsewhere: vacuuming, washing, cooking, straightening up. Sick of picking up after her brothers, she finally complained to her mother. "Mom, they're just, just being lazy – lazy jerks."

"Sheila, I don't have time for this."

"But they don't even help, Mom. I'm doing everything, and they don't help." Sheila felt the sting in her eyes and blinked hard. Eleanor threw on her coat then struggled with the elastic fastener of her overshoe.

"Look, I've got less than an hour to stop at the hospital, find out whatever it is your grandmother is complaining about this time, and still make it to work. My supervisor is watching me like a hawk, the manager is giving me the gears, I've got to pay the bills, take care of my own goddamn mother and you can't pick up the duster once a week." She fixed Sheila with a furious stare, her mouth a firm, straight line. "Just do it, Sheila. For Chrissake, just do it!"

As her mother pulled shut the door, Sheila heard a snort from behind her. Alan stood in the kitchen, arms crossed, his long figure leaning against the wall. "Poor little Sheila, what are you whining about now?" He blocked the door leading to the rear hall.

"Nothing." She moved to the counter, adding hot water to the half-filled sink. She felt his eyes on her, then sensed him draw close.

"Nothing? What was that about those 'lazy jerks'? What lazy jerks?" He took hold of her upper arm with his left hand. "I think what we have here is a failure to communicate. Retard." A cup slipped from her fingers back into the bubbles and thudded against the plates stacked beneath the water. She hoped that it didn't chip.

"Don't." It was a plea; she tried to control the crack in her voice.

"Don't what?" He made a wedge with the bent fingers of his right hand. Knuckles sharp and pointed, Alan began a rhythmic beat against her upper arm. Sheila tried to pull free from his grip. As she struggled, his left hand clutched tighter but he was less accurate. One blow glanced off her shoulder and landed hard against her neck. She yelped and he let her go.

"Alan – you, you bastard!"

"Just shut up or I'll give you more." He strode to the rear hall and started down the stairs. "Quit your goddamn whining, or I'll tell Mom what a dirty little mouth her baby girl has." His words drifted up from the basement, and she heard the door to his room slam shut. She finished the dishes in silence.

The week continued to unravel. Friday was spent at school struggling through a geography quiz, pleading for an extension for her English assignment and ending with a practical test in music. Miss Clarke was in a rotten mood.

There was a split in Sheila's reed, but she didn't have the quarter to buy a new one from the music department's supply. Mr. Bernstein wasn't there to ask for a loan.

When Sheila knocked her music sheets from the stand, the whole class snickered. The loose pages wouldn't go back up in the right order, and Miss Clarke marched from behind her desk, through the tangle of chairs, stands and instrument cases to where Sheila sat in the third row.

"Are we ready yet, Miss Barnes?"

Sheila straightened, raised her clarinet, wet her reed and looked up.

Miss Clarke's arms were crossed over her chest, her lips were pursed. She raised one arched brow and spoke in a slow, loud voice. "We're all waiting, Miss Barnes."

The notes on the page kept jumping around, and her wet fingers slipped trying to find the right keys to push and holes to cover. She shook so much that her mouth trembled and the instrument's mouthpiece repeatedly clicked against her teeth. She stopped halfway through.

Miss Clarke dropped her arms to her sides. "Thank you so much for that wonderful demonstration of the full range of woodwind wails and squeaks. Please have a new reed next time. And please, try to practise at least once."

Sheila sat back in her seat and tried to make herself as small as possible. She listened to the others play their practical tests, chewing on the end of her reed until it snapped.

After school, she hurried the mop through the apartment. She left Mr. Maier's record untouched. She scrawled a short note:

Mr. Maier:

*I don't have time to listen today.
Granny is still in hospital and
Mom needs me to do a few
things upstairs. Sorry.*

*Your friend,
Sheila*

That evening, Sigmund twice read the note. *Your friend.* He hardly thought of her at all, except Fridays. Yes, and Thursday evenings at the record shop, and then, yes, at the library. He supposed that such a little mouse would have few friends.

He smiled. *"Mäuschen."*

* * *

Sheila realized what she had written as she got ready for bed that night. It was probably "completely inappropriate" as Miss Clarke would say, but she wrote it without thinking. She did think of him as a friend – well, sort of. At least he was nice enough to teach her about the music and stuff. It wasn't like she could really talk to him or go to the movies or a dance or anything.

She had at least a half-hour before her mother came to bed. Reaching up to the back shelf of their bedroom closet, she brought down the Volume V of *The Home University Bookshelf.* She ran her hand over the burgundy leather cover; it was an old book, the corners worn. None of the books at her school library had these kinds of old-fashioned pictures on the front: dorky-looking farmer kids smiling up at their farmer mother. One was mixing something in a wooden bowl. They all looked so darn happy. Retards.

She remembered when there had been other volumes with other old pictures on the front, but she had no idea where they were now. Her mother threw out so much stuff when her papa left and they moved. She managed to hide her Volume V, two Bobbsey Twins, one Harlequin romance, and her batch of Superman, *True Confessions* and *Hit Parade* magazines in the back of the closet, all tucked away up high behind the box of off-season clothes.

Volume V was her favourite book. *Aesop's Fables, Grimm's Fairy Tales* and *The Arabian Nights* all mixed in together. The cover smelled like an old coat, and the pages inside were like damp leaves and dust.

She opened the book. The first page, a sheet of tissue paper. Under the tissue, a coloured illustration on a page of shiny photograph paper. Scheherazade sits at the Sultan's feet, all covered in veils; tassels and jewels cling to her skin. One pale, slender arm is raised, the palm facing up; she is telling a story and the Sultan leans forward, eyes only for her, only for Scheherazade.

Sheila touched the page with her forefinger and traced the arm of Scheherazade. Then she held out her own arm and turned her palm to face the ceiling.

One day, her papa was coming back for her. Maybe he was in Arabia right now, sailing up and down that Suez River or Canal or whatever in a cruise ship, playing in the band. And when he could arrange things, he'd come and take her away to the ship. He probably had to wait until she was old enough. But that would be soon. She was fourteen; almost fifteen. Old enough to work on cruise ships. She was sure of that much.

CHAPTER SEVEN

THREE WEEKS AFTER SIGMUND TURNED twelve, the physician started to make regular visits to his grandfather. One evening, Herr Doktor and his mother stood just outside the bedroom door. Sigmund was lying on the trundle bed, pacing his own breath with that of his grandfather's low rasping wheeze. He heard snatches of phrases like "future provisions" and "family considerations".

The next afternoon, Sigmund studied at the kitchen table as his mother made some broth. It was raining hard outside, the wind pressing sheets of water against the kitchen window. Hilda was focused on the steaming liquid that she stirred, and did not hear his question.

"I am sorry, Sigmund, what is it you want?"

"I wondered if we should advise my father's family." Seeing her blank expression, he continued. "About Grandfather Mann – his illness. I think it would be something that they should know." He kept his voice even, returning his attention to his workbook and pencil.

Hilda put the ladle down and shut off the gas.

"Sigmund, this is not for them to know."

"Why should they not know?" He continued to copy his numbers, refusing to glance at her, determined not to be deflected.

Hilda looked up from the stove. She studied her son's profile for a moment. Then, as if she had made up her mind about something, she nodded and spoke. "Your father's family, they were … displeased that your father and I married so young. After he was killed, they said he would not have joined the artillery if he had not been so anxious to earn money." She lifted a china bowl from the shelf next to the small stove. "They were correct, I think.

His education at the Academy might have secured him a place in officer's training, but he would not wait. Poor Helmut. They would have nothing to do with me, with us, after." Taking a tray from beneath the cupboard, she draped a yellow linen towel over the japanned surface. Her mother had brought this tray from the big house; she needed to protect it from her father's spills. "I will take this to Grandfather. Please put your work away and set out our supper things."

Sigmund did as he was asked, considering her response while he worked. He was certain that his mother was not telling him everything. *Poor Helmut.* Her voice was sad when she said that, but there was something more. Perhaps his father's family would want to see them, if they knew that there was no one else. If they knew that he and his mother were alone. After all, he was the son of their son. He thought that his miserable grandfather was the reason; his father's family would not want to know them if it meant knowing his grandfather. That seemed reasonable. The more he considered, the more reasonable it became.

They were farmers. That much he knew. And he knew what his Grandfather Mann thought of farmers. Herr Schneider was lately the usual recipient of Grandfather's epithets.

At least twice a week, Herr Schneider knocked at their door to "ask after the health of Herr Mann". Holding his hat and turning the brim around and around as he spoke, he was attentive as Hilda recounted how much better or how much worse her father was that day. Schneider nodded sagely with each report, adjusting the wire-rimmed glasses on his narrow nose and sniffing in short, punctuated breaths.

When Grandfather knew it was Schneider, he would call out from his room and ask if they were letting the farmers in. "Give that farmer a handkerchief! Keep his pigshit boots out of here!"

Hilda always blushed and tried to get him to leave, but the man lingered in the doorway, smiling, making excuses for the ramblings of the elderly. Sometimes he suggested new treatments he'd culled from advertisements in *The New York Times*. His cousin sent him a copy every few weeks and Herr Schneider made sure anyone he spoke with knew that he could read it.

"As a student of languages, I will soon travel overseas. I will go to New York City and sit in the Central Park and read *The New York Times* every day." Schneider then signalled his departure from the doorway with a sombre, slow shake of his head. Patting Sigmund on the shoulder, he'd bow to Hilda before finally leaving. And every day, Grandfather would call out "Pigshit farmer!" as the door closed. The coughing finally subsided when Hilda brought him his water and the medicine from the small brown bottle.

Almost a week to the day Sigmund spoke of his father's family, Gunther Mann passed away. Sigmund was in bed, matching his breath with his grandfather's ragged wheeze when the old man stopped. There was no movement, no struggle – just a stillness. After several seconds, Sigmund commenced his own intake of air, waiting. His throat suddenly burned and he blinked back tears. Furious, he rubbed his eyes in the dark and dried his hands on his blankets. He did not understand the heaviness in his chest, and concentrated on pushing away this strange regret for a grandfather who hardly knew he lived. Tears started again and he shook his head.

This was not a time to be childish; he was now the man in the house and must prepare himself to earn money. If Bronfmann could not hire him at the grocery, there were other shops where fast legs and strong arms could be used.

He took a deep breath and cleared his throat. He would delay waking his mother until dawn. There would be nothing she could do until the morning. He listened all night for a resumption – a re-awakening; there was only blessed silence.

Hilda's grief was quiet, his grandfather's funeral modest and restrained. Still, some reminders of the old man's former position resurfaced. Their old priest from an der Frauenkirche came to perform the service held in the tiny church of the current neighbourhood. There was no tea afterwards. Herr Schneider and Herr Grimmel and a few other neighbours attended at the church, along with three black-suited former business acquaintances of his grandfather who sat together and apart from the few other mourners. Hilda said they came out of respect; Sigmund watched them from the corner of his eye. With quiet asides and almost imperceptible nods of their heads, they conferred, one even jotting a few notes in a small leather-bound book.

Sigmund was certain: these old Jews were sniffing for money. If the pine coffin was not enough to convince them, surely they had to notice how his grandfather's suit hung on Sigmund's shoulders. Even his mother's tailoring skills could not hide the worn sections. Those greedy birds did not linger after the service.

Returning from the burial, Hilda put the kettle on to boil and sat at the kitchen table. She had not removed her hat or coat, and held her black gloves in one hand, gripped into a tight ball.

"*Mutter?*" Sigmund placed his hand on her shoulder and she started.

"Ah, yes, Sigmund." She lifted her hat, placing it next to the crumpled gloves that were now unfurling on the table's surface. "Are you hungry, Siggy?"

It was his turn to start. She hadn't called him that since he'd begun classes at the Gymnasium. He shook his head and sat opposite her.

Sighing, she unbuttoned her jacket. "I must find work." Hilda stood and moved quickly to put her things away. "For now, we will economize." Noting his expression, she smiled slightly. "It will be all right, Sigmund. You will see."

A few days later, she was waiting on the steps outside as he returned from school. Even from a distance he could see that she was anxious, stepping down briskly to meet him on the sidewalk. She kept her sweater coat wrapped tight against her chest, the raw March wind struggling to lift the hem of her dress. She spoke in a low, breathless tone.

"Come inside, Sigmund, quickly. I have news."

Following her up the stone steps, Sigmund had sudden thoughts of a rediscovered family. Perhaps his mother had written to his other grandparents after all. He raced up the marble stairs and imagined a long road in the country, leading away from Dresden, past the cherry trees that lined the outskirts and out to where ploughed fields were intermingled with forests, hills, and valleys that sheltered small winding rivers.

There is no heavy traffic of barges, dirty little tugs, or paint-peeled skiffs and schooners. The rivers are travelled by sturdy rowboats and sailboats, steered by tanned and muscled boatmen.

The farmhouse is low and flat, with a large wooden door and a small bench set against the bricks outside. Two people rise from the bench as he and his mother approach: a grizzled, elderly man, with blue eyes like his and a full white beard, and a plump, grey-haired woman. The old man tries to be gruff at first, but soon reveals his happiness and pride. The grandmother's large arms bury his head in the odours of spices and rising loaves. There are cousins; some he will have to wrestle and scrap with, but he proves himself and they soon ask him about the wonders of the city ...

"Sigmund? Are you listening to me?"

He brought his mind back to the small apartment – his mother standing next to Grandfather's chair, the late afternoon light streaming in from the kitchen windows.

"I am sorry, *Mutter*. What did you say?"

She looked impatient. "I said that I have secured a position as a dressmaker. I will commence tomorrow at the Semper Opera House."

"But I thought ... "

"What? What did you think?"

"I thought that you would write to ... to his family." He pointed to the picture above the fireplace. "I thought if they knew I was, that we were, alone now ..."

Hilda exhaled heavily. "Sigmund. This must be the last time. The family of your father has no interest in you or me in any way." Hilda looked over at the mantel, and then back at Sigmund. She spoke in a quiet but firm voice. "I did write to them. Two times last year. The first reply was polite, but firm. They were clear that they would not receive us, or any petition for help." Her voice rose. "The second letter was returned, unopened. We are dead to them, you and I, and you must not insist in this matter. Now, help me with the table."

He felt the blood rise to his face, but did as he was told. Hilda had prepared a good supper, and there was butter for the bread and sugar for the tea. It was not long before her usual calm returned.

"This is a good thing, Sigmund. A position like this at the Opera House will bring me new clients, I am certain of it."

He kept his eyes on his plate, dipping the bread into the last of the stew. "Yes, *Mutter.*" He heard her small sigh and offered something more. "How did you find this job?"

Hilda was quick to respond. "Frau Ullman provided a letter of introduction."

Alena Ullman was no longer a simple shopkeeper's wife, and could easily afford the couturiers of Paris. Nonetheless, she remained a steadfast customer of Hilda's, brushing aside Gunther Mann's insults. "An old man, Frau Maier, and one must have patience for old men. God knows, we must have patience for them even when they are not old."

She was one of the few clients with whom Hilda smiled.

At the table, his mother raised her head a bit. "Her letter was addressed to the *Direktor.* She mentions my particular skill with silk and trims." She began to clear the table, hesitating with several dishes balanced in one hand. "I told them I would work for less than the others. To prove myself."

Sigmund could not see the point to this; the letter from Frau Ullman should have been sufficient. But he said nothing.

Whether it was the letter or her willingness to accept lower wages, it made no difference. Her new position meant that soon their lives took on fresh qualities and rhythms neither of them could have imagined mere months before.

Indeed, the years to follow became the best of times for them both. Europe was changing; for some Germans, the impossible seemed attainable. It was a time of intense contrasts. Unemployment and economic uncertainty were mixed with optimism, even wild abandon.

For Sigmund and Hilda, financial independence became their just reward. With time, the old man's presence faded.

After each day of classroom study in the Gymnasium, Sigmund waited at the Opera House to walk home with his mother. Books in hand, he tucked himself into an alcove just off the orchestra seating. He spent many hours immersed in the music. He learned how a single note sustained by an oboe could carry the heart of grief; how the rising swell of violins could convey the beginning of a romance. He watched as the cold and bare stage evolved into castles, countrysides, battlegrounds, or raging seas. Grand operas, ballets, and symphonies became as common to him as the sounds of the city. They formed the backdrop to his studies as he became a familiar sight to all the Opera House company. He was transported daily and left behind the rigours of mathematics and grammatical structure to enter this world of music and colour.

Once, during a rehearsal for *The Marriage of Figaro*, he was imagining what it was like to be the conductor, to lead and control the music, the musicians, the voices. Eyes closed, he saw himself at gala performances, royalty and the grand people of wealth smiling from the boxes, gloved hands applauding, cheers from the audience, the whole company acknowledging him from the stage ... Immersed in his dream, he didn't notice his atlas and pencil box slip from his lap. The book hit the floor with a loud *whump* and the pencils spilled out, along with several marbles he'd been storing inside. He jumped up and ran to the next row and then the next, trying to stop his rolling and clattering pencils and marbles. They travelled under a succession of seats before coming to rest against the lip of the orchestra pit. The music staggered to a ragged stop as the conductor stepped up from the pit and turned pointedly in his direction.

"Herr Dirigent," Sigmund's voice was just above a whisper as he stood in the aisle. He felt the impatient eyes of the stage company upon him.

He was banished to the farthest corner backstage for the remainder of the season. This did not, however, diminish his pleasure in listening to the music and watching the performers. He decided to speak with Herr Dirigent before the end of the season. He was determined to discover what he must do in order to prepare himself for such a position. He would study; he would do whatever was necessary. The glory of music would be his life.

Atto Primo: Scena Quinta

A me fanciulla, un candido
E trepido desire
Questi effigiò dolcissimo
Signor dell'avvenire,
Quando nè cieli il raggio
Di sua beltà vedea,
E tutta me pascea
Di quel divino error.
Sentia che amore è palpito
Dell'universo intero,
Misterioso, altero,
Croce e delizia al cor!

Violetta, *La Traviata*

Act I: Scene V

When I was young,
with an innocent, budding desire,
I dreamed a sweet image
of the master of my future.
I saw him in a brilliant radiance
and I lived on that divine error.
It's said that love is the
heartbeat of the universe,
mysterious, unfathomable,
now my heart's burden and delight.

(translation by Roy C. Dicks)

CHAPTER EIGHT

By the end of April, Sheila's Granny came home from the hospital.

The next Saturday, Sheila came in from delivering the papers and nearly stumbled as she walked into the kitchen. Sigmund Maier was at the kitchen table, sipping tea with her mother. A bouquet of pink and white flowers was in a vase on the counter. Her mother turned to watch her come into the room. She had the strangest look on her face, all smiley and kind of excited.

"Sheila, dear, go and wash your hands and come and say hello to Mr. Maier."

As she stood before her dresser mirror, Sheila's mind was racing. *Sheila, dear* ... Did she find out about the music and about the notes? She straightened her sweater and brushed the lint from her navy skirt. Reaching for calm, she entered the kitchen.

Her mother gestured for Sheila to take the seat next to Mr. Maier. She pointed at the flowers. "Mr. Maier has brought flowers for your Granny, Sheila. You can take them in to her when she wakes up." She turned to her guest. "Now, Mr. Maier, you must continue telling me all about your home in Dresden."

It was like one of those surreal paintings in the library art books. Her mother pouring tea and asking Mr. Maier questions about his life back in Europe – Mr. Maier giving answers, talking about the beautiful churches of Dresden, the cherry trees, the museums, the opera houses ... As she listened, Sheila relaxed. Her mother was just being nice after all.

As he spoke, she pictured his childhood city. She imagined Dresden to be very old and very beautiful. Everywhere – statues, fountains, wide sweeping staircases, crystal chandeliers, lovely old bridges crossing the river, and great huge pipe organs beneath stained glass.

"And your family, Mr. Maier? Do you have any family in Dresden?"

He smiled at Sheila's mother. "No," he said, "my family is no longer in Dresden."

"Oh. Did they leave because of the East Germans and all that?"

"No, Frau Barnes." He continued to smile.

Sheila watched her mother start to frown and shift in her chair.

"Well, where are—"

Sheila sat up and cut off her mother in mid-sentence. "Mom? Can I go on a field trip to Casa Loma?"

"Sheila – don't interrupt Mr. Maier and me."

He cleared his throat. "It is of no consequence. In fact, I must leave." He turned to Sheila and smiled. "Good afternoon, Fräulein. Frau Barnes, thank you for the tea. It was most refreshing."

Mr. Maier had just reached the door to the basement stairs when he stopped and turned back. "Frau Barnes, I was given tickets for the opera. For next Saturday. I wonder if you would care to attend. As my guest."

Eleanor put her cup back on the saucer, the china on china sounding loud and startled. "Oh, Mr. Maier – what day did you say?"

"Saturday, the 11th."

"No. I'm working 3-11 that whole weekend. I work afternoons every other weekend." She placed her hand against her throat, running her fingers along the neckline of her blouse. "But thanks for offering."

"Ah then, it is unfortunate. Another time, perhaps, yes?"

Sheila watched as her mother nodded and smiled, her eyes extra bright, her hand now at the back of her head, patting her hair. He was at the door; he paused, turned back and was now frowning. "I wonder, Frau Barnes," he said. "Perhaps Fräulein Barnes would care to attend in your place?"

Sheila swallowed. Eleanor turned and looked quizzically at her daughter.

He started to open the door and shrugged. "Unless you think that it would be too, ah, dull for her, Frau Barnes?"

Sheila held her breath.

She could see that her mother was thinking hard, her eyes darting from Mr. Maier to Sheila and back again. It was a moment before she spoke, but to Sheila it seemed to take minutes. "I guess that would be all right." Her mother squared her shoulders and crossed her arms over her chest. "Of course, she'll pay her own bus fare."

Sigmund Maier smiled. "Of course."

Sheila wasn't sure, but she thought Mr. Maier winked at her as Eleanor turned to set the cups into the sink.

Sheila didn't know what to expect; other than school plays, she'd never to been to a live performance. Opera. The word sat heavy on her tongue, like the music. Going through her side of the closet and drawers, she scrutinized her clothes. She blew a raspberry into the closet, and sighed aloud. "Just one measly pair of go-go boots. Just one."

Her mother had a couple of fancy dresses at the far end of the closet, covered in zippered plastic bags. One was black with rhinestones sewn into the skinny shoulder straps; the other was a long pink satin gown. She tried them on, struggling with unfamiliar clasps, side zippers and built-in bras. The straps of the black dress would not stay up, and the pink gown buckled at the ground, inches too long.

She thought about asking Mr. Bernstein what she should wear to an opera but he was a man. And he was Jewish. Granny said that all the Jews hate the Germans.

That night at dinner, Alan and Paul stared at her.

"Does this mean Mr. Maier and you are going out on a date?" Alan's smile was merciless. Paul mouthed kissy-faces when her mother's back was turned. Sheila ignored them.

For two days, she agonized over her outfit, flipping through the Eaton's catalogue. Carnaby Street was on every page; miniskirts and the mod look with bold psychedelic colours, long lashes and thick eyeliner peeking from beneath straight-cut bangs.

She decided to ask her grandmother's advice. Sometimes Granny could be helpful.

"Saturday evenings at an opera are bound to be pretty fancy, Sheila. Your school clothes probably won't do."

"But I don't have anything that isn't for school."

"Well, Dear, maybe you could use some of your newspaper money for a new dress to go to the opera."

Sheila frowned. Granny was more forgetful since breaking her hip.

Before Sheila could answer, Eleanor shouldered open the door and pushed into the room with a basin and towels.

"A new dress? If this is going to cost a bundle, then you may as well forget it." She began to yank at the buttons on Granny's nightgown.

"Oh no, Mom. I'll wear my blue dress. That'll be just fine, right, Granny?"

Her nicest dress was a light blue A-line style, made from hopsacking and it had a small white lace collar. It was a lined winter dress.

Granny said nothing but set her mouth into a firm line. Gathering up the dinner tray, Sheila noticed that her mother held her mouth in the same way.

The only dressy coat she owned was a camel hair hand-me-down from a second cousin. It was missing a button from the cuff but, still, it looked better than her nylon ski jacket.

After her mother left for work on Saturday, Sheila plugged in the hot rollers. They were last year's Christmas gift to her mother, paid for by selling Christmas cards and wrapping paper door-to-door.

On Christmas morning, her mother had held them on her lap, one hand on each end of the plastic case. Sheila especially liked that case – creamy white, with soft pink mod flowers splashed all over. The hot rollers were the same pink as the flowers. When set up and plugged in, the rollers were raised in stepping-stone style, the fat ones low and to the outside, and the thinner ones poking up higher. A small red light turned on when the rollers were ready.

While her brothers fought over who would put together the road race set, Sheila pointed out the various features to her mother.

Eleanor smiled and nodded and then said, "Well, Sheila, if my perm wears out, I guess I can always use these." She then turned her cheek to accept Sheila's kiss. For all of Christmas Day, the pink and white plastic case sat under the tree with the other gifts. On Boxing Day her mother put the rollers in the cupboard under the bathroom sink.

By four o'clock on Saturday, Sheila's straight shoulder-length hair had been transformed into a mass of soft bouncy curls. By six o'clock most of the curl was gone, except for one strand that stuck out in a half-hearted twist, even after she brushed and brushed it with a wet hairbrush.

At the last moment, she risked using her mother's lipstick: Pink Passion. Sheila put it on after popping her head in to say goodnight to Granny. She nearly knocked Mr. Maier over in her rush to exit the side door. They rode the bus in silence for most of the journey to the subway station.

"It's really warm tonight, isn't it, Mr. Maier?" She swayed in the seat next to him. "I guess I didn't need to wear my coat."

He smiled at her, saying nothing.

When they reached the subway station, he stopped just past the ticket booth.

"I will take your coat, Sheila."

"It's okay. I'm fine."

He held out his arm and tilted his head slightly. She took off her coat and he carried it the rest of the way.

Granny was right. Many people arrived in evening gowns and tuxedos. Some women had long gloves and fur stoles or fancy shawls. They all wore their hair in elaborate styles piled on top of their heads or teased into hair-sprayed upsweeps. Her own straight hair hung limp, the errant strand struggling to free itself from behind her ear. She was sweating, and there were scuff-marks on her shoes.

Mr. Maier took her elbow, leading her through the crowd. Climbing the stairs, they made their way to the balcony and their seats. They were just three rows back from the railing. People were not so stylish up here and Sheila began to relax a bit. Music drifted back from the front, some of it familiar, some of it rising and lowering scales, none of it blending nicely. She heard a clarinet squeak – somewhere, she was sure, Miss Clarke was scowling. Sheila hoped that they would sound better during the opera. Mr. Maier would be disappointed if they didn't.

She scanned the people nearby, trying to listen to the conversations, moving only her eyes to watch. They were a mix of men and women but, with few exceptions, all older. Many chatted quietly together, usually women with women, and men with men. Others were studying their programs; Mr. Maier adjusted his glasses and then leaned toward her.

"It is good to read the synopsis, Fräulein. It will assist you to follow the story. You will recall *La Traviata* is performed in archaic Italian – a language which is today dead." He took her booklet and opened it to the correct page. A grey-haired woman, sitting in front and to the left of Mr. Maier, gave them an appraising look over her shoulder. Sheila blushed, and the woman turned her attention back to the front of the concert hall. Mr. Maier was studying his program.

"Mr. Maier?"

"Yes?"

"Will this be like your records?"

He frowned slightly before answering. "If you mean the music, Sheila, well, then, yes, the music will be the same. If you mean the emotion, then no, you will feel different after seeing the performance." He crossed his arms and leaned back into his seat. "Each performance is unique and solitary. One may record opera to listen at will, but you cannot contain the whole on flat vinyl disks."

She puzzled over what he meant, once more listening to the conversations around her. She speculated about the others on the balcony, wondering if they came here all the time. Could people seem like they'd been there before, even if it was the first time?

At Ashbrook, there were Grade 9 students who started out like they knew exactly what they were doing and where they were going at all times.

Beside her, Mr. Maier opened his program and started studying it again.

A woman and man came in two rows just ahead of them, and moved over to their seats. She was beautiful, her long blonde hair all twisted up on top of her head; hot-pink ball earrings dangled from her earlobes. The man took his seat just after her, and as he leaned to one side to adjust his position, Sheila watched as he brushed his lips against the woman's neck, and then sat back, watching her. The woman didn't say a word, just turned and smiled at the man and then looked away, opened her program, and started to read.

Sheila placed her own hand on the left side of her neck. She ran her fingertips against the skin there and shuddered. Would a boy ever kiss her there? She closed her eyes and imagined how that would feel – imagined the things she had read in the *True Confessions* magazine. Some of it made sense, like the kissing, even if she thought the tongue stuff would be disgusting. Other things in the stories weren't clear to her, but she felt excited in her stomach and tingly when she read the magazine, trying to understand what they were really talking about. Maybe she wasn't supposed to feel that way but the girls at school talked about that stuff like they understood the whole thing. How did they know?

A soft bell began to chime and she opened her eyes, looking for the clock. People walking down the aisles began to quicken their pace, filling the few remaining seats. She leaned forward. The lower level was a sea of balding heads and blonde bouffant hair. The houselights caught the occasional facet or sequin. She wondered if there was any royalty there; it was obvious that they were all very rich and probably famous. Maybe some were millionaires or movie stars. Or rock and roll stars. Big-name musicians.

One day, she'd be able to tell her papa that she'd been to the opera. She smiled to herself, thinking that he'd be proud of that –

that being a musician, he'd be so proud that his little girl went to the opera. When he came back for her, she'd be able to tell him.

The orchestra stilled its cacophony and the lights dimmed.

The conductor entered the orchestra pit. Everybody applauded as he stepped up to his dais, bowed slightly and then turned his full attention to the orchestra. For the rest of her life, Sheila would remember the way her stomach got all tight and full of butterflies as the overture began, and then the lights completely darkened and then, finally, the thick red curtain slid upwards.

Inside – a swirling, marvellous party of music and singing and laughter and fancy costumes and colours. The star lady was kind of fat, but she had a beautiful dress on, and jewels that flashed in the lights, and a nice-looking man kept singing to her. Only for her, only for the lady in the jewels. The man couldn't take his eyes off her, and Sheila knew that the lady could make him jump over the moon for her. Soon enough, Sheila was completely and absolutely lost in it all.

CHAPTER NINE

AT FIRST, IT WAS SMALL things. The humidor was moved into the pantry beside the kitchen. Old, dark walls were gradually covered with colourful paintings Hilda purchased from street artists. His father's photograph was joined by a clock then a pair of Delft blue vases, followed by a small silver-framed mirror, and a tiny ceramic pot filled with painted china roses. Hilda even bought a Chinese fan from Herr Schneider.

One evening, as Hilda and Sigmund returned from a walk, they stopped in the foyer. Grimmel and Schneider were in their accustomed positions, but instead of worn, wooden chess pieces, the table held several silk scarves and linens, delicate fans and etched cigarette holders. Herr Grimmel looked glum. Schneider rose quickly and, opening one of the fans, waved it about as he enthused about his latest venture.

"Chinese," he explained, "is a language I will soon study. As I am sure you realize, Frau Maier, it is so necessary to immerse oneself in a foreign culture's everyday objects when studying a new language. They assist in the absorption of syntax and meaning."

Hilda nodded and smiled, but said nothing. Encouraged, Schneider continued. "As I purchased a few things, I realized that there is a market for such lovely items." He lifted a painted silk scarf then rearranged it carefully among its companions on the table. "I may start modestly, but in the spring I will take a stall in the market and eventually, I expect to lease a shop." He raised the open fan and pointed to the blank wall beside him. "Schneider's Fine Imports and Wholesale Goods."

Grimmel hunched further down into his chair, folding his arms across his chest as he expelled a short burst of air from his nose. He opened his mouth as if to speak, the gap between his front teeth almost comical – and then he closed his mouth again.

Ignoring his companion, Dietrich Schneider offered them a serene smile. "I have already written to my cousin and have asked him to keep an eye on suitable locations in New York City. A shrewd businessman must be prepared to expand overseas."

Sigmund looked at the few pieces on the table. "Has anyone bought any of these, ah, fine things yet?"

A slow grin spread over Lukas Grimmel's face, as Schneider shrugged and waved his hands with small quick motions. "Why, I have only just embarked on this journey."

Hilda stepped up to the table. "How much for this, Herr Schneider?" She opened a fan, and a spray of cherry blossoms unfolded from the ivory handle. A pink silk tassel swung from the end. Sigmund thought it looked cheap and silly. His mother purchased the fan, and its spray of painted flowers joined the other items on the fireplace mantel.

Gradually, the mantel filled to overabundance; eventually, Sigmund could barely see his father's photograph.

There were other changes. Hilda had visitors. Schneider and Grimmel were invited to supper once a month. Hilda's co-workers – a Frenchwoman, Giselle Baron, and one or two of the other dressmakers from the Semper – would come for coffee and cards on Monday afternoons.

Sigmund put up with the two from the foyer; conversations were mostly Schneider's monologues, but at least the topics could be interesting: travel, languages, and strange and unusual cultural practices. It was the other group, his mother's work friends, that caused too much chaos.

They always arrived together, chattering in quick bursts and punctuating the air with staccato giggles. Occasionally they brought sweet wine or small cakes. Younger than his mother, they would come close to shouting when the card game became exciting. Sigmund failed to see what interested his mother in these women. He usually stayed in his room and read, or slipped downstairs to observe Herr Schneider and Herr Grimmel at chess. He found the noise of his mother's new friends unsettling, the laughter incomprehensible.

Whenever he was present Giselle would toss her blonde head and make a fuss over him, hugging him, kissing his cheeks, giving him little gifts of chocolates and wine gums. When Hilda protested that she was spoiling him, Giselle would make little waving motions with her delicate hands and pretend to be annoyed.

"Hilda, only too soon this beautiful young man will break hearts, won't you, *Chéri*?" Ignoring his flushed cheeks, she chortled, "Take note of my words, Hilda, he is one to break hearts."

Sigmund was relieved when he could finally escape to his room. Giselle's kisses were always wet and her breath sugary and warm. One time, after her usual greeting, she did not let him go. She hugged him close and pressed her lower body and thighs against him, her hands patting his back, her breath on his ear. The others were clustered in the kitchen, helping his mother. Ashamed, he felt heat in his groin. He pulled away and stepped back. Giselle's eyes were bright. She was laughing at him, laughing at the boy she teased, he was sure of it. But she was his mother's friend; he said nothing.

The other women returned and, thankfully, he was able to leave.

Sometimes he wondered if it had not been better before; there was order and quiet. He knew what to expect, and if he had had more time, his grandfather may have yet begun to see him, if not to like him, at least to acknowledge what his grandson would accomplish as a young man. But then he thought about his grandfather's anger and decided that some of the change was good.

There was the music. Hilda purchased an old gramophone. The wax cylinders played two- and four-minute highlights from operas and symphonies that Sigmund had come to love. Often, they listened to the radio. On Wednesday and Saturday evenings their station broadcast all sorts of music, including jazz and ragtime. Sigmund was less certain of this music; it reminded him of Giselle's and the other women's laughter.

It was to a jazz tune that Hilda began to dance that February night. At first, she was content to spin and kick on her own while Sigmund watched warily from his seat. Laughing, she took his two hands into hers.

"Sigmund – come! Dance with me!" Pulling him up, she led him around and around the small space, their shadows travelling over the walls and furniture. Keeping his eyes on her feet, Sigmund tried to follow the steps. The scent of her perfume competed with the smell of her body. His hands and neck were wet. He felt dizzy, exhilarated and terrified. Never before had his mother behaved in such a way; he wondered if she were ill.

He wanted to dance all night. He wanted her to stop.

Just when he thought he would fall to the floor, the music finished.

"Ah, Sigmund." She was breathless, flushed and smiling wildly. "I have not danced in years. Not since that last time at The Terrace. With your father."

He sat down and waited. She pressed a lace-edged hankie to her upper lip, and then dabbed behind her neck. Despite the short bob her hair had recently undergone, errant tendrils hung damp and loose.

"That was a long time ago." The smile was changing, moving to softness, to longing. "We were going to the opera – but first supper at The Terrace. And there was a small orchestra. A very small orchestra." A slight laugh. "So many young men. So many fine, young men from all over Europe." A pause, and then, "From all over the world. I wore my green silk dress, with Maltese lace so and so." She brushed a hand over her shoulders, her neck.

"*Bitte, Mutter.*" Sigmund kept watching her face. She was not looking at the photograph but out the window, toward the western sky. Hilda moved her hands over her eyes, and again, down to her neck. "*Mutter,*" he tried again, "tell me, please."

She shifted to the old man's chair and stood leaning forward against the back, her hands gripping the top. "He said I had beautiful eyes, but I have never seen eyes like his. They shone so that when he looked at you, it was as if all of Heaven was inside." She blushed and laughed with a sigh. "When I was with

him, I thought like a poet." Her hands relaxed and she stroked
the top of the chair. "We met at the Zwinger. He was a student,
you know. Did I ever tell you that he read Goethe and Schiller?
Studying Mine Engineering, you understand, and he read
Goethe and Schiller, imagine. He was visiting ..." She stopped,
looked directly at Sigmund, and began again. "He was a student
in the Academy at Freiberg. They were visiting the Zwinger and
I was there, with my father and mother and cousin Helga. He
was so polite, he and the other young men. They invited us all to
supper. My father was so impressed, one of the students was the
British ambassador's son, and another was a cousin to a Russian
prince. My father was so impressed." She stopped, lost in her rev-
erie, dancing once more at The Terrace.

"*Mutter.*" Barely breathing, Sigmund waited.

She looked at him again, seeing him at last. "Siggy. Tomorrow.
We will talk again tomorrow, but now, it is time for bed." The
atmosphere faded, and Frau Maier returned. "Yes, Sigmund, it is
past time for bed."

Arriving at the opera house the next day, he stepped from the
daylight of the afternoon and into the dark hallway. He blinked to
sharpen his vision, and breathed in the familiar dust and musky
backstage odours. It was February 20, 1930 and just one week
from his fifteenth birthday. Today, he would ask Herr Dirigent
for an appointment, to tell him of his passion for music, to request
music lessons. Explain that he would clean lavatories, polish brass
door handles – do anything to pay for those lessons. But he would
have them. He would learn the secrets of all the great conduc-
tors, one way or another. Today, he would tell Herr Dirigent of
the grand Semper Opera House that he, Sigmund Maier, would
no longer be banished to the wings. Today he would demand ...
Sigmund stopped walking, leaned against a doorjamb and gathered his thoughts. No. Today he would ask for an appointment.
Ask, not demand. He would be polite and respectful. He nodded
and then straightened. But if the man would not listen, then, yes,
then Sigmund Maier would demand.

He was coming close to the corridor that led to the costum-
ing department. He could hear voices from around the corner.

The main hall dead-ended and he turned to his left. Ahead, just outside the sewing room entrance, he saw several of the staff clustered together. They stopped their excited chatter as one of them tapped another on the upper arm and pointed in his direction. They all turned and faced him. Several looked away, either down at the floor, or somewhere past his head. Giselle stepped forward and called to him in a strange, tense voice. She raised both arms and ran in his direction.

"Sigmund – Siggy, come, *Chéri*. Come to Giselle." She held him close, crying, her words spilling out and falling onto his shoulders. He could not, would not hold on to what she was saying.

Myron Klauss was a gruff, heavy-set stagehand. He pried Sigmund from Giselle's arms and held his shoulders in an insistent grip. Klauss' eyes were fierce, and Sigmund noticed for the first time that they were a peculiar shade of green. The man's hands, he also noticed, were shaking. Sigmund shifted his focus to the stagehand's mouth and the several days' growth of beard surrounding it. He began to hear the man's words.

"Sigmund, are you listening to me? Your mother – your mother is dead – run down by a truck. She had gone to find some thread or ribbon or something else, no one is sure. She stepped from the curb. Giselle saw it all. There was nothing to be done." Myron's breath smelled of the sausage he'd eaten for lunch, his voice held acceptance and resignation. He was a solid, reliable man; all denial sat frozen on Sigmund's lips, unuttered. Giselle continued to sob behind him.

For the remainder of this day, and the day following, Sigmund kept himself busy. There were arrangements to be made and, while there was no shortage of willing helpers, it was essential to oversee each detail. When Giselle announced that she would stay at the apartment, he was polite but firm.

"I can care for myself, thank you, Fräulein."

"Oh Siggy, *mon pauvre, pauvre* Siggy!" Her eyes welled with tears. "You are just a boy, and your dear *maman* ... *ma chère amie*, Hilda ..."

For the fifth time in as many minutes, Giselle prostrated herself across the kitchen table, burying her face in her arms. Sigmund restrained himself from reaching across the table to hit her. "Fräulein Baron. Mademoiselle – please." When she finally slowed her sobs and sat back in her chair, he struggled to produce what he hoped was a kind smile. "I appreciate very much your concern, but I wish to be alone this evening."

Her lower lip began to quiver and he hastened to add, "I will need your help in other ways. Would you assist me with my mother's dresses, her things?" The distraction won him a few minutes of peace, and when other visitors from the Semper arrived, he discreetly enlisted their help to convince Giselle he could take care of himself. She was almost out the door when, for one terrible moment, tears began to fall once more while she moved back toward the kitchen.

"I need to put the dishes away. Oh, no. I must not leave you with all that."

Thankfully, Myron intervened. "Come, Woman. He wants to be alone tonight. You only make him sad, with your tears and your nonsense." Steering her towards the door, Myron looked back at Sigmund for a moment and nodded solemnly. Sigmund nodded in response and closed the door.

He was just sitting down in the kitchen when a short, quick knock startled him. He imagined Giselle waiting on the other side; somehow, she must have escaped Myron and returned to rescue him from his grief. Resigned, he walked to the door. He supposed it would not be so bad after all – at least her tears gave him something else to consider besides the silence of the small apartment.

It was not Giselle. Instead, it was Lukas Grimmel. He was pale, and Sigmund could see that his eyes were red; around his nostrils and upper lip it was raw-looking. His mouth opened and closed several times before he said anything.

"Sigmund. I – Dietrich and I, we want to know if you need anything. If there is something ..." He shrugged and tried to smile. "May I come in?"

Sigmund moved from the door and motioned him to enter. Grimmel went straight to the kitchen and filled the kettle, calling out over the gush of running water. "My mother always said coffee for the mind, but tea for body and soul." He moved quickly and quietly about the kitchen as Sigmund watched from the doorway. In a few minutes, the dishes and cups on the drainboard were put away on the shelf. A pot of tea steamed on the table and, like magic, a small bundle appeared from Grimmel's pocket. He unwrapped several sugar-sprinkled biscuits, which he arranged on a plate.

He nodded toward the table. "Sit. You will have tea and biscuits." Silently, Sigmund did as he was instructed. The tea was hot, and the biscuits sweet and tasty. He looked across at his neighbour. "Thank you."

They drank tea and ate together in silence. When they finished, Grimmel washed and put away the dishes. He placed his hand on Sigmund's shoulder. "Now, you must sleep."

Sigmund nodded and went to his room, closing the door and moving quickly to the bed. Taking off only his shoes, he pulled the eiderdown over his head and almost immediately fell asleep.

When he awoke, it was still dark and he could hear noises in the other room. For a moment, he thought that his mother was sewing. He rose quickly, cracked open the door, and peeked down the hall. He could make out a pair of figures near the closed apartment door – silhouettes in the dark. He recognized the two profiles, Grimmel and Schneider. The apartment door opened and the dim light from the hall confirmed their identities. Schneider put his arm around Grimmel's waist and spoke softly.

"You can come back before he gets up."

Grimmel shook his head. "No, I should be here."

"I am missing you." Schneider had a playful smile on his face. He bent forward and kissed his roommate on the lips. Grimmel's arms moved around the other man's shoulders and he returned the kiss.

Sigmund felt the floor shift under him, and pulled his head back from the door, his mind racing. He knew about homosexuals, but not once had he thought that these two were anything but old friends. He imagined them together, naked. He imagined Schneider trying to kiss him, Grimmel watching. He heard his grandfather's voice. "Pigshit farmer. Filthy pigshit farmer." Silently closing the door, he returned to bed and buried himself beneath the covers. He waited for the sun to rise. He would not think about it.

At breakfast he was polite when he asked Grimmel to leave. "I wish to be alone now, to sort out my mother's things." He smiled at the man. "You understand."

Sigmund pulled back when he tried to hug him at the door, offering his hand instead. "Thank you for the tea, Herr Grimmel."

As he listened to the man's footsteps retreat down the stairs, Grandfather Mann's voice echoed with each footfall. "Pigshit. Pigshit. Pigshit."

Sigmund found the small wooden box that was in the bottom drawer of his mother's rosewood dresser. After his grandfather's death, they carried the low, narrow dresser from the parlour, down the hall, and into the bedroom. But Hilda had continued to sleep on the little cot. No longer wheeled in and out each day, the cot remained where the dresser had been. During the day, she covered it with several small cushions and a green spread that she had made. It was edged with a matching green fringe. The cushions had tassels on each corner, tassels that she had brought from the sewing room at the Semper.

Sigmund sat on the cot with the box in his lap, his back resting against two of the cushions. With his finger, he traced the initials carved on top: S M. He had never seen this box, and assumed his mother had it made for him, for his birthday. It was new and unused.

Lifting the small brass clasp, he opened it and looked inside. There was a letter, folded and flat; a pressed rose, once pink or red; and a small gold straight pin with a miniature leaf at one end. He lifted the rose and it broke from its brittle stem. Placing it back inside, he removed the letter, carefully unfolding the paper.

8th October, 1914
My dearest H,

Helmut has agreed and it will be for
the best. In name only, until I can came
back for you. This cannot last much
longer, six months at most, and we will
soon be in much better times. I would
send for you both as soon as it is safe. I
am certain that your family will under-
stood and, in time, accept what we had
to do. Until then, I am always and ever,

Yours –
S

Sigmund struggled to make sense of the enigmatic message. "H" must be his mother and his father must be this "Helmut", but he stopped at the signature, "S". And what was it, this thing that "H" and "S" "had to do"? Whoever "S" was, he – or she – had some difficulty with grammar, as Sigmund found no less than three errors in the few, hasty lines. Hasty. He wondered why he thought that. Perhaps he assumed a rush because of the mistakes, the brevity of the note, the informality and mystery of the initials.

After a few minutes, he re-folded the letter and replaced it in the box. It would remain a mystery. There was no one he could ask.

CHAPTER TEN

SHEILA AND MR. MAIER WENT to the opera once more, once to the ballet and finally, to a brass quintet performance at the university. Each time, Mr. Maier's tickets were for evenings when Eleanor had to work.

That last time he came with the tickets to the top of the stairs, and spoke with Sheila's mother. Sheila waited in her bedroom, holding absolutely still to hear everything that was said. Sheila did not like her mother's tone. Not at all.

"I'm not sure a young girl should be gallivanting around with an older man, Mr. Maier." She paused for a heartbeat before starting again. "And it just seems to me that every time you get these tickets, it's for a night when I'm on afternoons or nights." She imagined her mother was crossing her arms. "It's like you plan this."

Sheila felt sick.

Mr. Maier's voice was low, almost soothing in response. She heard "next Saturday" and "dinner first" and then her mother giggling.

She held her breath; she could not remember ever hearing her mother giggle. Did she ever sound like that with her father? Maybe if they had laughed more together ...

"Well, Mr. Maier, I suppose if you're taking me to the show next Saturday, Sheila can go hear this brass band on Friday night."

It was a short performance and Sheila and Mr. Maier came home before 10:30. He stopped at the landing and offered to make tea.

Sheila had her hand on the knob of the upstairs door. She looked back over her shoulder. "That's very nice of you but I don't think I better. I have to look in on my Granny, Mr. Maier."

He smiled at her. "Yes, Fräulein. You are a good girl. Just so. Another time, *ja*?"

She nodded and then went through the door. She heard his footsteps head downstairs.

Granny was asleep. And snoring. Paul was in his room, the light off.

Before she even understood what she was doing, Sheila made her way back downstairs to Mr. Maier's door. She stopped before knocking and took a peek behind her. There was no light coming from under Alan's door. He often stayed out late on nights when their mother worked. Although she sometimes heard him sneak down the stairs, Sheila never told. Seemed he was out again tonight. She turned back. Should she knock or just go back upstairs?

The door to Mr. Maier's apartment opened, and he looked down at her. "You have come for tea then?"

He must have heard her come down the stairs. "I, ah, Granny's asleep, and I thought, I just thought—"

"Just so. Come in, come in. The kettle is almost ready."

They sat at the little kitchen table. He brought out a small plate of cookies; plain digestive ones, sprinkled with sugar crystals.

He saw her looking at the plate. "These biscuits. I have enjoyed these biscuits since I was a young boy." He poured their tea while she nibbled on one of the cookies.

They weren't chocolate chip or double fudge, but they were nice. She lifted her cup to take a sip of tea, blowing first to cool it. It was not as strong as her Granny always made it. She glanced up over the rim of the cup. "Nice tea."

"Thank you, Sheila. It is from Ceylon. Sometimes, you understand, I have Chinese tea, but not tonight." He sat across from her and sipped from his cup.

She took another tiny bite of her biscuit then glanced up again. "It was my birthday on Thursday. May 30."

"Ah, Sheila, your birthday. I did not know. Happy birthday."
He paused. "You are fifteen now, I think so, yes?"

"Yeah – yes, I turned fifteen."

He nodded and smiled. "Ah. Just so. Fifteen."

"Thank you again for taking me tonight. It was a beautiful
concert."

He thrust out his lower lip. "The trumpet was weak in the
final piece."

"It was? I thought it was all great."

"Yes, he started strong, but lost his way. It was unfortunate."

"Sometimes when I play the clarinet in school, Mr. Bernstein
says I start strong, but that I lose my way."

"You lose your way when you do not concentrate, Sheila." He
took a cookie from the plate and peered at it. "You must focus;
you must always focus and hear nothing else but the music." He
looked up at her. "Keep all things from your mind, Sheila, except
the notes on the page and the baton of the conductor – then you
will never be lost."

His expression was so, so fierce. She felt the hairs on her
arms rise. He kept staring at her. She should say something, but
what?

He smiled and the fierceness went away. "Young people, you
do not always understand, yes? I am just an old man, Sheila, with
strong ideas. But," he fixed her with those eyes again, "strong
ideas kept me safe. Remember that as you grow into a woman.
Strength in the mind is power in this world. Power."

The hairs on her arm rose again. "Sure. I'll remember."

He sat back in his chair and appraised her. "You are almost a
woman now, Sheila. You are so small and quiet, I forget that."

She looked down at her tea and shrugged. "A woman? I
dunno. My mom thinks I'm just a kid."

"You think so? Why then does she let you take care of so
much?"

She shrugged again.

"Why do you do most of the work here, and must still keep
to your studies and such?"

There was this great lump in her chest. Sheila could feel it, and a stinging in her eyes. She tried to swallow. She had to explain it to him, that she did the work because it was the best thing right now to help her mom, that the boys didn't know how to do the stuff, that Granny was old, that Mom was, Mom was, Mom was ... and Papa, he was ...

She couldn't stop it. The stinging in her eyes and throat kept growing, and then great huge sobs choked out of her mouth, tears fell from her eyes, and she wanted to crawl under the table and hide. He was looking at her, his mouth saying things, and she was crying, and she couldn't hear him and then he moved his chair and put his arms around her and pulled her close and she cried and cried and cried into his chest.

She could have stayed there forever, in his arms, her cheek pressed against his clean white shirt, leaning her weight against his warm chest, her fingers clutching his upper arms. She felt his hands pat her back, and heard deep soothing sounds from his chest, odd foreign words she didn't understand but liked the sound of.

She had never felt this safe.

Gradually, her sobbing slowed and Mr. Maier kissed the top of her head. She felt his warm breath on her hair, and one hand moved from patting her back to stroking her head, his large palm moving against her long hair. His other hand remained on her back, no longer moving, just holding her.

She felt so embarrassed. She'd just turned into an absolute baby, and here he was treating her like the little girl she really was. Almost a woman, he'd said. She pulled away and ran the back of her hand against her wet face. Taking a paper napkin from the table, she wiped at her eyes, at her nose. "Oh Mr. Maier, I, I was only, oh gosh, I am sorry. I didn't mean – I really didn't, I'm sorry."

He had such a strange look on his face. His eyes were wide, and his mouth slightly open. He was breathing hard, like when her mom was about to explode over something she'd messed up again. She knew she'd really done it this time. Crossed the line – no more operas, no more records and books. This was going to be like the Newtons. Done. Finished. Over. She sat right back in her chair and waited.

Sigmund struggled to keep himself very still, to slow his breathing. This was – it was so strange, he only held the *Mäuschen* for a moment, to quiet her. That mother of hers would go mad if she saw him holding the girl. Sheila. The *Mäuschen*. A child. And yet not a child, or else how did this happen, this rising of the blood in his ears, in his hands, his groin? *Gott in Himmel!* He dropped a hand into his lap. He went to speak, but his throat was thick and hot. He swallowed, and tried again. "Sheila. I only meant to, to comfort you, *ja?*"

"Yeah, I'm so sorry."

He could see she was miserable. She was apologizing to him. Yes. So she did not notice, did not know. Sigmund felt the blood leave his hands; his ears stopped ringing. But he remained stiff in his groin. For one split second, he imagined her soft white hand on him, and he blinked hard.

"So. You are feeling better, yes? A crying is a good help, I think. Yes?"

She nodded again, eyes down, her face so sad.

He wiped at his mouth with his hand. "Sheila, you have much to make you sad, but you must learn to take that sadness and put it away. Control it, Sheila, or it will control you. Make you weak. You are a strong girl, strong and smart." She started to protest but he continued, "No, now you must listen, Sheila. You wash your face in the bathroom here, you go upstairs and you remember that you are the strong one. In this house of snivelling baby boys and weak, foolish women, you are the strong one." He pointed at her. "You, yes?"

She nodded.

"And next week, I will try for the tickets to *Aida*, yes? In July, they are coming for three days to the big arena – with elephants, Sheila, and a chorus of hundreds. There has been nothing like it, and we will go. Yes?"

"Oh yes, Mr. Maier. Yes." She rose from the table, and raced into the bathroom. He carried the dishes to the sink; from the bathroom he could hear her running the taps. He hurried through the dishes, nearly dropping two cups before placing them on the drainboard. The toilet flushed. She ran the water again for a moment. He walked over to the kitchen door, folding his hands before him, hiding his erection. He tried to think of the music, tried to clear his mind of all the strange thoughts.

The bathroom door opened and she stepped back out and into the kitchen. She ran her fingers through her hair. "How do I look?" She shrugged and glanced away for a moment. "I mean, do I look like I've been crying?" She added, "Much?"

He smiled then stopped when he felt the corners tremble. "You look fine, Sheila. Fine."

She grinned then moved past him to the door. She stopped and turned around. "Mr. Maier?"

"Yes?"

Before he could say anything, she rose up on her toes, put her hands up on his shoulders and pulled him down to kiss his cheek. She whispered into his ear, "You're a really nice man. I love you." She released him, and then ran through the doorway and up the stairs.

He closed the door and leaned his head against it. *I love you.* Love. Love like that of a daughter?

He'd never been a father. He had always been careful, even with prostitutes. A father? Surely that was the love she meant. Her *I love you* was the love of a daughter or a fond niece. Uncle Sigmund. He had never been Uncle Sigmund either. He closed his eyes, saw her naked.

Call me Uncle Sigmund and touch me here my *Mäuschen*, and touch me here and here.

Mein Gott! He must be careful, these ideas were foolish, madness. The stuff of dark nights.

Holding himself through his pants, he walked into his bedroom. The dishes could wait; he would finish with these thoughts, find release in his bed. Alone.

CHAPTER ELEVEN

THE NIGHT THEY CAME HOME from *Aida*, Sheila did not hesitate when Mr. Maier invited her in for tea.

This time they sat in the living room, he in the rocker recliner and she on the couch. Chopin was playing softly on the stereo, but Sheila was still so excited by the spectacle they had just seen that she could barely sit still, let alone listen to Chopin.

"It was so great, Mr. Maier. Those elephants made me feel like we were in Africa. And those costumes." She thought of Scheherazade.

He thrust out a lower lip. "Showmanship, Sheila. The music was lost in that – that sports arena. The sound was poor and the soprano was weak. Yes, very weak."

She frowned. "How come you always do that?"

He raised an eyebrow.

"You always seem like you want to find things that are wrong. Don't you like going?"

"Bah. If you want to see opera, true opera, you must hear it in Europe, go and see it there. Here, they imitate. In Germany they have the echoes of all who went before. It is so much richer."

Sheila was silent for a moment. "Where did you used to live? Back in Germany."

"Dresden. I grew up in Dresden."

"Yeah. You said that to my mother." She paused. "Do you ever want to go back?"

He raised an eyebrow again. "To what, Sheila?"

"Your home, I guess."

"My home? Yes, my home." He laughed. It was a hard and dry sound. Sheila didn't like it at all.

"Sorry. I didn't mean—"

He interrupted, "Let us speak of other things, Sheila. How is your practising?"

"I don't get much chance—"

"Ach. You must make time, Sheila. You will never do well in the fall if you are not practising your instrument. Every day. Four hours at least, every day."

"I can't. My mother—"

"Your mother, your mother. *Bitte.* She is not going to be with you all your life, yes? You must be strong with your mother. Practise every day, and if she questions you, tell her you will one day be a great musician – and then, you will buy her lots of beer so she should leave you alone."

Sheila's mouth fell open. She closed it. What was wrong? Pretty much since they'd come into the apartment, every time she'd said anything, he just cut her off. He sounded so – so sarcastic and mean. "I ... I think I should go now, Mr. Maier." She picked up her teacup and moved toward the kitchen. As she passed the recliner, he reached up and grabbed her free arm.

She glanced down at his face. He looked so angry, so odd. What had she done now?

She tried to tug her arm away. "What?"

Suddenly, he pulled her down, down onto his lap. Her empty teacup and saucer fell from her hands. She heard them clatter and roll on the linoleum as her feet left the floor and he gathered her into his arms. She held herself still as he kept saying her name, over and over. *Sheila, Sheila, Sheila.* His hands were moving over her arms, her shoulders, her back, her hips, her legs. Against her bottom, she felt a lump in his groin. She kept still, arms at her side. What was he doing? He was kissing her, kissing her face, her lips, her nose, her hair, his lips soft, his hands moving everywhere, now one hand holding her tight against him, the other hand moving over her chest, rubbing, squeezing first one breast then the other, and at the same time his tobacco-and-tea breath hot on her face, his lips now hard on hers. She felt his mouth open and his tongue press against her lips, her teeth, trying to move them apart.

There was a heat in her chest, a fire in her belly and between her legs. She could no longer hold herself still. She opened her mouth and took in his tongue, gingerly moving her own against it, tasting tea and tobacco and spice, tongue meeting tongue. She pulled away, gasping for air, and he kissed her neck. It was terrible and yet, and yet … as his hand moved down from her chest, over her stomach and she felt him cup her through her dress … Her legs moved apart as his hand moved slowly against her. From her throat, a deep low sound escaped. She didn't understand where it came from but it felt so good to let it out, to feel him rub and press against her there. The fire inside got hotter. He stopped kissing her and his hand reached up under her dress to the top of her panties and pulled them away, down over her thighs, her knees, her calves, to dangle from her feet. She kicked and her sandals and then the panties fell away. He was struggling with the buttons on the back of her dress. She knew she should not do this. She should not. But it felt so nice, so warm, so exciting. He looked at her with hooded eyes, his cheeks flushed. He was breathing as though he had been in a race. "Sheila, undress me, undo my shirt, *Mäuschen*."

She did, fumbling with the buttons and pulling the white cotton aside. His chest was covered with hair, soft curly man hair, some of it white and some of it grey and dark. She brushed it with her fingertips and she heard him draw in his breath.

She leaned forward and kissed his chest and he moaned. Like she had moaned. She. She had done this – made him call out like that.

He guided her to move so that both knees were on either side of his hips and she faced him. He pulled her dress up and off her body. Chopin was playing softly behind her and she was naked except for her bra.

She should be ashamed, but he looked at her in such a way, she had his eyes on her, only for her, only for Sheila. He reached and pulled at the hooks and then her bra was off and on the floor.

His mouth fell open, his blue eyes widened. "Beautiful, my *Mäuschen*, so beautiful." She was beautiful. She was. And she was on fire, the top of her head ready to explode.

With his index finger, he traced a slow, tingling line from her lower lip, over her chin, down her throat, between her breasts, over her belly and down, down toward the opening between her legs. He whispered, "Such a sweet treasure here, *ja*." She drew in a sharp breath between her teeth and held it. He smiled and touched the hairs with his fingertip, slowly, and then two fingers, and then his hand pressing against her, his fingers teasing. The tip of one moved just inside her and she closed her eyes. This was so wrong, so wrong. She raised herself and felt his finger move farther inside. Good. So good. She moaned and then said it out loud: "Good, so good."

He grunted, and reached with his free hand to undo his belt. She looked down as he opened his pants and his penis rose up, stiff and large. "Touch me, Sheila, touch me here." He reached for her hand and guided her. All the while his other hand was rubbing her, the one finger moving inside her.

His penis felt strange. Strong and stiff and yet soft. She traced her fingertips up and down the shaft and he growled in a low and thick whisper, "Tight, *Mäuschen*, hold me tight." She gripped him and he smiled – oh, his smile, his smile for her. She leaned forward and kissed his mouth. Her lips opened and his tongue moved inside her mouth, tongue tasting tongue. When she released her grip and put both hands on his shoulders he removed his finger, held her hips in his two large hands and guided her up and then down so that the tip of him was resting against her.

He pulled his lips away from her mouth, gasping, struggling to speak. "I – I can stop – stop now, my Sheila, I can if, if you don't want—"

She took a deep breath and pressed herself down, deliberate and slow, and felt him, large, stiff and soft, felt him fill her. Despite what they all said in the girls' washroom, it did not hurt. Something so big pushing up inside her did not hurt. Instead, she felt the heat of him mix with the heat of her; she knew she would soon explode. She moved now, raising and lowering herself, slowly at first, then faster, and he too was moving, pushing up to meet her.

Mäuschen, Gott, Liebling, meine Sheila, Gott. Sheila, Sheila.

This was being strong, she decided. Oh yes. And he loved her. She watched him, his eyes closed, his mouth saying her name again and again. He was hers. All hers.

His eyes flew open, and he pushed her off him and to one side. She felt hot liquid spurt over her thighs and belly and, at first, thought he was peeing himself. He looked at her, shock on his face. "Oh Sheila, *mein Gott*, I did not mean—"

"Why did you stop?" She was breathing hard and still felt all tingling hot. "Didn't you like it?"

His eyes widened and then he smiled. "Oh yes. I did, but you ..." He stopped smiling. "You are so young and I could not, Sheila." He raised a hand and stroked her cheek. "I could not risk ..."

She reached for his penis with her fingertips. It was so small now, small and limp and wet. "Again," she whispered. She wanted to see if she could make him big again. She liked that so much, being in charge.

He pushed her hand away. "No, no. This is not right. It was an accident."

"Please." She grabbed again, rubbing harder this time. She felt him stir, felt his small penis shift in her hand.

"*Nein!*" He pushed her away again and held her back by the shoulders. "What are you doing?" He frowned, and then nodded. "I understand. You need to finish. Here then." And he moved his hand back to between her legs and stroked her. She opened her mouth slightly and sighed as she closed her fingers around his penis again. She felt him grow thick and rise up. She closed her eyes and leaned back her head.

"Sigmund. Tell me you love me."

He pulled her towards him and buried his face in her neck, kissed her again and again and cried out, "I do, *Liebchen*, God help me, I do."

Later, she curled into his lap, her cheek against his chest, listening to the rhythm of his heart. His one hand stroked her hair, the other rested on her bare thigh. She would stay there forever. She almost fell asleep.

A cat meowed outside in the night and he stirred. He shook her. "Sheila. You must leave." He shook her again. "Now. Get up and put on your clothes."

His voice had changed. She sat up, wary. "Can't I stay a little longer?"

"*Nein*, no – you must put on your clothes. Go up to your room – before your mother comes home."

She moved from his lap and stood up. Her things were all over the floor. She found her panties and was putting them on when he spoke again. "Go to the bathroom – wash yourself first."

She tilted her head. "Wash myself?"

"*Ja.* You smell of sex. Down there." He pointed.

She felt colour heat her cheeks. "Oh." She gathered up her dress, her bra, her sandals, and went into the bathroom and closed the door.

When she came out, the living room looked as if they had never been there. The tea things were all washed and put away; the hi-fi was silent, the lid closed. He was as neat as ever, his hair smoothed back, every shirt button in place. He stood in the kitchen, waiting by the apartment door.

She remembered those women from the James Bond movies and tried to look sexy as she came over to her lover. She slid her palms up against his chest and lifted her chin. "Sigmund, Darling, when will we do this again?"

He reached up, held her wrists and pulled her hands away. His eyes were cool, far away. "Fräulein, we will not speak of this."

Her throat closed and there was a small black weight in the back of her brain. "Wha–what do you mean?"

"I mean that we will not speak of this. Ever."

The weight grew larger, and her throat smaller. "But I thought—"

"Sheila! Listen to me. Tonight ... this ... all this was wrong. A mistake."

"No!"

"You are only fifteen, my God, barely a, a woman. And I – I am more than fifty, Sheila. This was a terrible mistake."

She felt hot tears burn in her eyes but refused to allow them to fall. "I don't understand. You love me. You called me sweet things and you kissed me, and you said you loved me."

He pressed a fist against his forehead. "You misunderstood, Sheila. Control was lost and things happened which should not have happened." He took a step backward. "We will not make that mistake again, understand?"

She, too, took a backward step and peered up at him carefully. He was scowling, angry. A thousand thoughts jammed inside her head, and then, with a cool calm, she understood.

He was afraid. That was it. Her big strong lover man was terrified, and he was hiding it. She considered that for a moment. This would be a good thing. He was afraid she would tell someone and he would be in such trouble. And she realized another wonderful terrible thing. He was afraid because he still wanted her arms around him. She thought about undressing again, slowly, just to see what would happen – what he would do.

The floor tilted beneath her. She bit her lower lip and then nodded. "Okay, Si– okay, Mr. Maier. I understand, I do." She glanced down at her feet. "Don't worry, I won't tell anyone." She looked up again. "I don't want you to get into any trouble, so I won't tell anyone."

His eyes were still wide and afraid.

She felt sorry for him and it was weird, so strange. "Honest, I won't tell. My mother would kill me, and Granny . . . well, I just won't, okay?" Sheila moved to the door and then turned around, her fingertips resting on the handle. "But just tell me this."

"Tell you what, Sheila? What do you want?"

She tried to smile. "Just tell me that you'll . . . that you'll still bring me the music."

He looked like he was in pain, one hand back up against his forehead, the other hand clenched at his side. "Yes. Yes, Sheila, I will bring you the music. Now *bitte*, please. Just go." His voice was almost a whisper at the end.

He stood in his apartment and listened to the sound of her footsteps overhead as she crossed the kitchen floor and down the hall to her bedroom.

Sigmund did not hear her get up a half-hour later and move into the bathroom, where she held herself over the toilet and retched until her sides ached and her throat felt like acid had been poured down inside.

Nor did Sheila hear him, as he lay in his bed and clutched his covers hard against his mouth and moaned and sobbed long into the night.

CHAPTER TWELVE

THE NEXT AFTERNOON, SIGMUND MAIER had a visitor. Sheila opened the front door to an older woman who was looking for "a Mr. Sigmound Mayor". The woman was dressed all churchy, in a navy blue seersucker suit. Tufts of silver hair poked out from beneath a hat covered with blue flowers. At first glance Sheila thought she was a Jehovah's Witness.

"Mr. Maier lives in the basement apartment." She pointed around the side of the house. "There's a door down there, at the side. Just go in and his apartment is to the left at the bottom."

The lady looked a bit confused, so Sheila ended up going around with her to make sure that she didn't knock on Alan's door. She didn't want any friends of Sigmund's thinking he should move or something because of her family. It looked like maybe she had money; her big car was parked in front of the house. Almost as soon as she knocked, Sigmund opened the door and looked first at Sheila, then at the lady, and then back at Sheila. He didn't say anything, but his eyes widened and he took a half-step back. Sheila spoke quickly. "This lady came looking for you, Mr. Maier. I don't know her. Or what she wants."

He took a quick shallow breath and then nodded. "Just so." He turned to the woman. "Yes. So. What is it?"

The lady glanced over at Sheila and spoke up. "Thank you, Dear. You can go now."

Sheila looked back at Sigmund. He was also looking at her, his head tilted ever so much. She held back her smile, knowing that she was coming by Thursday night when her mom started back on afternoons. She'd read a story in *True Confessions* that giving a man time to think was the best way to handle it when he was confused. Thursday seemed to be enough time.

The lady spoke again. "Mr. Maier, I have information for you – good news, I believe." She glanced over at Sheila. "It's private. May I come in?"

Sheila strode back to the stairs, but she took her time going up each step. She heard him let the lady in and close the door.

* * *

Sigmund, too, thought the old woman appeared ready for church. Somehow, the odd little bird in the blue hat was now standing inside his living room.

"My name is Florence Morrison." She smiled; her teeth were yellow but seemed her own. "You have no idea how long I have searched for you."

The old woman was one large smile, this Florence Morrison, her stretched lips outlined by bright pink lipstick. Two dots of rouge sat like stop signs on her powdered cheeks. She looked expectantly at the couch and he gestured for her to sit and then sat on the recliner opposite. "What is it that I can do for you?" He sat forward, feet firmly on the floor.

"You were born in Germany? In Dresden – February 27, 1915?"

He frowned and then nodded.

"Your mother was Hilda Mann?"

"Mann was her maiden name. Yes."

"And she died February 20, 1930 in Dresden? An accident?"

After a moment he nodded, more slowly, carefully.

"Mr. Maier. Sigmund – I am your aunt. Your father was my brother, Stanley Morrison."

He did not move a muscle. Not one.

She tried again. "Your father, Stanley Morrison, was my brother. I was 17 when Stanley came back from Germany, from the Freiberg Academy, and he told us he'd been married in Dresden, to Hilda Mann." She opened the clasp of her large purse and took out a yellowed piece of paper. "The certificate of marriage. He needed it to arrange to bring her here." She held out the paper. He glanced at it. She stretched her arm further and he took it. It was in German. The long, narrow paper felt as dry as dust; the inked words were brown and slanted.

"Stan was so excited. I don't think he noticed how disappointed Mother was." She quickly added, "She missed the wedding, you see. She was so disappointed. Mother had such plans for all of us. Stanley, Harold and me." Florence Morrison chuckled, her dry voice cracking slightly. "Stanley had to promise to do it all over again when Hilda came over." She tilted her head.

He noted the faint tremor. "Miss Morrison. You are mistaken. How could my father be this Stanley Morrison? My father was Helmut Maier." The photograph.

"All my research has led me to you ... I don't know what to say."

Sigmund kept his expression unchanged. It was difficult to control the muscles. He peered at the certificate again, searching. His mother's name – Hilda Mann. The family address in the Altstadt. He dared a quick glance at the elderly woman across from him and a clear vision of his imaginary farm family rose up. The large grandmother's flour-dusted apron, her arms gathering him to her bosom ...

The paper trembled in his hands, so he put it down on the coffee table. His guest cleared her throat. "Mr. Maier. Sigmund. If I'm wrong, then I'm truly very sorry for intruding." She paused, searching for words. "After my brother died in the war, my parents didn't know if they should search for Stanley's Hilda. It was a difficult time; Germany had been, well, after all, the enemy." She looked away and then back. "It was long ago. My father died in the spring of '28 and Mother, three years later. They left a fair estate. I decided to spend some of it looking for Hilda. I think Stanley would've wanted me to." Removing a tissue from her purse, she dabbed at the end of her nose. "Of course, I had no idea that there was a child. I think that Stanley knew, though. When the Kaiser, well, when the Great War broke out, he was beside himself. He blamed himself, you know, that he did not insist that Hilda come with him. But he wanted to prepare, you see; Papa could be a bit testy. I think Stanley thought if he came home first, you know, got everyone comfortable with the idea of a foreign wife. Oh dear.

"I can still see Stanley pacing the hall, slamming his fist into his hand. He tried everything to return – lawyers, our Member in Parliament. He even tried to contact the Prime Minister's office, and then the Governor General. I think he would have gone to the King if he could. Anything to get back there, to get a message to Hilda and get her out – but, of course, the war simply got larger and was full bore by then, and I'm afraid there was little sympathy for his situation." Her voice had begun to quaver and she coughed. "Do you think I might have a glass of water?"

Sigmund leapt to his feet. "Yes, yes – of course."

He struggled to put it all together as she sipped from the glass. The photograph. His grandfather calling his mother "Frau". The box and its letter: *always and ever, yours - S.* Her evasiveness that he took to be some terrible secret, that he had been "a bastard". Was this worse? His mother married to two men. Two. He stared at the back of his hands, at the raised veins that held a stranger's blood. "You say that you have researched this, Miss Morrison. If you did not know that there was a child, how could you be searching for *me*?" He held his hand to his chest.

"Well, Sigmund, that's a story in itself." She took another sip of water. "I remember that Stanley received a wire from abroad. It was the fall, perhaps September – I didn't want to be in school. It was so exciting. Every day, parades and bands and speeches, and all the young men in their uniforms... It was..." He watched her drift in memories.

... so many fine young men... His mother staring out the window, looking to the west.

Sigmund coughed.

"Oh my, oh yes, where was I? Yes – Stanley received a wire. I think now that it was from your mother about her pregnancy, but at the time, he just told us it was from a friend abroad. Someone who was helping, he said. He had one or two American friends – students still at the Academy. Of course, the States were not in the war as yet, and could get letters through, I suppose." She stopped, and smiled. "I see that I'm confusing you again. I'm sorry – it is a difficult story because I don't have all the pieces."

Someone moved a kitchen chair upstairs.

"Miss Morrison, I do not see—"

"Oh Sigmund, you are so like your father – be patient." She glanced away for a moment. "I think that's why he enlisted. All he wanted to do was to get over to Europe, get back to Germany for Hilda, your mother. I often wondered, if he'd only waited, continued to try through official channels – oh dear. He didn't, and that was that. But I had your mother's name, and your grandparents' names from the marriage certificate. I started with that, making inquiries, and it took only a few months before I was able to locate where your grandparents once lived, and then, where they moved. I took a chance, and sent a letter to Hilda Mann Morrison. I had things from Stanley and there was also his part of the estate. My brother Harold thought it was better to leave it all alone. But it was only right that I find her. Only right, eh?" She shook her head, remembering. "I'd nearly given up hope when I got a reply some six months later. It was very short. I think someone helped her write the letter."

Hilda, Chérie, you must learn more of this English, you can never tell when you might need it ... Giselle fixing her mother with that look, his mother stealing a glance at him, at Sigmund, and then back to Giselle and nodding.

"*Meine Mutter*, my mother, she had friends who understood some English, speaking and writing."

"I thought so!" The old woman looked so pleased with herself; another piece of the puzzle in place. "So I wrote and told her that I would come to Dresden to meet her. I had a student from my school translate so she would understand. Did I mention that I was a teacher? No, eh? I used to teach music, Sigmund, at high school. In any event, I sent her both letters – mine, and the translation. I came over on my own and stayed at a very nice hotel in Dresden. Very ornate, very lovely – it was quite old, I think ... It was, let me see ... Oh, I'll think of it later.

"Anyway, I waited at the hotel for your mother to contact me. She sent a note; I think her friend helped her again. We were to meet at the Zwinger Museum, by the fountains, and then we would go for lunch. I was to look for a woman in a short grey coat and matching hat." She ran a blue-veined hand over her skirt and gently cleared her throat.

Sigmund could almost see this Miss Morrison, a prim, earnest woman in her early thirties, pacing in front of the Zwinger, carefully searching the women's faces as they passed.

"I waited until almost 4 o'clock, there at that lovely palace, but she never came. I sent a note to the address in the morning. There was no reply. I went 'round myself the next day." Another sip. "A very nice man met me in the lobby of the apartment, and with my bit of French and his bit of English, I finally came to understand that Hilda had died in some kind of accident." She blinked, owl-like. "The day before, while I was there, waiting to see her. I could hardly believe it." She stopped, dabbing her eyes. "It was as if Stanley died all over again."

She sipped some more water and cleared her throat. "Just like he had gone once more, and there was nothing I could do. I thought about attending the funeral, but I lost my nerve. I couldn't speak German, I didn't know anyone there and, of course, I didn't know about you." She stopped. "Oh, Sigmund, if only I had gone. Instead, I took the train to Paris and stayed several days with friends before coming back home."

This was so fantastic yet Sigmund knew every word was true. The light grey coat and cloche his mother wore. Schneider's mutterings in French and English.

Why did Schneider not say anything? And Giselle. Did she know? Did she want to keep her *pauvre Siggy* to herself? He put a hand to his forehead, remembering. For a time, he did stay with her. But her mood swings – one minute laughing, the next crying – it was all too much. He could only withstand six weeks before he left for Freiberg and secured that foundry position. Giselle. He never wrote to her. Later, he held some regret. He might have been able to help her before ...

"Oh Sigmund, it wasn't until I received a letter from Charles Gleason that I found out about you."

Sigmund looked up. "Gleason?"

"He was one of the Americans who studied at the Academy with Stanley and Helmut Maier and the others. He was from Illinois, I think; they were having a reunion. They had some kind of graduates' club in New York, and they were coming from all over North America. Someone had the idea of a tribute to those who died in the Great War and they wanted all the families there." She pulled another piece of paper from her purse. It was typed and had International Mining and Refineries Ltd. on the letterhead.

February 3rd, 1938

Miss Florence Morrison
229 Avenue Road
Toronto, Ontario, Canada

Dear Miss Morrison:

The North American Chapter of the Royal Mining Academy of Freiberg graduates is holding a reunion for all its members on September 15th, 1938. Our records indicate that your brother, Stanley Russell Morrison, a graduate in June 1914, gave his life at Ypres on April 23rd, 1915. It is our sincere desire to hold a memorial tribute during the reunion for our fellow graduates who lost their lives in the Great War.

The Memorial Committee, of which I am Chairman, requests the honor of Mr. Morrison's family to attend, and I have enclosed an invitation for yourself and your brother, Harold Morrison. We would appreciate your kindness in providing us with Mr. Morrison's wife's address, so that we may prepare an invitation for her.

Unfortunately, we have been unsuccessful in locating either Mrs. Morrison or her son in Germany, and trust that you may be able to be of assistance in this matter.

We thank you in advance.

Yours very truly,

Chas. C. Gleason,
Chairman of the Memorial Committee,
Royal Mining Academy Graduates of Freiberg,
North American Chapter,
Eastern Division.

"I thought it was a mistake and wrote to him immediately. I assumed that they had someone else's information or that your mother had remarried. It took two more letters and a telephone call to confirm that Hilda had borne Stanley a child. Mr. Gleason himself, and a Wilfred McGowan from Connecticut, actually saw the baby – er, you – when you were quite small. When Mr. Gleason told me the story of how Helmut Maier married your mother – in name only, God bless him – I knew I had to look for you." She cleared her throat and paused to take another sip of water. "He must have been quite wonderful, this Helmut Maier. Imagine, taking Stanley's place so that your mother would not, ah, suffer any embarrassment."

Sigmund wet his lips. "I never knew him." He could no longer remember what the man in the photograph looked like.

"Well, Sigmund, I wish I had." She leaned forward and patted his knee. He tried not to flinch. "I had such a time trying to find you. Things became quite difficult, what with Hitler and everything. I could only pray that you were all right during the war years. And then after, my goodness, there were almost no records. With Stalin taking over, it has been dreadful trying to get information of any sort from that bunch, eh?" She winked, startling him. "They didn't expect such persistence from an old woman, I imagine. And here I am. And here you are."

Sigmund could only look at her – her yellow-hued teeth peeking out from between the smiling lips with their coat of bright pink – and try to breathe. The glass on the coffee table was empty, vibrant lip shadows decorating the rim.

He swallowed. "And you discovered my location, how?"

"I hired a private detective, Sigmund. You were a machinist. When he discovered that, he tracked your last known employment in Germany and they had records on file that a transcript had been required for immigration." She chuckled. "And he found where you emigrated to, and then, where you worked. From there, it was simple."

He stood up.

"Yes, just so, Miss Morrison, this has been much of information. *Bitte* – please. You will leave your telephone number, and I will contact you at another time. Soon, yes." He smiled his acquaintance smile, polite.

She blinked once, twice. "Oh, yes, I suppose I can understand that, Sigmund. This has been a lot to take in." She laughed; a nervous twitter. "It's been a lot for me to take in. So much excitement, eh? Perhaps you would like to come for a visit next week? I have some photographs and things you might like to see. Here's my number and my address."

Rising from the sofa, she dropped her purse. Sigmund bent quickly to retrieve it, bowing slightly as he held it out for her.

"Thank you, Sigmund."

He took the piece of paper she offered as she stepped through the door. She looked back at him. "Next week, then? You'll come next week and meet the family, eh?"

It was not until Florence Morrison was driving away that she realized he had only smiled in response.

CHAPTER THIRTEEN

ON WEDNESDAY, ELEANOR BARNES STOOD before the apartment door, a set of keys in her hand. "Sheila, have you seen Mr. Maier this week?" Sheila was halfway down the stairs, folded sheets and a pillowcase for Alan in her arms.

"No, Mom." She continued to Alan's door. She kept her voice as ordinary as possible. "Not since Sunday." She didn't like her mother's tone. Surely to God she didn't – couldn't – know. "Why?" A small knot was forming in her stomach.

Her mother clicked the keys together in a terse, short rhythm. Not bothering to answer, Eleanor unlocked the apartment door, flung it wide and marched through the kitchen. Her heels echoed across the linoleum. Sheila felt, more than heard, her mother's sigh.

"Well damn it all; isn't this nice for Chrissakes. Sheila!"

Sheila stepped in behind her mother. Her throat tightened as she heard her mother call from his bedroom. What if he was home ill? She was sure she'd heard him on the back stairs very early this morning, but what if she was wrong? What if it had been her brother sneaking back in? On TV, a man had a heart attack and he was only thirty-five. Dr. Kildare saved his life. Her Sigmund could be lying on the bedroom floor, all blue and gasping.

He wasn't. In fact there was absolutely nothing of Sigmund Maier left in his bedroom. Everything was gone. His clothes. His shoes. The hairbrush. Sheila ran back into the living room. Even the albums and the gold rack had vanished.

"Mom, wh-where's he gone? Where's Mr. Maier?" ... *falling, she can feel her feet leave the floor, hear the clatter of the cup and saucer, the squeaks of the recliner ...*

"If I knew that, I'd chase him down and give him a piece of my mind! Rotten Kraut! He had the money to take you to that – that big show, but what about my rent?"

Sheila was going to throw up. Or maybe she would just fall down on her knees and scream. Yes. That was it; fall down on her knees and scream. Her Sigmund. Her darling Sigmund. Her mother was looking hard at her, seeing something, frowning. Sheila reached out and gripped the doorway between the kitchen and the living room.

Her mother pointed at her. "What do you know about this?"

Sheila shook her head. She swallowed. "Nothing."

"You know something, you do. I can tell. Who was that woman who came here? Mother said somebody came to see that goddamned Kraut on Sunday. Who was it?"

"I don't know, I don't." She was close to crying and should not must not could not let her mother see how upset she was. Sheila tried to think – did she do something wrong? Did he hate her? Did he think she didn't care? She was just giving him distance, like the article said she should. What if Sigmund was just getting himself some time away – surely then he'd come back for her. He couldn't leave her here. He loved her. And he knew she loved him.

An idea formed in the back of her head and Sheila spoke as it took shape. "I think that lady was an old friend or relative or something. She probably just wanted him to visit for a couple of days, and he's coming back. Oh, he'll be so upset that we've come in like this."

Her mother looked over at the open door. Then she shook her head. "A couple of days and take all his stuff – take *everything* with him?"

"He didn't have much, Mom. It was all he had and he needs it to feel safe wherever he goes. Everybody needs to feel safe." Her voice faltered. "Even on vacation ..."

Her mother's face changed. Her eyes narrowed and she took a step forward. "What do you know, Sheila? What've you and him been planning behind my back?" She took another step. "You and him. You were jealous when he took me out to the show. You didn't like me being with your special friend, did you? What did you say to him, Sheila? What?" Sheila was moving her head back and forth, back and forth, trying to say something. She thought she was saying *No, Mom, No* but she wasn't sure. Her mother now had hold of her arm and was shaking her, her hand gripping Sheila's flesh like a monster, her face all twisted. "You and that rotten Kraut. You planned this. To humiliate me. You ruined everything. You did." Her voice rose and now she was screaming at her, accusing her of other things, horrible things.

"You little slut, you wanted to steal him from me, didn't you? Just when he was getting interested, you told him terrible things and made him leave. You bitch. You nasty little bitch." Her mother kept screaming, one hand shaking her shoulder back and forth, back and forth, flecks of her spittle punctuating the words that Sheila would not listen to, would not hear. She would not. And her mother's other hand grabbed her hair and yanked so hard that Sheila's tears finally flowed, unchecked. And then her mother shoved Sheila and her head cracked back against the doorway.

As she fell to the floor, she felt the rush of the air around her. The linoleum rose up to meet her. In the moments before she landed, in the split second before the cold flat surface of the floor reached up and slapped hard against her arm, her legs, her hip, the side of her face, knocked the breath from her lungs and threw her deep into unconsciousness, she thought she could smell him, smell tobacco and spice.

And she knew he would come back for her. He would.

SONATA IN C SHARP

HILDA MAIER LED HER GUESTS to the nursery. It was nearly three o'clock and the baby was still asleep. She could scarcely believe how perfect he was, his long fair lashes skimming the tops of his flushed cheeks.

"He has Stanley's eyes," she whispered.

Wilfred McGowan stood by awkwardly, glancing from the baby to Charlie and back again. He was not at all confident of his German, unlike the dapper Charlie Gleason, so at ease in many languages.

Charlie grinned, leaning close to Hilda and whispered, "He must return them, *schnell!*"

Hilda laughed, her hand quickly covering her mouth, as she ushered them out of the room, and back to the parlour. The clock struck the hour. Her parents were soon to return, and she wanted to speak freely.

Her hands trembled as she poured the sherry. Passing them each a small rose-tinted glass, she sat on the edge of the settee, next to Wilfred. Her right hand played with the amber brooch at the top of her blouse.

"Are you soon returning to America?"

"Yes. We're booked for passage next month." Charlie smiled.

Wilfred started in, nearly spilling the contents of his glass. "April 15th. For New York. By steamship from Italy."

Hilda set down her wine. "You should have returned last summer or fall. It is so dangerous now."

Charlie leaned forward and chuckled. "We'll be fine, Hilda, just fine." He grinned at his companion. "Wilf and I don't think the Kaiser's navy will sink a passenger ship bound for America. President Wilson would be more than upset."

They heard a tiny cry from upstairs and Hilda felt her breasts tingle. She hoped that her milk would not leak through. She leaned forward and gripped one of Charlie's hands. "You must tell Stanley. He needs to know – he must understand that, that this marriage with Helmut is in name only, a show, for my family." She looked down at her left hand clutching a lace handkerchief. "He needs to know that Helmut and I, that there is nothing legal, that we have not, that the baby is not ..."

Charlie stood up. "This damned war will be over soon, Hilda. It will not last beyond the summer, in God's name." His ears pinked. "Oh, excuse me."

She stood also. "Charlie, you will get this message to him?"

"Hilda, there is no need. He knows. Helmut told us before he left for the front. He knew Stanley should be told." He glanced over at Wilfred. "I, er, we were all worried that it would be difficult for Helmut or you to send a message. Freddie and I wired Stanley when we were in Greece last September."

Before Hilda could say a word, Wilfred jumped into the conversation. "We wanted Stanley to know so, so he would understand. Because of the child, ah, the baby. It was so soon, and he might have thought that Helmut, that it appeared that Helmut might have ... We had all been such good friends ... we think, er, we thought it was the right thing, for Stanley to know ..." Wilfred blushed, quite red. It was the most he'd spoken in the thirty minutes they had been there.

Charlie clapped him on the back. "Good old Wilf, always trying to keep the peace."

Hilda remembered how Wilfred had been so awkward dancing with her; tall, lanky and always a half a step behind the orchestra. She had not appreciated back then how sweet he was. Dancing at The Terrace Café; was that only a year ago? She smiled at him. "*Danke*, Wilfred. *Danke schön.*"

Nearly seven months later, Hilda received a note from Mr. Wilfred McGowan of Stafford Springs, Connecticut. His written German was nearly flawless, and his penmanship was steady and precise. He was so very sorry, but he had "received word from the family of my dear friend, Stanley Morrison, that Stan had fallen" – *mein Gott*, my Stanley, *mein Gott* – "in Ypres" – months ago, dead months ago – "shot whilst trying to rescue two others overcome by fumes. He would be awarded a posthumous medal" – last April *mein Gott* – "a brave man. A good friend and a good man."

There was ice tight around her heart, keeping it from beating. She was dying. She was. She blinked away tears, and watched them fall onto the inked words. Wilfred's words.

There was more.

Would she, Wilfred McGowan of Stafford Springs wondered, wish to have him tell Stanley's family about her and about their son? He understood that Stanley's family did not know that she had borne him a son. He was certain that the family would welcome them both. Did she wish for him to tell them about the boy?

Hilda pressed the note to her breast and rocked; the room moved around her. She held a fist against her open, silent mouth, spittle and tears falling to her lap.

Sigmund stirred in her bed, and Hilda dropped her hand from her mouth, rose and crept to his side. He remained asleep, his long fair lashes resting on his cheeks. Damp tendrils of his blond curls were plastered against his temple. So healthy, this boy. So strong.

Like his father. His father, the Canadian student she met that April afternoon and waltzed with at The Terrace Café. His laughing eyes, so blue; his terrible, perfect German. Their secret meetings, those few blazing afternoons in the apartment of his friend, their marriage, so rushed, barely time to kiss to hold him to feel his arms around her, his heat against her chest, her belly. He left her, left her with this boy growing inside. So long ago. She put a clenched fist to her forehead.

She looked back at her desk. A letter from Helmut was propped against the inkwell, still sealed; unopened, waiting. Helmut was a good man. He wrote every week. He asked after her health, and the health of the child. He wrote with pride of his progress in the military.

She whispered to the room. "This Canada, this strange place of cold winters and wild Indians, would I go there with my son, cross the ocean and go to my Stanley's family – to strangers? To the land of enemy soldiers?" She swallowed. Would they want her to come to them now, a woman of the soldiers who shot and killed their son? She cried out, "Oh *mein Gott*, my Stanley," and reached out to clutch the bedpost for a moment before straightening her back and shoulders.

She returned to her writing desk. Outside, the trees on the avenue were just changing colour, the street a bustle of carriages and motorcars and motorcycles. Her eyes rested on the distant spire of the Kreuzkirche and the tower of the Rathaus just visible. Her eyes dropped to the desk, to the letter that waited, unopened.

Helmut was a good man. He would be a good father. He would take care of her and take care of Sigmund. Raise him as his son. When Helmut came home, they could marry legally and quietly – somewhere in the country. Sigmund would never know. He would not grow up with the shame of being a son of the enemy.

She sat at her desk and pulled out a tissue-thin piece of paper. With a steady hand, she wrote back to Mr. Wilfred McGowan of Stafford Springs, Connecticut to thank him for his kindness, to bless him for his kind heart. To ask him to say nothing, please nothing at all to the family of Stanley Morrison. That it would be too painful, especially in these dreadful times between their nations. It was best.

She posted the letter. She prayed it made it safely into his hands. Returning home, she took Wilfred McGowan's letter from Connecticut and burned it in the fireplace, watched as the flames moved in from the curling edges and ate his kind words. Then she prayed for the strength never to think on this again.

CODA

HILDA FOUND STANLEY'S LETTER QUITE by accident, in her mother's sewing chest.

8th October, 1914
My dearest H,
Helmut has agreed and it
will be for the best ...

She was searching for a small button for Sigmund's nightshirt; she thought there might be one in the ragbag tucked in the bottom drawer. Her hand touched the paper beneath a pair of her mother's woollen stockings. When she pulled it out, Hilda knew the handwriting in an instant. She read the letter to herself, over and over, searching the words, savouring the scent of the paper, the colour of the ink. Carefully re-folding the thin, almost transparent paper, she carried it to her dresser where she removed the small wooden box from beneath some linens. Opening the carved lid, she took out the gold pin, kissed the tiny leaf and placed it with the letter inside the box, just under the pressed rose.

A rose for a rose, my dearest heart.

How the letter came to be in Ilse Mann's possession, or why she hadn't shared it with her daughter, Hilda would never know. By this time, her mother had been dead two months.

A few months before the end of the war, her father's investments and the family business failed. They were forced to move into the small apartment just off Pragerstrasse. Her mother perched stock still on the ottoman in front of the small fireplace grate, clinging to her valise, her jacket still neatly buttoned up.

Her father had gone for a walk, leaving Hilda to cope with her mother, a young Sigmund and a jumble of furniture, crates and bundles left by the two men hired to load and unload the cart.

Ilse's distress was palpable. "This is a temporary setback, Hilda. We do not belong in this place and I will not remove a single dish, not one dish, until your father returns us to our home." Ilse turned to face the cold grate. "Not a solitary item until then."

Hilda began the process of making order. By the time her father returned, her parents' bedroom was unpacked, and she was almost finished in the kitchen. Sigmund sat at the small table, intent on re-folding the linens that had been wrapped around the china and cutlery, his small hands methodical in following his mother's direction. Ilse was beside her daughter, silently wiping each plate before placing it on the worn, painted shelves.

Gunther Mann grunted, walked to his chair before the fire, raised his feet to the ottoman and opened the newspaper. He read silently until tea and bread were served.

Ilse never settled in the apartment, drifting during the day from parlour to kitchen and back again. Any sudden or unfamiliar noise startled her, and she moved anxiously to the windows, watching lest an acquaintance might somehow discover them and arrive for a visit. No one ever did. Other than brief forays to the market and once a week to church, Ilse rarely left the building. It was a surprise that she, alone, contracted influenza.

Hilda struggled to cool her mother's fever, to soothe her rasping throat. Within a few short hours of first falling ill, Ilse was delirious and grasping at her daughter's hands.

"An orange, *bitte*, an orange."

"Yes, *Mutter*. I will do my best."

There was no money for medicine, let alone fresh fruit. Had there even been money, there was little medicine available at the end of the war. Oranges were not to be found in the market stalls of their new neighbourhood.

In less than forty-eight hours Ilse was dead. Hilda washed her mother's body and dressed her in her second-best tea dress.

Her best dress and Hilda's amber brooch were sold to pay for the coffin. Her mother's several pairs of shoes and gloves were bartered for the gravediggers.

Hilda arranged for the mass with a priest from the small church a few blocks away. She knew her mother would be ashamed to have the priest from their old parish on an der Frauenkirche. There was a graveside service with Hilda, her father and little Sigmund in attendance.

Stone-faced, Gunther bowed to the priest and strode back to the apartment. Hilda, with Sigmund in tow, could hardly keep him in sight as he wove his way through rear alleys and side streets.

Hilda was never sure if he was angrier about his business losses or the loss of his wife of twenty-six years. He never spoke of it.

On the other hand, he had rarely missed an opportunity to point out to her the folly of her matrimonial choice.

"After promising you marriage, he enlists in the army. A foot soldier, no less – not even the cavalry. He is a farmer's son, without claim to inheritance." Helmut was the third son in a family of five children, his Academy tuition paid for by a maiden aunt. "You want to marry a nothing!"

Ilse, to Hilda's surprise, had taken her daughter's side in the arguments.

"Husband, there is a war on. If they wish to marry, it is best to be done quickly so that Helmut can begin to earn a married soldier's pay. When he comes back, he will have learned skills that may prove of use in one of your warehouses. No doubt he would be grateful for your consideration."

Hilda's father warmed to his new son-in-law, even hiring a car to take Helmut to the mobilization unit. He stood and waited at the curb as the young man stowed his gear.

Hilda wanted to see him onto the train, but Helmut refused. "It will be a madhouse there. You stay here." He reached to take her chin and, leaning close, whispered against her ear. "Be patient. He will send for you."

Her father called out to Helmut as the carriage pulled away. "You must write to us."

Hilda prayed that she and Stanley would be far away when her father finally learned the truth.

After a few short weeks, her father's mood shifted back. "A farmer's wife – breeding right away." He looked pointedly at her belly. "Will it be a litter, or merely triplets?"

By Christmas of 1914 it was apparent just how far advanced her pregnancy was, and her father no longer spoke to her. When Sigmund was only hours old, Gunther Mann stood at the foot of his daughter's bed, peering through his pince-nez.

"Not even six months," he said, and left.

He took to calling her "Frau Maier" after that, and would have nothing to do with his grandson.

When Hilda found the letter, she understood it all. Her father's disgust was not driven by his belief that Helmut had impregnated her before marriage. Her mother must have told him what Stanley had written, and they assumed the worst. That "S" was her secret lover.

But by then, it seemed pointless to tell him the story, to try to explain that she was truly married to the young man from Canada. Stanley was dead. Helmut, too, was dead. And Hilda knew that she, also, was dead.

All You Need is Love

– The Beatles

CHAPTER FOURTEEN

SHEILA RAISED HER HEAD FROM the steering wheel, peering out into the dim garage of her house. A glance in the rear-view mirror confirmed that she looked terrible. Beth would take one look and know something was up – Sheila hadn't cried in years, and never in front of her daughter. And tonight – a houseful of people coming.

She took another tissue and dabbed under her eyes. She winced. Even if she managed to avoid being cornered by Robin tonight, she was going to have to go in tomorrow. And then Robin would fly into her office, perch on the corner of her desk, fix her with that I-am-so-involved-in-this look, and demand that she report. She blew her nose. Kenneth, if he thought of it, might look up from the newspaper tomorrow morning and say, "Did you go meet that fellow?"

She pulled herself out of the car and through the garage entry to the laundry room and pantry. She made it to the main floor bathroom. A cold cloth on the back of her neck and water splashed on her face brought the sting in her eyes and throat under control.

She sat on the toilet and cooled her head against the Italian tile that lined the bottom half of the walls. Slipping off her shoes, she allowed the marble to work on the soles of her feet. Then she used the breathing exercises Ardith taught her in therapy. That much, at least, wasn't a complete waste of money. Eventually, calm returned and she spent a few minutes repairing the mess of her face. She hoped Beth hadn't heard her come in, or listened in the hall as she fumbled into the powder room.

She glanced at her watch as she stepped out of the bathroom and listened. The house was completely silent; no one-beat thumping bass from upstairs. She walked quickly down the hall and checked the phone in the alcove between the kitchen and the great room. The red message light was flashing. She hit the speaker button and sank onto a stool at the breakfast bar to listen.

One message. Sent today, at 3:23 p.m. *Sheila, it's Ken. I tried your cellphone, but you must have it off. Vivian ran into a problem with the grant projections and I'll need to meet with Production and Marketing to talk about the fall lineup. It may mean moving some titles to next spring. I'll have to pass on your party tonight. Sorry.*

She shook her head. "Business. Yes, sure. I bet Vivian ran into some projections all right. All I asked of you was to run the bar." She shook her head again. "Next time, I'll hire a bartender." She hit the erase button. "And I'll bill you." Sheila rose from the stool just as something bumped or fell in the basement. She froze, head cocked to the side. Something else drifted up and echoed from a heating duct – voices, whispering perhaps. After a moment, she nodded. She marched from the great room, back through the kitchen and across the foyer. She stopped at the top of the staircase that wound down into the lower level. The lights were off.

"Beth? Is that you?"

There was no response; and then, "Yeah. It's me. I'll be up in a minute."

"Did you do your homework?"

Again, silence for a moment. "I said I'll be up in a minute."

Sheila gripped the smooth wood of the banister. There was some whispering. "Who is down there with you, Beth? You know you're not to have people over until you've done your homework and practised." No response. "Come up here, Beth. Now."

More whispers. Then the top of her daughter's head came into view as she rounded the curve in the stairs, followed by another head. This head did not belong to a girl. Beth was not holding the hand of some Tisha or Ashley or Danielle. A tall, slim boy trailed after her daughter, his big awkward hand firmly clutched in Beth's as she nearly dragged him and his large, awkward feet up the off-white carpeting that blanketed the stairs.

Beth gave her the nasty smile. "You're home early."

Sheila firmed together her lips. She nodded. "Yes. And you don't have my permission to entertain your friends here while I'm at work. Who else is down there?"

"No one."

She swallowed and took a good look at the two of them. The young man was mildly embarrassed, his cheeks nearly the colour of Beth's pink top, which, on close inspection, was inside out. Her white belly winked from between the bottom of her tight tank top and the low rise of her little plaid skirt. The boy was all in black, and his wavy blond hair was longish – unusual these days. The kid ran his fingers through it, trying to smooth it out. Beth stood her ground, her chin raised, one hand on her hip, the other still clutching that awkward boy's hand. On some level, Sheila had to admire her daughter, who was nothing like she had been at that age.

Sheila thought about her last therapy session. Ardith would probably suggest that Beth's defiance is normal at this age. "She needs to challenge you. How you choose to respond is what shapes your relationship with your daughter." Ardith was such a pain.

"So I should just smile and accept what she hands me?"

"No, Sheila. I'm not suggesting that at all. I do think that talking things out, calmly discussing your concerns for her, is one way to keep the communication open between you two." Well, even a painful, cliché-spouting therapist could have a point.

Sheila took a deep breath and kept her focus on her daughter's face. "Beth, we need to talk about this."

"No, we don't."

"Beth, I—"

"It's my life. Stay out of it."

"Just a minute here. House rules are not to be ignored."

Her daughter turned to the boy beside her. "C'mon, Colin, let's get out of here." She tried to pass her mother, but Sheila reached out and grabbed at her arm.

"Listen here, Young Lady. You don't have a clue what life is all about. You didn't have to work your way through school, hold down *Mcjobs*, live off macaroni for weeks on end."

Beth pursed her lips. "Oh yeah? How many pairs of shoes do you own, Mother?"

"What does that have to do with—"

"You have it all."

"I work for all this, Beth. I work my tail off at my business—"

"Dad got you started, Mother. He helped you – gave you the money. You don't even look at him, but he did everything for you. Everything."

Sheila struggled not to scream that Beth didn't know what she had to pay for that bit of start-up – how much she paid even before Kenneth came on the scene. For a moment, she closed her eyes, watching headlights streak by in a heavy night's rain. Where was that? Just outside Medicine Hat. Or was it Fort McMurray?

Beth yanked her arm away from Sheila's grip. "C'mon, Colin. Let's go."

"Don't you dare, Beth. You are going nowhere."

Her daughter strode through the hallway to the door. Colin followed close on her heels, the sound of their footsteps echoing up the cathedral ceiling above the foyer. Beth yanked open the door, then turned back to face Sheila, her expression full of disgust and dismissal. "Mother, I am sixteen. I don't have to listen to you. I don't even have to stay here." The two of them walked out and the door slammed shut.

Sheila stared at the closed door. Tried to imagine what would have happened to her if she had done that, if she had given her mother lip and walked out. And then she remembered. She did. She reached her 16th birthday and was out of there. And nobody tried to stop her.

How dare you speak to me like that, Young Lady? Don't you dare.

And don't you dare, Mother. Don't you ever touch me again. Ever.

She shook her head, shrugging off the words.

She watched the brass handle for movement, for some sign that Beth had a change of heart, that she was coming back inside so they could talk it all out, discuss their concerns, keep those so-called lines of communication open. Beth used to like staying home for Sheila's parties, carrying trays of hors d'oeuvres, chatting with the adults. Charming, everyone said. Why didn't she ask Beth to stay – instead of yelling, she could have ...

Letting out her breath, Sheila went upstairs to take a bath. That, and the inhale-exhale exercises, would hold her together.

By 7:05 the caterers had arrived and it was all under control in the kitchen; Sheila felt she could leave them to go upstairs and finish putting herself together. At 7:30 she was ready, and spent a few minutes double-checking the details, lighting the wall sconces in the powder room, switching the bird of paradise arrangement in the foyer for the white roses in the living room. Two minutes later, she switched them back again. Drama at the entrance was better than classic elegance.

At twenty minutes before eight, like a whirlwind of organized fuss Robin rushed through the door, blew her a kiss, and marched over to the bar in the dining room. After surveying the contents of the wall unit he popped up the lid on the ice bucket. "Sheila, did you stock up on ice?"

She eyed his black slacks and white open-necked shirt. How thoughtful to dress like a bartender! If she weren't already married and if he weren't completely gay ... She grinned and called out as he passed her on his way back through the foyer, "Well, hello to you too." She pointed into the kitchen. "Two large bags in the side-by-side, and four in the freezer downstairs if you need more. But I don't think you'll need them. Costair likes his wine, and the rest of his crew will probably follow the leader." She didn't need to add that the invited staff would nurse their drinks for most of the night.

At ten to eight, the doorbell rang for the first time. Margaret Wilson and the rest of the marketing team arrived together. Margaret wore a European look for the evening – vintage coat dress and Italian shoes. Smart girl. They were all smart, that marketing bunch. Sheila surrounded herself by those who understood nuance and Margaret certainly filled the bill. Sheila cast her smile on all of them, but focused on Kim Lee, the nervous little

Internet guru. She touched his shoulder and lowered her voice. "Listen, when Costair gets here, I want to make sure you have time with him. Generate some chat about the plans for cyber-space – what is it you call that – online retail services, right?" She straightened and took a step back.

Lee nodded but Sheila wasn't at all convinced that this kid understood his role. She took Margaret aside in the kitchen.

"I want Costair landed tonight and signing on with a ten-year lease for the Montreal store. I want his commitment to the cash reserves for a second store in Quebec City. Can Lee handle this, Margaret? He's so damn young. Stick close to him, and come get me if I'm not there."

Margaret frowned. "Sheila, you hired him. You've seen his work. Just let him alone on this. He's brought his laptop all set with the proxy looking as good as the real thing. Relax. At the right time, he'll pull off the show, I'll do the yak yak and Armand Costair and company will be sold. As a matter of fact, Kim's put in some of our hot promos aimed at the Quebec market—"

Sheila was no longer listening. The doorbell was ringing again, and she left Margaret in mid-sentence. Had to be Costair. Everyone else had their arrivals organized; Paul and Bunny Williams would be watching from across the street for Costair's arrival. Such wonderful neighbours. Before she opened the door she took a deep breath, and exhaled. If she looked anxious, she knew they'd all smell it on her.

Her palms were sweaty and she wiped them on her dress. She took another deep breath and fixed her smile at the right level. She'd done this so many times before; everyone loved Sheila's parties. It was all perfectly planned. That was the secret. Hardly one thing unfolded unless she set the pieces in motion first.

She opened the door and ushered in Costair and his group. He brought along three bright young things who apparently spoke little English. She wasn't fooled. It was good business to hold back. Her lessons in French and Spanish had made her privy to asides not meant for her, and she expected the same to happen tonight. Her art appreciation seminars, ballroom dancing

lessons, golf and tennis lessons, interior decorating workshops –
it was all of it useful over the years.

"Your home is magnificent, Sheila." Costair was a large man,
and dressed all in dark grey he seemed to fill even her oversized
entry. He raised an arm and gestured up the staircase to a large
painting on the first landing. "Is that a Morrisseau?"

She nodded. "Yes, Armand. I was the lucky bidder at a fundraiser." The door opened and Paul and Bunny walked in, smiling,
ready to gather up the rest of Costair's team and keep them busy.
"Come in, you two. Just in time for the first bottle of shiraz." She
waved them in as she took Costair's arm. He smiled at her.

"*Félicitations*, Madame, on your fine taste. I have an interest
in Aboriginal art." He smiled, smoothing his tight-to-the-scalp
greying hair with his free hand and adjusting the small ponytail
that ran down the nape of his neck. "My mother, she was Métis,
you know. Marthe Montcerf, my *maman*."

Sheila smiled right back. "Well, then, you might be interested in having a look at a soapstone sculpture we have in the
living room. It's fairly primitive – I just love its energy." She led
him into the living room, peering over at Robin, who was busi-
ly working the bar at the far end of the dining room. Her right
hand had once more done all his homework. And it didn't hurt
that Robin's gallery connections allowed her to lease the sculpture and the Morrisseau on such short notice. She may, however,
hang onto the painting. It might make a great investment.

As she led the Quebec investor into the room, the energy was
already in great form. Margaret had switched into her performer
role and was playing a jazzy blues number for several guests gathered around the baby grand. Sheila could breathe again. Even
without Kenneth and Beth, she knew her night was absolutely
on track.

CHAPTER FIFTEEN

THE LAST GUEST LEFT SHORTLY after midnight. It took little time to tidy up; the caterers took care of the dishes, and Mariella would tackle what was left in the morning. Wired from the night and the commitment from Costair to sign the deal next week, Sheila lay in her bed and listened for Beth to return. She did, finally, close to two o'clock. Kenneth was still not home, so Sheila went to the top of the stairs.

Beth took one look at her mother and raised a hand, palm out. "Not tonight, Mother. No way."

Sheila watched her retreating back as she strode down the upstairs hall. "When, Beth? Just when will we deal with this?"

Her daughter didn't even turn around before she went into her room, flicked on the lights and slammed shut the door. Within seconds the noise of some half-talent gang of wannabes throbbed from the other side. Sheila went back to her bedroom, closed the door, and got into bed with a pillow over her head.

The next morning Kenneth sat at the breakfast bar, his beefy face buried in *The Globe and Mail*. As Sheila poured herself a coffee she could hear Beth running the shower.

"Ken."

"Hmm-mm." No other sound, no movement.

"Kenneth, listen to me. I had a real problem with Beth again last night."

"Hmm-mm." The paper remained raised.

"She was here while I was out. With a boy."

The paper shifted and his wide eyes appeared over the top. "Alone?"

"Yup."

He knit his dark eyebrows into an almost frown then the paper went back up. "Well, I imagine you put a stop to that."

Sheila thought that if she threw her bagel with enough force she could hit the newspaper and maybe it might rip right through to his face. Instead, she took the cream out of the fridge. She was about to pour it when she put it back and reached for the 1%. "Yes. Of course. I put a stop to it all right. So she and the boy went someplace else."

The paper came down, bunching and crackling as he lowered it. "For pity's sake. You can't let her walk all over you, Sheila."

As if she had anything to do with what Beth did and didn't do. "I agree. I can't let her walk all over me. So I am asking her to leave."

"Oh for heaven's sake, Sheila. We're not going there again."

"And why not? She does nothing around here – she comes and goes as she pleases and when I dare even attempt a discussion, she gives me the finger. Or worse." Sheila put her hands onto her hips. "Exactly why should I have to put up with that?"

He folded the paper and released a deep sigh. "First, you have a woman who arrives here three times a week, cleans out the bathrooms, does the laundry, washes the floors, the windows, polishes the furniture – Mariella even cleans out the air ducts, for God's sake. From March to November, you have Wilson et al dropping by to cut the grass, trim the hedges, fertilize, plant, dig up, prune, thin, weed-whack and rake. Every other year, you have Sally Whoozits swoop by and wave her magic colouring wand so that *poof!* we have a nice fresh look."

It was the most he'd said in weeks. Sheila ran a hand through her hair and fixed him with a look. "Sally does wonderful work. Everyone loves our place. We were written up in *Modern Homes* because of 'Sally Whoozits'."

"Lemon chiffon in the powder room. Oh please, Sheila." Kenneth raised his chin, his eyes challenging her. "Why in God's name do you need Beth to be doing things around here like some sort of washerwoman?"

"Chores, Kenneth. They didn't hurt me. They won't hurt her."

"You had no choice, Sheila. My income offers her plenty of choices. And the way your business is going, it's looking like you've plenty of choices too."

She decided to ignore the comment and stick with Beth. "And what about respect? What if I choose to have some respect and she chooses not to give it to me?"

He crossed his arms over his chest. "Respect is earned."

She opened her mouth. She closed it. Opened it again. "Well. I guess it is, Kenneth. You'd know all about that, wouldn't you? And while we're on that topic, just how was your overtime? Went a lot later than usual, eh?"

He looked at her. But just as she had expected, he didn't dare head into the minefield she had ready for him. He just knocked back the rest of his coffee and pretended she had not tossed down the gauntlet.

She thought this might be the time she'd haul out his dirty laundry. Let him know what she knew. She heard Ardith's soft voice. "You should bring Kenneth in here; let the two of you discuss your concerns about your marriage in a safe place."

"Ardith, those are not concerns. Those are facts. Cold hard facts. And I don't think he could handle it if he had to face how much I know." Ardith's expression was all gentle concern. Such a soothing pain in the rear. Still, the breathing exercises helped. That much was useful. For $175 an hour.

She left for the office nearly half an hour after Kenneth had backed his Cadillac down the driveway. Beth had still not come down for breakfast and Sheila wasn't about to wait for the princess. Let her be late for school; Sheila had plenty waiting for her at work.

She pulled into the parking lot of Musicians' Clearinghouse. Robin's car wasn't there yet. Sheila swiped her pass card and walked through the front entrance of her store.

This was always the best part of her day. She'd loved it even when she had the little hole-in-the-wall music store on Queen Street East. She loved it more now that she had acres of retail space to wander in – here and the satellite stores. She revelled in being in first, before the staff and any of the customers showed up, before the noise.

Just inside the front door, stacks of her in-house newsletter waited. *MCNow* was chock full of local gigs, songwriting contests, band competitions, workshops, and juicy gossip. Her editor had a wild sense of fun, so lots of smart graphics, bright colours and amusing comics kept their customers reading. Kim Lee's web version would be ready before the fall. Sigmund Maier was right; the Internet was growing at a phenomenal rate.

An old man in tune with cyberspace. She smiled. So like him. He was always ... always knowing everything.

She shook her head, and turned to check out this week's giveaway. Her purchasers managed to pry goodies from a whole range of industry suppliers. She ran her fingers over a jumble of guitar picks, dust cloths, resin, reed cases, posters, score sheets in a bin at the checkout; most of it was seconds or old stock but the kids didn't care.

If walking through the doors was the best part of her day, deciding which way to travel back to her office was the most fun. It was her secret – completely unscripted. Inhale, close her eyes and then drop a pen. Her direction depended on which way the pen pointed. Head to the right, and journey through row after row of instruction books and sheet music – everything from jazz to classical, from Broadway to Bombay – then past CDs and posters at the back, collectibles up on the wall.

Take the left aisles, and she'd follow the paths through the instruments: strings, woodwinds, brass, percussion.

Accessories were down the centre aisle. The sound rooms up front and along the one side doubled for what the staff called the Spin Rooms. *C'mon*, they'd say, *why don't you take that baby for a spin?* Nobody bought an untried instrument at the Clearinghouse. It meant high labour costs, but it was what was behind so much of her success. Along with her willingness to rent instruments and gear to players with zilch credit. The dividends of loyalty and the power of knowing the breed: musicians would rather play than eat.

She stayed connected with all those music rats who used to hang around until they scored. And she called in the favours. Musicians' Clearinghouse brought in big names for special workshops, and the customers loved it.

Now everything was poised to go to a national level. She had built this huge business on her own – mostly – five stores from Ottawa to London.

A far cry from her first little place.

Long before the big box stores, she found a fabulous warehouse. But she had to fight so hard for her vision. She remembered how Kenneth shook his head to each argument she made.

"Sheila, it's out in the middle of an industrial area and off any main streets. In the suburbs – you hate the suburbs. There's no retail in the neighbourhood – the closest houses are several streets away. Who will go there?"

"Kenneth – three different bus routes are within less than a block, and it's only four blocks from the highway. I don't need 'drive-bys' if we market this right."

"It's a huge gamble. Huge."

"Christ, you are so negative. What about its sale price? The building's a steal."

"It's still a recession, for God's sake. Everything's a bargain – real estate is barely moving. How will you unload this?"

She stared at him for a moment. "You already think I'm going to fail. You have no faith in me." She nearly hit him. "Kenneth, you can't deny that I have built my store up from nothing."

"I didn't—"

"Ken Martin!" She was going to explode. She was still that girl in the schoolyard, and the sound of her mother's voice filled her head. She took a step toward him. "Try to deny that I have a huge following and need more space. Deny that everything I have done in this business has paid off and paid off brilliantly. Go ahead you – you damned soda cracker you. Deny it." For a moment, for just the briefest of moments, she thought she had gone too far. She shifted her stance and inhaled before starting over. "Ken – I need your faith in this. Just for once, can you share in my vision without all this hesitation and second-guessing? Can you not see what I am doing here?"

She was sure he was going to continue to fight her on this. Raise more excuses. But then he nodded. When he spoke, his voice was flat, without expression. "Okay. Okay, Sheila. You are right about your accomplishments. You are always right." He looked down at his shoes, then back up at her. "I'll find the backers you need. I'll help you get this set up. And then ..." his voice trailed off.

"And then?" she prompted, not at all certain she wanted his answer.

He shrugged. "And then we'll see. That's all. We'll see."

In early 1983 the small voice in the back of her head told her that he would get her started and then leave her.

Five days after they negotiated the purchase of the building, Sheila was told by her doctor that she was pregnant. She must have looked sick because Betty Wong immediately started talking about abortions and choice.

Sheila waved a hand in her direction. "No, no. I don't know what I want to do yet. I'll need time to think about it."

And she did. For most of that night, while Ken snored upstairs in their bedroom, Sheila sat in her kitchen drinking tea and snacking on biscuits. While the clock in the hall ticked off the early hours she considered her options. Baby. Business.

And then, probably because nobody would think she could, Sheila chose both.

It was a gamble. A music store on the scale no one had ever before visualized. The brainchild of a pregnant woman.

Ten weeks before opening the Musicians' Clearinghouse, she gave birth to Beth. Three weeks premature, but still a healthy 6 pounds, 2 ounces, Elizabeth Antonia Martin was a perfect baby.

At the memory of the labour pains, Sheila stopped walking and put her hand out to grip a display case. She looked up at the sign overhead: STRINGS and remembered negotiating an exclusive with one of the big guitar names. Tying up the only public phone that worked on that hospital wing, she had covered the mouthpiece with each contraction, pretending that she was consulting with her partners.

Partners. She snorted. There were no partners. Kenneth lent her some upfront cash to start the little store – which she paid back, with interest – and from then on, her own judicious investments and careful bookkeeping meant she went to the banks with an impeccable business plan and a big chunk of her own money. And for what the banks couldn't do, Kenneth brought in other investors. But no partnerships.

For the first five years after opening Musicians' Clearinghouse, she had to question if she was out of her mind. But all the years of trusting musicians who couldn't get their gear elsewhere meant two things: they came to her first, and 99% of them paid their bills. It was her secret weapon.

As she made her way to the stairs that led up to her office space in the back, she wondered if Sigmund Maier had ever come in here. He may have come into her store and looked over how she had this set up. Perhaps he knew it was her store. Or maybe he'd admired it without knowing it was hers. What did he really think? Maybe that she shouldn't appeal to the young kids so much. She shook her head and quickened her pace.

She picked Mozart after she settled in to her office. Mozart to help her clear her head enough to deal with Robin.

Robin Borson was her other secret weapon. Sometimes she wondered at how she nearly passed him by, but then she'd remember the interview in the back of the little east end store. While not flaming, Robin didn't bother faking either. Sheila almost couldn't get beyond that.

Brilliant, intuitive and with organizing skills she learned to rely on, Robin became her personal assistant and worth his weight in every raise, incentive bonus and special perk she sent his way.

And he never hesitated to remind her.

It was Robin, not Kenneth, who coached her through Beth's birth on September 28, 1983. Ten years ago, it was Robin, not her brothers, who made her mother's funeral arrangements.

And Robin who took the message from Sigmund Maier, and understood immediately that this was no ordinary phone call.

She was in her office less than twenty minutes when, true to form, Robin scurried in. He closed the door and perched himself on the edge of her desk. He raised his eyebrows, Groucho Marx style, and grinned. "Okay, I did not ask last night. I waited for you to bring it up. Patiently. You decided to play the tease and I can't stand it another minute. Now dish. What happened yesterday afternoon with the mysterious Sigmund Maier?"

She shrugged. "It wasn't much of anything."

"Come now, Honeybun. Thirty-two years and your old boarder just calls you up out of the blue?" He put on a dreadful German accent. "*Sheila, jawohl, und how izt zings?* Right. I'm not settling for anything less than you telling me that he declared undying admiration for you and wants to put you into his will." He leaned forward and stage-whispered, "He is rich, right?"

She dismissed him with a hand wave. "God Almighty, Robin. You read too much trash." She shrugged. "He just needs me to write a letter for him, that's all."

He slumped back and released a huge gust of air from between his teeth. "A letter? And that's all?" Then he sat up again. "What's the letter for?"

She sighed. "Just a letter – for the government. Something that confirms he lived at our house, and when. A character reference, I guess. You know, 'he's a nice person. Nobel Prize material', and so on." She took another breath. "There's some mistaken identity thing and he needs documentation. Immigration stuff."

Robin was quiet for a moment. "Immigration? Maier – a German in Dutch with Immigration?" He started to chuckle, then noticed her expression. "Sorry."

She glanced at her watch.

Robin frowned. "And he came over to Canada when, exactly?"

She shrugged. "How would I know?" She sat back in her chair. "Look, Robin, he's got a lawyer working on this. It's the government. They need fifty affidavits – and in triplicate." She rummaged in her purse and pulled out the business card. "You'll be helping me with that letter; you may as well have this for the address."

He peered at the card. "Kris Douglass, eh?"

"Yeah? So?"

Robin gave her that look. The one that said she was dense. "This 'misunderstanding' with Immigration is way too vague. It must be something bigger than that. I know this lawyer's name. Douglass defends a lot of creepos and keeps getting them off – Sheila, I'm afraid that maybe your old sugar daddy is—"

Sheila hit her desk with the flat of her hand. "Don't you call him that, Robin. Don't you ever call him that."

He stood up and took a step back. "Whoa, Nelly. Sheila, I was only—"

"Just leave it. Leave it." Her hand was stinging; she looked at it, the palm red. "As a matter of fact, Robin, why don't you just leave my office? I need to get some work done around here." She busied herself with the papers on her desk, the last chords of the symphony fading. She knew he was waiting, waiting to see if she was going to calm down. She did not want to calm down; she just wanted not to think about Sigmund Maier.

When she lifted her head back up, Robin was still there. He looked so guilty.

"Sheila, honest to God, I didn't mean anything. You were so – so intense about this guy, I was just trying to make you laugh."

She sighed. "I know. I know. Christ Almighty, I don't know what's wrong with me." She leaned back in her chair. "Mr. Maier meant a great deal to me as a kid. He was more than just some boarder, you know? I was such a nobody, a pathetic little dork. He introduced me to music, to culture in fact. He took me to a couple of operas and concerts, he got me books to read, he ..." She swallowed. "I had so little. I was a nothing, Robin. My mother, you know. At a time in my life when my walls were collapsing, when my choices were fewer and fewer, he shored everything up." She blinked. "I can barely remember my childhood. But I remember him being nice to me. So kind."

The muted rush of passing traffic from outside was the only sound in the room. Robin was staring at her. He had the strangest expression on his face. She thought he was going to cry at any moment. And then she realized that it was she who was crying, and she fumbled in her drawer for a tissue. "Christ. What is wrong with me?" She wiped at her eyes, furious and bewildered.

When he spoke, Robin's voice was low-key and without any trace of humour. "What do you need me to write in that letter, Sheila?"

She shook her head and smiled. "Oh, I'm going to have to draft that up myself after I speak with the lawyer. But I need you to look it over for me."

He nodded, still serious.

"And Robin. Help me make sure that I don't sound like a blubbering fool. This is important to the man and I want to be nice."

He nodded again. "Don't worry, Sheila. It will be so excellent they'll be offering him tea and a tour at the Governor General's place. Okay?" He handed her back the business card. "You'll need this to call that guy. I'll get it from you later."

He was almost out of the office when he stopped and turned around. "Sheila?"

"Yeah?"

"Are we still on for tonight?"

She frowned. "Tonight?"

He put his hands on his hips. "Good grief, Sheila Martin. Skydome. Level 100. Two tickets, third baseline."

She slapped her forehead. "Oh my God! I almost forgot. The game."

He nodded, grinning. "Yup. The game."

"Yeah, we're still on. This is going to be the year, right, Robin?"

"World Series. All the way," he agreed as he left her office.

It was the strangest thing and they had shared it every year since 1992: a pair of seasons' tickets and a passion for the Jays. Music may have been her life, but something about the boys of summer, those fields of dreams ... Cito Gaston and the back-to-back Blue

Jays' championships hooked her, and she went year after year, waiting for them to prove it once more.

Of course, Robin went along to check out the tight uniforms and speculate about all those Bay Street suits in the stands. They had a lot of fun together, Robin speculating and Sheila waiting.

Sitting at her desk, she smiled just thinking about the game. Okay. She reached behind her and opened a CD case: time for a little Oscar Peterson. Maybe the day would end up okay after all.

CHAPTER SIXTEEN

KRIS DOUGLASS RETURNED HER CALL close to six o'clock that evening. She was clearing off her desk and almost didn't pick up the phone. Robin had left to get the car gassed up, and the retail end was winding down.

"Ms. Martin, this is Kris Douglass. Thank you for calling." His voice was almost too high-pitched for a man, but he spoke with authority.

"I understand you need something from me about Mr. Maier," Sheila answered.

"Yes. That's correct."

"That I need to confirm Mr. Maier was a tenant in my mother's home."

"Absolutely correct. We need to verify that Sigmund Maier lived there, the duration of his stay, his rental payments and anything else you can add about his reliability – anything that helps establish his work history, his activities in his community. My notes indicate a residency from September 4, 1967 to July 8, 1968."

"Yes, well, I can confirm that." Sheila bit her lower lip. "I guess you don't want me to mention that he skipped out owing the last month's rent."

His response was immediate. "It was the only time? The only occurrence of, uh, unreliable behaviour."

She couldn't remember him ever missing his rent. But her mother told her almost nothing. She chewed at her lower lip.

"Ms. Martin – are you there?"

"Yes – yes, it was. The only time."

It was his turn to pause. "Well, perhaps there were circumstances that forced his uncharacteristic behaviour. But overall, he functioned well as a tenant? Paid his rent and so on?"

"Look. I won't add that last bit to the letter. It was long ago. He was a good tenant. The best we ever had, I guess." She swallowed. "And he was kind. Generous." She added. "At least, he was kind to me."

"That is useful information, Ms. Martin. It will be helpful if you can attest to his character. Can you tell me more about his kindness to you?"

She sighed. Where to begin? And where to end? She decided to give him the Reader's Digest version. He picked up on the encouragement of her music.

"Ms. Martin, would it be safe to say that had Mr. Maier not introduced you to music and art, you would not be the person you are today?"

"Absolutely. Sigmund Maier saved my life, in a way."

"Saved you?"

"Well, perhaps that is extreme. What I meant is that my life was pretty circumscribed when he started renting the apartment. He opened up aspects of the world to me that I simply would never have experienced."

"And your life in music – your success in the music industry. You owe it all to him for starting you on that path?"

The cover of the Tchaikovsky album; the cavalry officer astride the horse, sabre at the ready. *You may think that this is pretty also* ... "Yeah. I guess that's a fairly safe bet."

"That information is as important as the verification of his residency. I thank you for sharing it. It will certainly help his case if you attest to all of this."

"Okay. So who do I send this letter to, Immigration?"

"No, no. I will have the document drawn up here. I'll need you to come in and sign it, have it notarized and so on. And as soon as possible."

"Wait a minute. I thought I was just writing a letter for him. That this would be my letter."

"It will simply be what you have told me, Ms. Martin. I've taken notes. There is a time factor here – we are waiting for a hearing date, but I anticipate it won't be too long now. There's a real push on to get these cases through the system."

"Cases? Mr. Douglass, what cases would that be?"

"The government has targeted certain individuals. There is a group that is somewhat fanatical; they've hired lobbyists to apply pressure on the politicians, and I'm afraid Sigmund Maier has been caught up in that."

"Group?"

"Yes. Really, just a special-interest group. This is a case of mistaken identity – some old photographs, a few faded memories and archives that list names – common, ordinary names – that Mr. Maier has the misfortune of sharing with an unpleasant character."

"What is he being accused of, exactly?"

"You'll have to ask Mr. Maier."

"No. Now you wait a minute, Mr. Douglass. I'm not about to sign anything unless I know everything that is going on here."

There was a pause, and she heard the squeak of a chair that clearly needed oil. "It has been suggested that Mr. Maier misrepresented himself when he immigrated to Canada. A group identified him as being involved in criminal activities during the war, but they don't have enough evidence to support their ridiculous claim. Unable to proceed, they have lobbied the government to put together this little dog-and-pony show. They'll stop at nothing, these people, to make the lives of honest, hardworking Canadians a misery."

Sheila was going to remind him that his client was not a Canadian citizen but thought better of it. He continued, "Immigration charges are just another way to harass my clients."

The buzz of an intercom sounded in the background. "Ms. Martin, I'm afraid my next appointment is here. Can Mr. Maier count on you to come in and sign the document?"

Just write a letter, Sheila. That is all.

Sheila pressed her lips together. "No. No he cannot, Mr. Douglass."

"But—"

"What Mr. Maier can count on me to do is to draft my own letter, in my own words, to support all that I've said here."

"Ms. Martin, this is just standard practice. I would not be asking you to sign something inaccurate. After all, I am a lawyer."

"That is hardly my concern here. I simply choose not to sign things drawn up by other people when it relates to information that I can provide, clearly and accurately, on my own."

She heard his sigh. "I see. But if I may be permitted to offer you some direction?" She didn't respond and he hurried on. "Not to tell you what to say, but to suggest that certain facts, and the order in which they appear, may be critical to my client's defence."

She nodded. "Okay. Can you email me something and I'll keep it in mind while I write this thing up?"

"Yes, that will work out just fine."

She gave him her email address.

"Will you be able to have this letter to me by tomorrow?"

"I'll courier it over tomorrow or first thing the following day. Okay?"

"Fine, then. Thank you for your co-operation. Mr. Maier is fortunate to have your friendship."

"Yes. Yes he is." She hung up and checked her watch. 6:18. Robin would be waiting out front in the car and he would be antsy. Just over an hour to get downtown, grab some food and settle into their seats. They would barely make it.

At the start of the seventh-inning stretch, Kenneth called her on the cellphone. She'd forgotten to turn the damn thing off.

"Beth isn't home yet."

"It's Wednesday. She has music lessons until 8:00. Did you call and check with Jane Hockley if she said she was going anywhere afterward?"

"Well, that's just the thing. I dropped by Jane's place. Beth hasn't been in for her piano lessons for nearly two months. Jane said Beth told her she was moving on to another school."

Sheila lowered her voice and hissed into the phone. "See! She's been off with him, that Colin boy."

"We don't know that."

"Damn it, Kenneth, what do you think she's been doing? Crossword puzzles?" Robin was working hard at studying the crowd but she knew he was listening to every word she said. "Kenneth, are you at home?"

"Yes. I said that."

He hadn't but she didn't bother to correct him. "Take a look downstairs, even if the lights are out. Especially if the lights are out. I guess if she's not there, you can just wait to see if she comes home. Then you can ask her how her music lessons went. She's been telling me to mind my own business every time I ask. It's your turn." She hit the END button.

He called back at the bottom of the ninth. Jays were at bat. They were down five-zip.

"Beth is over at her friend's house. She called just after you hung up on me."

Sheila ignored the swipe. "Friend's house?"

"Yeah. Her friend Tessie or Tessa or something like that. Beth and I are going to talk about the music lessons when she gets home."

Sheila rolled her eyes, stood up and stepped in front of Robin to squeeze out into the aisle. Maybe she could find a dead spot and lose their connection. "That's nice."

"Well, I was thinking maybe you should be here too."

Here we go, handing it back to her. She shook her head, knowing he couldn't see her. "I think you can cope with it, Kenneth. Just ask her what she's been doing with the money that she was supposed to be handing over to Jane Hockley."

He didn't say anything in response.

"Look, she sees me as the enemy. I think you'll get further without me there. Just don't let her hand you any nonsense; she gives back the money and the boyfriend stays out of the house when nobody else is home. Period."

He sighed. "I'll do my best."

"Okay. Gotta go. José Cruz is up to bat next and I don't want to miss it." She was about to hit END when Kenneth spoke.

"Did you see that man?"

"What?"

"Maier. Did you go see him?"

"Yes, yes. I went to see him."

"And?"

"And nothing. I went to see him. We had a visit."

There was a long pause. Then her husband spoke again. "Look, Sheila, I'm just interested. Just asking. You're in charge of your own life, but I just thought – well, I just thought it was odd after all these years. That's all. Obviously, I've *overstepped the boundaries again and—*"

"I went to see him. We had a visit. He needed a bit of help, nothing much. He wasn't asking for money. Just a letter; a recommendation for Immigration."

"Immigration?"

She heard the same tone as Robin's. She glanced to her left. Robin was busy trying to get the attention of the kid hawking the beer. "Yes. Immigration. No big deal. An old man who screwed up his paperwork nearly fifty years ago and he's got to fix things. Government. You know."

Another pause. "What things, Sheila?"

"Jesus Murphy, Kenneth. Immigration things – forms, documentation, government paperwork." She started pacing the aisle, heading toward the inside of the stadium. A few people were openly staring. Others were taking sideways glances. Why did she answer the damn cellphone? He was like a little old lady half the time – fussing about this and that. The rest of the time, a cold fish. Except, she supposed, with the others.

The only reason she stayed married was ... She glanced up at the television screen. Cruz was stepping up to the plate. It had been an up-and-down season thus far, but it was still early. The Jays could be a summer and fall team this year. She could always hope.

Kenneth started to say something as the cell connection cut out, came back on, cut out again, came back, and then he was gone. She turned off the phone and went back to her seat.

Robin leaned over to her as she sat down. "Sheila, dear, do you think next time you could leave that yakking thing in the car? We've got a game to watch here."

"As if you watch the game. It's those uniforms, Robin, and you know it." She gave him her best withering glance moments before Cruz hit a line drive far into the outfield and made it to second base.

CHAPTER SEVENTEEN

Two days later, Robin popped his head around her office door. It was just before lunch. "Got a minute?"

She nodded and gestured for him to come in. He stood close to her desk, but did not take his usual perch. It was a moment before he started talking.

"Sheila, I've been working on your letter, you know, and I'm thinking you should know a bit more than what this Douglass is giving you."

She frowned. "What do you mean?"

"Well, if Maier's been charged with falsifying his immigration application, you should know what those false things are exactly."

"He said they have the wrong man. I don't see how knowing makes any difference to me."

"Yeah. I know." He scratched his head and looked at her in an odd way. "You sure you want to write this letter?"

"Of course I'm sure. I already told you, Robin. He made a real difference to me. I owe him."

Robin nodded. "Okay. Well, at least do one thing for me, okay?'"

"What?"

"I've got an old friend. He works in Ottawa in an MP's office – can't tell who he is, so don't ask, but I called him yesterday afternoon and told him what was up with you and this Sigmund Maier. He got all intense. His boss is on some committee and, anyway, he said you maybe should, you know, know more than you do."

"You told somebody else about this?"

"He would never—"

"You told somebody about my personal life?"

"Listen, Sheila, wait. I've been worried about you and about this Maier thing. He just shows up, I mean ..." He put his hand out to touch her shoulder and she rolled her chair back. "Sheila. Before you get all freaked just listen to me for a minute."

She took a deep breath. "Okay, Robin. I'll listen. But I am not happy about this. Not at all."

His eyes narrowed. He was angry – angry with her when it should be the other way around. Her mouth was suddenly quite dry.

He cleared his throat. "Look here, I'm sorry but you'd just better listen. I called my friend because I was not at all happy either. And since I spoke with him, I'm even less happy."

Sheila kept her expression cool, distant. Inside, her stomach was flipping. "Go on." Her voice was so cool, so together. Sometimes she impressed herself.

Robin pulled up a chair to the other side of her desk and sat down. "This guy in Ottawa, he's an old friend." The corners of his mouth lifted. "We probably would still be together if I hadn't been so, so young and stupid, but that's another story." He smiled more broadly now. "I had to promise to spend the weekend with him if he'd look into this for me." He stopped smiling. "The point is I trust him. Absolutely. And when all this started with Maier, I could see that you weren't really looking at it too hard."

She opened her mouth to say something and he held up a hand.

"It's okay. I understand you're involved in this thing and looking clearly is not something you're doing too much of right now."

She remained silent.

"My friend has access to things, to people. His boss, she's on this committee – something about immigration. So he called me back today – on a secure line. God – that was when I really got freaked. He said, 'Robin, I'm calling you back on a secure line, but we can't talk for long.' Then he told me."

Sheila wet her lips. She kept her voice tightly even and low-key. "Told you what?"

Robin looked down at the floor and then back at her. "Your Sigmund Maier is not a nice man, Sheila. Not a nice man at all."

"Go on. I already know they've got him confused with somebody else."

"Sheila. They have pictures. Documents. Testimony. Sheila, he's a Nazi."

She focused on his mouth, struggling to understand his language, the words he was speaking. Robin was always so clear. What was he saying?

"All through World War II, Sigmund Maier was up to his Nazi ass in gas chambers and mass executions. And he lied when he immigrated. And that's what they're going to use to get him out of Canada and extradite him to Israel."

"Israel! What the hell are they sending him there for?"

"They're going to try him over there; once he's had his status here revoked. Like that Demjanjuk guy. They want to put him on trial for war crimes."

Falling ... Nazi? She can think of nothing to say. Nothing.

Robin rubbed his eyes. "And Sheila – Douglass doesn't really want your letter."

She frowned. "What do you mean?"

"Look. It's his modus operandi. He starts small with the character statement thing, gets the person hooked, and then the next thing you know, he'll pull you in to be a witness, parade you in front of the media. He'll subpoena you if he has to." He looked away for a moment, and then turned back. "You end up between Maier and the press, Sheila. It will be your face all over the news. Sheila. Think of the business here, of all the bad publicity."

It was too much. Robin had to be watching too many B movies.

"Sheila? Look, Mar— ... my friend thinks you should talk to somebody about this. He connected with a man who has information. My guy called this man and he said he'll talk with you." He narrowed his eyes and tilted his head to one side. "If you want to talk to him, he'll meet you. Here in Toronto."

There was a loud ringing in her ears. Robin must hear it also. How could he not? There was not enough air in this room either.

She'd written her letter; he was just supposed to check it, fix any typos and courier it to that lawyer.

Robin was watching her carefully. She shook her head. "And if I don't talk with him? If I don't listen to what he has to say?"

He nodded, thinking. "Well, I guess you have to decide what you want here, Sheila." He took a deep breath. "I'm sorry if I upset you. But I'm not sorry that I called. Not at all."

She closed her eyes. It would be easier just to send the letter, like she was asked to. Douglass was expecting it, and what would she say if he called? *I'm just looking into Sigmund's Nazi past, Mr. Douglass. Be right along with the letter.* She thought about Douglass trying to get her into court, to use her. No way. She needed some ammunition here. Poor stupid Sigmund Maier. At his age, he'd be lucky not to have a heart attack. He was no more a Nazi than she was. She opened her eyes. "Okay, Robin. I'll talk with this person. But you know it's all smoke and mirrors, eh? That they have the wrong man. Or the wrong information. It was a long time ago, right?"

Robin stared at her for a moment. "Sure. It could be a mistake." He rose from the chair. "And if you meet with this guy, you'll be better able to decide that for yourself, right?"

"Right." She raised her chin and stared back. "So, do I call him or what?"

"No. He's calling you." Suddenly, he looked almost sheepish. "I gave him your number."

Either Robin knew her better than she did, or he wasn't getting enough excitement in his life lately. She made a mental note to hold off telling him any deep bits from her life for a while.

When Robin left her office she called Sigmund Maier.

"Sheila." He sounded pleased. "It is good to hear your voice again."

She looked down at the scratch pad on her desk. John Demjanjuk's name was written there with bold, dark pencil lines. Around the name, a solid square box, the lines thick and unbroken. "I spoke with Mr. Douglass."

"Good then."

"I'm going to write the letter, Mr. Maier."

"Just so. Good."

"I was just wondering."

There was a pause. She heard him breathing. "Yes? You are wondering?"

She couldn't just say what she was wondering. She couldn't just say, *Mr. Maier, I was wondering, you know, if you were a Nazi and all because somebody says they have pictures and stuff.* She wanted to. But she couldn't.

"Sheila? What is it?"

She wet her lips. "I was just wondering, you know, if you had anyone else to write letters for you?"

Silence for a moment. "*Nein.*"

"What about your co-workers? The people you used to work with. And where did you go, you know, after and all? You must have worked at other places. With other people."

Silence for another moment. "Sheila, I stayed. At the same factory, after."

The ringing in her ears started up again, and she fought to keep focused. "You didn't leave your job when you moved away? You stayed at the same place? That same factory?"

"Yes. It was a good job. They were stable, yes? At least, I thought so." He gave a short dry laugh. "My employer bankrupted in 1981. I lost my pension. People left and took work in other provinces, the States. It was a recession, you understand?" He paused, and when he spoke again, his voice changed. "I – I tried, yes, but I cannot find anyone who knew me. No one." She imagined he was looking down at the floor, his shoulders slumped. He sounded so lost. "I was not, you know, close to anyone there. My supervisor, he was older than me. The others – I am not sure that anyone ..."

His voice quavered and she heard him breathing hard. He truly was an old man. She wanted to hold him and that idea frightened her. "It's okay. I was just wondering. I'll have the letter done tomorrow. Don't worry."

"Tomorrow?" The quaver was gone. "It is hard for you, Sheila? To write this letter?"

She frowned. "No. Not at all. I just want to be sure I have it as good as I can. I know it's important. That's all."

"Ah, just so." His old voice again. "You are a good girl, Sheila."

"Mr. Maier, I only know that a letter going into court needs to convey just the right information. I have to be accurate. Absolutely truthful."

Silence.

"Are you still there, Mr. Maier?"

"Yes, Sheila. I am still here."

She'd upset him. She knew that tone. Why did she say that? God, this was getting creepy. "Look, I don't intend to put anything in that letter other than the length of time you lived in our apartment, and that you paid your rent, and ..." She paused just for a moment. "And that you were kind to me. Nothing more. Okay?"

"Yes. Just so, Sheila."

"Mr. Maier?"

"Yes? What else?"

She had to ask. She had to. "You weren't, um, I mean, you didn't, back in Germany ..." She swallowed. "You weren't part of the Nazis, were you? Back then?"

He coughed. There was a pause. "Sheila. I was not. Not a Nazi." Another pause. "I was with the resistance, in Germany. I fought against the Nazis, Sheila. Against them."

If she could have leapt through the phone and hugged him, she would have. "The resistance? In Germany?"

"Yes."

"I had no idea there was a German resistance."

He laughed. "Oh yes. It was small, you understand? Too few were left. But it was there. And I was there too."

"Oh, Mr. Maier, that's great. That's just great. I didn't think that you could have, you know, been one. I was so sure."

"Good, Sheila, good. Thank you for helping me. It is good you called. I have some papers; I sent them to your office today by courier."

"Papers?"

"Yes. I realized that you may have questions. You should know about my life, how ordinary it is – was. I have copies of my papers when I arrived to Canada, and I want you to have them also, Sheila. They should arrive today."

"Okay. I'll look at them. Now I really have to go. I'll call if I have any problems with this, okay?"

She stared at the phone for a long time after she hung up.

The package arrived at the office just before 4:00 that afternoon. She glanced at the courier slip on top. *Pick up: 13:16. Status: Priority Rush.*

At least half an hour after she'd finished talking to him. After she'd hung up the phone.

Clearly, he decided to send her the papers while they were speaking. Or maybe he was confused. Thought he'd sent them to her, and then after he hung up, realized he hadn't. She decided not to call and ask.

Adjusting her reading glasses, Sheila went through the photocopied contents in the large brown envelope, placing them on her desk one by one.

One transit pass for Sigmund Gunther Maier, formerly of Aachen, West Germany, duly stamped and processed through Canadian Port of Entry, Saint John, New Brunswick, December 30, 1950.

One boarding pass for the *S. S. Beaverbrae.*

One faint copy of a document, transcribed and translated into English on an attached paper – his machinist training certificate.

One handwritten record of previous addresses attached to copies of numerous rent receipts for various Toronto locations over the years – there were dozens of addresses.

One Separation Certificate from Nikoma Tool and Die, Ltd. of Scarborough, Ontario, paper-clipped to a letter of recognition for "twenty-five years of service".

One Canada Pension Plan application, and annual statements from Nikoma's pension fund for 1978 to 1981 inclusive.

She stared at the letter of recognition. *Twenty-five years.* All that time; he'd been there all that time. She was upset by that, but she wasn't sure why. And then she remembered something, almost. And then it was gone.

Taking a deep breath, Sheila ran through all the papers once more. A dull and unoriginal packet of documents: the sum total of forty-nine years of residency, reduced to a small stack of paper. There was nothing of his music, nothing of his relationships with others. Despite what he said, there were relationships; she heard again the voice of that old woman: *I am looking for Mr. Sigmound Mayor* ...

That visitor had stayed a long time. Sheila remembered how she hoped the woman would come back after he'd left, but she never did. Sheila had forgotten about her until now. How could she forget the woman coming to find Mr. Maier, looking for him?

Sigmund Maier. A private person or not, if she was going to get any further with writing on his behalf she knew he'd have to be more forthcoming about his personal life. And she would have to be more aggressive in getting that information from him.

CHAPTER EIGHTEEN

IT WAS NEARLY 10:30 WHEN she pulled into the driveway. Kenneth's car wasn't in the garage. The day's mail was still stuffed in the box by the door. She wanted nothing more than a hot bath and cup of tea. Sigmund Maier and his personal life could wait until the morning.

The message light was flashing on the kitchen phone; while the kettle came to a boil, she took off the messages. There were only two. Kenneth, who was sorry, would be late again; the second voice was unfamiliar.

"Ernest Szabo here. I would like to speak with Sheila Martin. It is regarding Sigmund Maier. I can be reached at the Carleton Hotel until 2300 hours tonight and between 0800 and 1100 hours tomorrow." His voice held a soft European accent she couldn't place. She called the number right away and he answered on the first ring.

"Ms. Martin, I understand that you are, uh, assisting Sigmund Maier. A mutual acquaintance suggests that we should meet." He paused a moment. "I have papers you may wish to see."

"Are you with the government?"

"I am – a researcher. I gather information."

"I'm not sure I should be even talking with you."

"It is your choice. I regret I have little time for uncertainty. If you want more information about Sigmund Maier, you will meet me tonight. Or not."

"Your message said you'd be available until 11:00 tomorrow morning."

"I have switched to an earlier flight. I'll be gone by 0700. If you want to meet, it will have to be tonight."

"Where? It's twenty-five to eleven already." She had no desire to head downtown this late, and all this mystery – yet, she was intrigued. And Robin had arranged this.

He broke the momentary silence. "There is a coffee shop downstairs. It's open quite late. Can you be here in forty minutes?"

A coffee shop was public. And at a hotel – bound to be people around. She nodded. "Okay."

"Please don't be late. I have a long flight." He hung up before she could answer.

It rained all the way down the Parkway, a soft mist that softened the headlights of oncoming cars and trucks. Ahead and beside her, Toronto was spread out like a postcard.

The lobby was nearly empty, the bland décor on the verge of faded. Sheila took a deep breath before she crossed the front reception area to the coffee shop. She was beginning to fade herself, and she caught her reflection in the mirrors. Her confused expression made her stop mid-stride. She stood there in the middle of the lobby and organized her thoughts while she ran her fingers through her hair and straightened her suede jacket.

She never did anything for which she was not at all sure of her reasons. But she had to admit that she had no idea what she was doing here.

Besides an overly made-up waitress, there was only one person in the coffee shop. Towards the rear, an intense and thin-faced man sat in one of the booths lining the windows. The man looked up from his cup as she entered. He raised his hand just a bit, and nodded. Adjusting his glasses, he stood as she approached.

"Ms. Martin, I presume?"

"Mr. Szabo?" She took his hand, his palm was warm and dry, his handshake firm. His brown eyes were set beneath a pair of dark eyebrows that shot up and down every time he spoke. She tried not to look at them waving at her with almost every word that came out of his mouth.

"Please sit. Coffee, or perhaps a tea?" She nodded and he called over the waitress. The woman took her order, pleased to have something to do.

Sheila folded her hands together on top of the table. "You wanted to see me, to discuss information about Mr. Maier. What exactly is it that you wanted to discuss, Mr. Szabo?"

He didn't respond at first, taking a sip of his black coffee and dabbing at his lower lip with a paper napkin. "What is your involvement in this?" He looked at her quizzically.

She wondered what to tell him, weighing her curiosity against this man's role. Who was he working for that he'd even have a job with the government?

"I understand that Sigmund Maier is someone with whom you had, perhaps, a close relationship?" His smile and tone were bland, but his eyes carried something she found distasteful.

Sheila stiffened. "He's an old man – just an old man. Years ago, he lived in our basement apartment and we became …" She paused, searching. "We were friends, in a way. We both liked music very much, and he talked to me. He was a nice man." She watched his face as she spoke, his half-smile – his hard eyes. "Just who are you anyway?" His expression did not change. "My friendship with him is none of your business. I can see that I've been foolish to travel all the way down here," She began to slide out of the booth.

"Sigmund Maier is a murderer, Madame."

She stood at the end of the table and froze.

"A taker of lives. Women. Children. Old men just like him now. It didn't matter."

"What – why are you saying those things?"

He shrugged. "Because they are the truth. If you are at all interested in the truth, then you will stay to listen. If not …" He shrugged again. "I have some photos and papers that relate to Mr. Maier's activities during the war. You may want to see them."

She eased back into the booth, shaking her head. "Those are terrible accusations, Mr. Szabo. Terrible."

Up went his eyebrows. Down again, and then up. "I know, Ms. Martin, I know." Reaching to the seat beside him, he angled up a brown portfolio and removed a large black and white photograph. "You have, I imagine, seen films and photographs from the concentration camps?"

She shrugged and then nodded.

"Well then, I trust that this will not be too distressing." He passed her the picture.

She put on her reading glasses. The photo she held was of a haphazard stack of clothed bodies; visible parts of coats, dresses and shoes mingled with arms, legs and heads. Absurdly, at first she could only recall that in the pictures and film clips she'd seen, the emaciated bodies of victims were either naked or dressed in concentration camp rags. In this picture, there was no evidence of starvation, no shaved heads. On top of the heap and lying on its back, was a baby, no more than eight or nine months. The perfect picture of a sleeping cherub in smocked gown and bonnet – until Sheila looked closely at the half-opened eyes, the darkened cheeks rosy-looking.

He spoke as if he could read her mind. "A sign of the gas used. A lack of oxygen, suffocation, and the capillaries burst. But through the soft lens of distance, she is peaceful-looking, isn't she?"

Sheila looked up quickly. His eyes were cool, his expression controlled. He resumed his narration and Sheila heard tender fury in his voice.

"When I saw this picture, I thought she looked asleep. At first. In truth, hers was a terrible death. Spasms. Vomit." He pulled on the picture to take it back. Sheila noticed that his fingers were long and delicate, the nails carefully trimmed and filed. "This picture was taken by a young technical adjunct, part of a group sent to 'problem-solve' mechanical difficulties at some of the camps. Execution of the Final Solution order was not going well. Trucks with rigged exhausts and firing squads were simply not efficient. The cause of slowdowns, backups. Gas chambers were built. They improved the process, but were still less than perfect. And so experts came to develop and put in place certain efficiencies. See, here is the 'before' picture."

He passed her another photo, also black and white, this one slightly out of focus. It showed a small group of men, women and children, bewildered and wary-looking. They were herded together at the entrance of a long barracks-like building. No windows. The baby, alert and one little fist in her mouth, was in the arms of a dark-haired woman who stood towards the front of the group. The woman wore an attractive fur coat to which a young boy of four or five was clinging. "Incredibly efficient to arrange before and after shots, don't you think? Such a penchant for detail – it left a massive record that allowed for some to hide within the minutiae." He passed her another photo. "At least, for a time."

This picture was obviously another 'before' shot. Most of the people from the original group were still in the frame, some in the act of turning as if to move inside the building. The change revealed more of the background. Standing next to the building's open doors were three men, two in uniform and one in white coveralls, a clipboard in his hand. She knew it was Sigmund Maier without even a close look.

"My source tells me he was instrumental in adjusting the flow problems they were having with the vents. He cut the time between gassings by over 27%." Szabo took another sip of his coffee. "*Remarkable.*"

Sheila heard a car pass out on the wet street, followed by an engine starting up nearby. She glanced out the window next to the booth. Her reflection stared back in the glass, but she could also see outside areas lit by streetlights. It had stopped raining. She turned to face Szabo. "Has he seen these?"

"Not from me, but he knew they existed. He likely thought they were destroyed or lost years ago. Just one or two pictures among thousands and thousands." He removed a sheet of paper from the portfolio. "Now, this report is interesting. It is about moles within the German resistance and, in particular, one Sigmund Maier is identified as being a brilliant Gestapo agent. Apparently, someone felt he should be given special recognition by The Fuehrer for saving his life and wrote this to start the wheels into motion. Do you see the date?"

He held the paper before her. It was a photocopied report, with the symbols of Nazism and the Third Reich across the top. It was in German. It might as well be gibberish for her.

Szabo smiled ironically, his finger jabbing the paper, beside the date. "Two days after the arrest of three resistance members in 1945. The remnants of the trade unionists they were, betrayed by a person or persons from within their own organization." He removed another photo, this one in front of a narrow old-fashioned railway station. Men in long dark coats shoving other men into dark cars. He pointed once more. "They were arrested here. Right here. Executed the same day."

She tried to focus, to follow what he was saying. He continued, relentless.

"It is ironic, don't you think? Not only did Sigmund Maier function as an agent for the Gestapo, he also worked quite diligently as a machinist and technician. It was his mechanical skill that got him that choice little assignment at the camps. A busy man. Murderer. Betrayer."

Sheila raised both of her hands and held them, palms out, before her. "Now just a minute, Mr. Szabo. There could have been more than one Sigmund Maier. That agent or mole or whatever you called him, he could have been anyone." She narrowed her eyes, lowering her hands to the table. "I never even heard of a German resistance, until Mr. Maier told me." She stopped, suddenly wary of saying too much.

Szabo paused as the waitress arrived. He stirred the refill she poured for him, mixing in three spoonfuls of sugar. After she moved away, he resumed, "Sigmund Maier was always a pleasant man to chat with. Dietrich Schneider told my uncle of the many fine conversations he had with the young Sigmund. Sigmund and his mother Hilda lived in his building. In Dresden. Interestingly, my uncle was Dietrich's bunkmate at one of the camps." He paused and laughed bitterly. "One of nine bunkmates at the time. It was cozy. My uncle said Dietrich recognized Maier at the camp when he came to perform his, uh, maintenance duties. Schneider was sure that Sigmund Maier would help him. My uncle never forgot watching Maier turn and walk away as Schneider called out his name – *Sigmund Maier, Sigmund Maier.*" He shook his head. "The Kapos kicked him to death that night. Kicked to death because he called out Maier's name." He took a sip of the black steaming liquid. "Ah yes, a pleasant man to chat with."

She tried to reconcile all the information with what she knew. Mr. Maier told her he wasn't a Nazi and yet, here, proof he was at the camps. But not in uniform, just holding a clipboard, making notes perhaps, perhaps even plotting ways to end Hitler's regime.

And Ernest Szabo's stories were his uncle's memories. One old man pointing his aging finger at another old man. European hatreds still ran deep; the tendency to lump all Germans as Nazis was nothing new. She heard her grandmother's lowered voice: *Is he German, Eleanor?*

"Mr. Szabo, what is it you want?"

"I was, uh, retained by certain parties to conduct investigations and to bring that information to the attention of your government. The past activities of several Canadian residents are of interest to my clients." He adjusted his glasses. "And Sigmund Maier is of special interest, given my family connection." He folded his hands, resting them on the table. "Maier is a frightening man, Ms. Martin. Your friend believes that your involvement is, well, misdirected – born out of obligation and kindness. He suggested that I share some of my material to help you review your position."

She tensed. "Mr. Maier is also my friend."

He ignored her. "Your government often prefers a – how do I say? – a low-key approach to conflict." He did not hide the sarcasm. "Do you know how many war criminals have been successfully tried in your country, Ms. Martin?"

She shook her head.

"Not one. Not a single prosecution to bring justice to those who rained horror down on others. Fortunately, there are one or two people within the process for whom this still mattered. And so, you have the immigration hearings." He smiled. "I suppose it doesn't matter what starts the process as long as justice arrives. But it has been, for some, too long."

She was having trouble keeping it all straight – who he was and why she was here. "One minute you're part of the government, the next, you're not. I'm having difficulty with this, Mr. Szabo, a great deal of difficulty. I'm not even certain if you even are Ernest Szabo."

He coughed. "Please, Ms. Martin, you speak as if this is some secret spy film. I assure you I am who I say I am. As to your friend in Ottawa, I imagine that he felt concern for you and your connection to this man and his, uh, situation. And I agreed that you should have a better understanding of the facts." His expression was bland, almost bored.

Sheila was so done with this. No way was she going to be some patsy for shadow clients. Szabo could even be a crazy person and she had nearly fallen for his whole clever show. She lifted her chin. "You know, it is entirely possible your 'facts' are less than accurate, or a clever fabrication. The man you accuse of being a part of all that horror taught me a lot. Sigmund Maier opened my eyes to the world around me, showed me where to find beauty in music and art. I was just some dumb kid and he took an interest in me. Because of him, I've read literature, history – attended opera, symphonies, sat on arts councils – things I never would have done without his help. You tell me he is capable of murdering children, of betraying friends? I think we speak of two different men, Mr. Szabo, and you have the wrong one. My Sigmund Maier is not, I repeat, not your Sigmund Maier."

He said nothing at first, keeping his gaze level and direct. The waitress moved towards them, coffee pot in hand. His eyes never left Sheila's as he raised his left hand, palm out; the waitress retreated to the cash register up front. He turned and reached into the portfolio once more. "I do understand how difficult this must be to you. I understand the pull of loyalty, friendship ..." He paused. "Of affection, Ms. Martin."

He handed her a thick file folder. "These are just copies. I think you should have them ... all of them. Maier's lawyer has these as well but you have not seen them, have you." It was not a question. "I suggest you review the file, give your full attention to it, and if you still feel secure, then so be it. I have done all I can." He stood, picking up his portfolio in one smooth motion. "With you," he added.

Placing some cash on the table, he held out his hand. "Madame," he offered. His hand was still warm, the palm without any hint of moisture; nonetheless, she couldn't hold the handshake for more than a moment. He started to walk away, and then turned back for a moment. "Should you have questions, my email is on the inside of the folder."

Sheila watched him cross the lobby and step into an elevator before opening the file in front of her. She didn't want to look, really. But she would. And she'd look with hard eyes, not ready to be swayed by heartbreaking photos. It was terrible what happened. But the world has always been full of terrible things and there was always room for interpretation. She had no long history of family lines extinguished in the ovens. Yes, it was terrible. Awful, really. But she'd look at this file with a clear vision of what she knew. And she knew Sigmund Maier was not capable of what Szabo said.

Before she finally took off her reading glasses and got up to leave the coffee shop, before she gathered up all her dread and horror, before she repacked the papers and photos inside the file, before she could lift her eyes to the face of the waitress asking if she wanted anything else, Ma'am, anything else, before she fumbled in her purse, fishing for money to leave next to her cup, it was nearly 2:00 a.m.

She had no recollection of the ride home, and was almost surprised to find herself turning into her driveway. Kenneth's car was in the garage, the hood still warm. She knew there would be no sleep tonight and, for just a moment, considered going upstairs, perhaps waking him if he'd already fallen asleep. She took a walk to the fridge instead. Eventually she went to bed, not at all comforted by the warm milk. Just before dawn, she fell into a kind of sleep haunted by rosy-cheeked babies and the sound of hissing gas.

CHAPTER NINETEEN

Sigmund Maier opened his apartment door before she could knock. A linen napkin tucked in at his throat, he welcomed her with enthusiasm. "Come in, Sheila, come in. I – I am just completing my lunch. Are you hungry?"

She shook her head. Her coat was slung over her arm; she gripped the large file folder in sweating fingers. "I met a Mr. Szabo yesterday." She kept her tone even, noncommittal. "Mr. Szabo is a kind of private detective, Mr. Maier."

For a brief moment, his eyes widened. "Ah yes, just so." He gestured for her to come in.

She stepped though the doorway and followed him down the hall. He crossed the living room and took his seat in the dining nook. The remains of a sausage and boiled potato lay on his plate. He smiled pleasantly, signalling with his hand that she should sit. She remained standing. He steepled his fingertips and waited.

"Mr. Szabo's been to Israel and to Europe, investigating. Talking with people. Researching. He brought me some documents and photographs. They're all about you, Mr. Maier."

"I see."

"Do you?" She looked at him and then at the file folder she held. She shook her head, trying to clear it. "I need to understand what these documents mean." Her voice was flat, leaden. She tossed the file onto the dining room table and it fell open. Several papers fanned out, a photo on top. A young Sigmund looked out from the small black and white picture, his arms slung casually around the shoulders of two other laughing young men.

They wore the uniform of the Brownshirts; Sigmund's soft cap was tilted far back on his head, the visor rising up on top like a halo. His smile was broad, confident, his tall figure trim and electric. The three men stood together among the broken glass and strewn contents of a storefront.

"They mean what they mean, Sheila." He remained seated, now a coffee cup in hand.

"Mr. Maier, I have worked on your behalf. When this Szabo started in telling me all this, I was prepared to write dozens of letters, contact lawyers, even the goddamned Prime Minister's office. On your behalf. I would have done this, all this, because you asked for my help. Because you said they had the wrong man." She took a step back from the table. "I need to understand, Mr. Maier, I need to understand and sort through what all this means."

He put the cup onto the table. Hesitating just a moment, he reached across and lifted up the top picture. He had a slight smile as he adjusted his glasses and peered closely at the photo.

"This means, Sheila, this means that Gerhardt and Anton have just told me the most interesting joke and Heinz took the picture just after." She took another step away from the table. "This also means that I, along with Gerhardt, Anton, Heinz and many others, was caught up in the time, Sheila. The time. It was a magnificent time to be German, to be young back then. Everyone," he paused, straightening his shoulders, "everyone was filled with a kind of fever. It was power like we had never known, Sheila."

"You were a Nazi. God." It was a relief to say it out loud.

"Of course, of course. Everyone was, you understand. Almost everyone."

"You said that you were never one of them. Never."

"Sheila, that is true also. The person I am today was never a, a Nazi. The person I am could not be one. Sheila, people change, situations change. I left the National Socialist Party long before 1939, emotionally left them. It had been a game, a youthful game of which I tired."

He coughed and put a hand to his chest. Pausing long enough to sip at his coffee, he continued, "As I told you, I joined the resistance. I connected through my machinist work with what was left of the trade unionists. We wanted to make changes. For a long time, I did not see what could be done – but I knew that Hitler was a madman. In time, there was a plot to assassinate him. I was involved, but only in a small part. The leaders were betrayed and arrested. I was fortunate to escape. Soon after, they began to call up even the skilled workers, and I was sent to northern Italy." He put the picture down. "We surrendered to the Americans, and I spent the last few weeks of the war in a prison camp."

"These papers and pictures prove you were involved in con-centration camps." She looked out the apartment window. "That you helped with ... maintenance. Two separate witnesses – living witnesses – can place you there. Their statements are here. There are pictures; you can see for yourself." She closed her eyes but the baby's face was still there. Even in black and white: the telltale flush on the soft round cheeks, the whites of her eyes through just-open lids, the wisps of hair contained by the starched and pleated bonnet.

"To begin, Sheila, I have seen this, seen the statements, the photographs. Those pictures and documents are all with my law-yer. I know what these people are saying I did. But, Sheila, it was war. We all did things, Canadians, British, Americans, French, all of us did things because we had to. I had to survive, and yes, once, I was sent by the foundry to fix problems they had at a camp. Design problems. I could not refuse. I would call atten-tion to myself and perhaps that would betray others. Those in the resistance – their work was important, Sheila. I did not stay there, only went to fix things. It was ... difficult ...

The air dark and ripe with such a stench. Razor wire beside and now behind as the gate closes after the last one.

Toward the end of the line, he thinks he recognizes one of the women. It cannot be. Older. Thinner. Perhaps ... he is almost certain it is Giselle.

He watches until he can no longer see her.

... Difficult."

Sheila pulled out a chair and sat down. She moved her hands through her hair, resting them for a moment on the back of her neck. The stack of photos and papers waited expectantly. "I see." She was capable of nothing more.

Sigmund stood up and went to his stereo. Schubert began to drift through the apartment in sweet, quiet notes. Sigmund sat back down, covering his eyes with his hands as he spoke, his voice frail and trembling. "Ah, Sheila. It was not so easy then."

She looked at him, his liver-spotted hands over his eyes, his thin white hair, his tremor. She supposed that it had not been so simple. What would she have done? *Following orders.* Always a convenient response, but he did have to protect his friends in the resistance – that part made sense. Given the same situation, given the same set of circumstances, what decision would she have made?

She stood up. "Look. This is all a lot of information for me to understand. To process." She gathered the photos and papers back into the folder. "I guess I can see how this might have happened. How you had – had bigger things to consider – your resistance work. But I think you better write all this down. Take some time and get all the facts written down and give it all to your lawyer."

"Sheila, forgive me, but do you not think that I have done that?"

She crossed the living room, moving towards the hall, incredibly tired. The file was in her hand, pressed against her chest. "Mr. Maier," she began, "please. There's nothing else, you've told me everything?" He took his hands from his face.

"I am sorry that I did not tell you about the camps, but I was not sure that you would understand. It was wrong not to tell you before this, and I am sorry." He rose from the table and walked over to where she stood in the hall.

"I need to think all this over."

"Of course." He placed his hand on her arm, gently. "If you do not wish to return, I understand."

"I'll call you tomorrow. I need to read this over again and think about what you've told me and then I'll call you. Okay?"

"Yes, just so."

After she left, he returned to the living room and stood for a moment staring out the window. He moved over to the stereo, switched tracks on the CD and then returned to his seat at the table. With the full power of Beethoven in the background, he slid the photograph from under his plate. He smiled broadly at the expression on Gerhardt's and Anton's faces.

"Ah Gerhardt, it was good to laugh, *ja*? Even then?"

Placing the photo on the kitchen counter, he filled the sink with water and poured himself one more coffee.

* * *

When Sheila arrived home, Beth was in the great room. She was on the couch, wrapped tight inside a quilt, and didn't look up as Sheila came into the kitchen. No TV. No headphones. Just sitting there, cocooned.

"Beth?"

Nothing. Not even a glance her way.

Sheila considered ignoring her, but then, "Beth. What's wrong?"

This time the eyes came up. They were Kenneth's eyes. Beth mirrored just about all of Sheila's features, but she inherited her father's large brown eyes. His best feature – and hers.

She looked back down. "Nothing." Her voice was so small, Sheila could almost close her eyes and imagine that her daughter was five years old again.

Sheila walked into the great room. She sat on the edge of the big chair opposite her daughter. "Look, I'm not trying to be nosey—"

"Then don't be and just leave me alone."

Jesus. Slapping her would be too easy. Maybe just buy her a one-way ticket to BC. Let her go 'find herself'. Sheila remembered finding herself. Hitchhiking all the way out west after she left home. Sixteen. On her own. Easy. A little feel-up here, a little deep throat there, and it was pretty much a free ride. Meals. Beds. Truckers. Whatever. Whoever. And sometimes, just conversation.

"Okay, Beth." She stood.

Her daughter looked up, her face screwed up into a tight little fury. And something else. Sheila knew that something else. Knew it like she knew which steps on the basement stairs creaked all those years ago. She moved to where Beth sat scrunched up, and lowered herself beside her daughter. Put her arms around Beth's shoulders, ignoring how she tried to pull away. Just gathered her child into her arms, patted her back and rocked her. After the barest hesitation, Beth let herself go, allowed herself to be rocked and held. And then the crying started.

Sheila said nothing. She just kept hanging on. If she opened her mouth, if she said anything at all, her little girl would disappear, vanish. So she just held on. And they stayed that way, Beth's heaving sobs eventually fading to sniffles and sighs, until the phone rang.

Sheila was prepared to let the machine pick it up, but Beth pulled away from her, flung off the quilt and ran to the phone.

"Colin?" Her daughter's voice was almost frantic as she answered. Beth frowned, and then held out the phone in Sheila's direction. "It's for you. It's some man."

Sheila took the receiver. "Yes?"

"Sheila." It was him. Calling her at home. When did she give him her number? "I regret that I did not talk with you before. I do not – I wish not to have you angry, Sheila. Please. Can you come back and I will tell you all of my story?"

He sounded so old again. One minute Mr. Vigour, the next Mr. Geriatric. She took a deep breath. "Yeah. I can come back." She glanced over at Beth who was doing her best to look like she wasn't listening. "But not today. Today I have things I need to take care of in my family."

"Just so."

"Tomorrow. I'll come by tomorrow."

"Good. You will stay for a long time, Sheila? We will talk, and I will tell you all of the story and you will not have appointments or meetings?"

She sighed. "That's right. I'll book off the entire afternoon. I'm all yours."

There was silence on the line. And then, "*Bitte*. All mine, Sheila. For the afternoon."

She said goodbye, hung up and turned to face Beth, who was back on the couch, not quite entirely wrapped up in the blanket but still scrunched into the corner. Sheila sat beside her. Not so close this time, but close enough that she could reach out if the opportunity arose.

Beth spoke first. "Who was that?"

"An old friend. Someone who needs my help." And then because she thought she should say more, she added, "When I was young, he was kind to me. Changed my life, really. So I owe it to him, you know?"

Beth nodded. "Yeah. Changed your life, right?"

"Yes. He did. I didn't have a great childhood."

"You've said that." She looked down at the floor. "You remind me of that every chance you get."

Sheila took a deep breath. "Well. Maybe I just figured you should appreciate what you have here is a lot more than what I ever had."

"You've mentioned that too." She turned and faced her mother. "Every chance you get, I'm reminded what a lucky little girl I am." She licked her lips. "Lucky Beth."

"I guess I tell you that a lot."

Beth said nothing.

"Look, Beth. I'm not a perfect mother. God knows my role model was—" She stopped herself. How many times had she told Beth this one too? She started again. "I guess because I'm hard on me I'm hard on you. Ardith says I need control in my life because I had so little of it when I was growing up."

"Ardith?"

Sheila chuckled. "Six years of biweekly therapy appointments with Ardith and I can finally admit I'm a control freak. What a surprise."

"You have a therapist?"

Sheila sat back and looked at her daughter closely. "You knew that. Surely you knew that?"

Beth shook her head.

Was this possible? Could Beth not have known? Of course, it wasn't like she discussed her life's intimate details with her daughter. But this! Why not this? The ringing in her ears started up, and she leaned forward, shaking her head to clear it. "Beth, I'm – I'm surprised that you didn't know." She tried to laugh. "Don't any of your friends' mothers go to therapists?"

"Yeah. I guess a lot of them do. But they aren't strong like you."

Sheila sat back again. "Strong. Like me?"

Beth nodded. "You always know what you're doing. Where you're going." She looked down at her fingers. "Not like me. Not like me at all."

"Beth. You are so wrong. You are absolutely strong – look how you go for things. You're on the student council, the debate team."

"I haven't been on the council since Grade 9. Two years ago. And the debate team was last year. I quit after Christmas."

Sheila licked her lips. "Oh." She blinked a couple of times. Started again. "Well, you went out for them. Gave them a try. Strong doesn't mean succeeding at everything, you know. Just having the guts to see how things are, to try them on. That's strength, Beth."

"You always say you have to stick with things. Be strong you say, and stick with it."

Sheila shrugged. "Oh, don't always listen to what I say, for heaven's sake."

They looked at each other. Sheila realized how ridiculous she'd just sounded, and she chuckled. Beth smiled, and then she, too, was chuckling. The more Sheila struggled to stop laughing, the more she let go. It was a minute or so before she had herself calm enough to speak.

"I think what I meant to say is, 'Don't listen to *everything* I say.'" She sighed. "After all, no mother is always right, eh?" She thought of her own mother. Of how she worked so hard. Of how she'd been handed so many disappointments. She constantly carried her fury, and held close her distrust, her dark vision of the world. "I remember my mother bringing home a stray cat this one time. Scrawny little thing. All black except for the patches of white at his throat and on his toes. We called him Tuxedo. My mother loved that cat, and it was the strangest thing. All of us kids had asked and asked and asked for a pet – for years. A cat. A dog." She smiled. "A pony. But Mom always said no. 'Too much bother. Can't afford it. They carry germs.' You know." Beth nodded. "But that cat was her cat, and for four years, from the minute she came home to when she had to leave for work, Tuxedo never left her side." She wet her lips. "So one day, I was washing up in the kitchen and my mom was sitting at the table, drinking tea. The cat was on her lap, purring. And I said to her, I said 'Mom. I'm glad you changed your mind about pets.' And she looked up at me with the oddest look on her face. And she said, 'You know, Sheila, sometimes mothers are not always right.' She sounded like she wanted to say more. I didn't know it at the time, but I think she was trying to say she was sorry. Back then, I figured she was talking about her own mother, my Granny. But it has just come to me now, that maybe she was talking about herself. And me." She blinked.

Beth reached across and put her hand on Sheila's hand.

Sheila took her other hand and covered her daughter's.

Beth cleared her throat. "I'm sorry, Mom."

"Me too, Beth. Me too." The phone rang again. Sheila glanced over at her daughter. "Want me to get it?"

Beth nodded.

It was Colin, and Sheila brought the portable over for her daughter. "We'll talk some more later, okay?"

Beth didn't say anything, but as she left to go upstairs and change, Sheila caught just a snippet of Beth's side of the conversation. "No! I didn't. Not yet." Beth spoke in an almost furious whisper, and Sheila fought the temptation to go back and find out what she didn't do.

When she returned downstairs to the kitchen, Beth was gone. Sheila called her from the top of the basement stairs and then she hollered up to the upper floor. The house was silent.

So much for quality time.

Kenneth came home before six. When she got over the surprise, Sheila asked him if he was hungry.

He shrugged. "Yeah. Do you want to order in?"

Sheila looked up from the notes and papers on her lap. Though Kenneth always wore his hair short and neat, it looked a bit messed up tonight. Wind-blown. For a moment she saw the Kenneth she had first married, when he used to rumple up his hair just to make her laugh. When was that? How long ago? She shrugged. "How about I toss something together tonight? I'm hungry too." She realized she hadn't had lunch today. She rummaged in the freezer for a couple of packaged salmon filets, threw on some pasta and mixed up a salad. Then, without being sure why – maybe because it had been so long – Sheila decided to set the dining room table and open a bottle of wine. Kenneth walked past the opened French doors and did a double take. "We're eating in here, Sheila? What's the occasion?"

"No occasion. I just thought, you know, it might be nice for a change. You being home and all."

He didn't say anything. But he did find the matches and light the candles.

It was her turn to do a double take.

Dinner was pleasant enough. They didn't talk about Beth. They didn't discuss Sigmund Maier. They kept it all to business. She asked him about the fall lineup of books; which titles were pegged as being likely successes, which ones were clearly a mistake. He shrugged. "That's the thing of it, I guess. Just when you figure we've got the readers all sorted out, something comes along and knocks the whole thing out of kilter." He took a sip of his wine. "Take that Rowling woman. If anyone suggested that a book about an orphaned boy wizard would take the reading public by storm, they would have been laughed right out of the editorial meetings. And I guess more than a few were. And yet, here she is with a monster hit on her hands, three books already in the series and there are more coming. Incredible."

"Does Laurentian have anything like that coming up? Books about a boy wizard?"

"No." He shook his head. "And adults are reading Rowling also. Bugger."

She ran her fingers down the stem of her wine glass. "It's the same in any business. Remember when I had a chance to partner with that group fixing up the theatre and putting up a little musical in Toronto? No, says I – Musicians' Clearinghouse is not into stage productions. How was I to know live theatre would become as popular as it did in Toronto in the last decade?" She rubbed her temple. "I wasn't asked again. Stupid."

"I remember when you told me they'd approached you."

"You said you'd lend me the cash if I thought I should do it." She stared at him. "We were just off the ground with the Clearinghouse, and yet, you would find me the money if I was ready to risk it." She swallowed. "I'd forgotten that, Ken. Forgotten all about it."

He nodded. "Like I always say – you always have to make decisions in business. Some you'll regret. Some you won't." He shrugged. "A real accounting philosopher, eh?"

She sat back in her chair. Where did this man come from? First Beth's little moment of mother/daughter-ness. Now Kenneth. Was there some strange convergence of the stars? Was she still in bed, dreaming? She stood and reached for the pasta bowl with one hand, and her wine glass with the other.

Kenneth shifted in his chair and touched her arm. "Let's not. Just let's sit here a while longer." He shrugged. "Let's talk."

"Talk?" She sat back down, appraising him. "How much wine have you had, Kenneth?"

"What?"

"Well, you haven't been home for dinner in weeks. And now you want to sit here and chat." She took a deep breath. "I just wondered. How much wine have you had?" She meant it as a joke. She'd really wanted to say something funny, to have them laughing together. It had been such a long drought between times of laughter. Between touches. But she didn't sound like she was joking. It surprised her, though she made no attempt to clarify – to make plain her intentions.

And then she knew. She was not joking. Not in the least.

He glared at her. "I should have known."

"What? What should you have known?"

"That you would not want to sit here, with me. That you would say something to set me off." He stood up. "So we argue."

"Well, at least that's something. That's something more than dead dry silence. More than constant absence. More than that, at least."

He stood up and strode from the room. She heard him head up the stairs, cross the hall, and slam the bedroom door. She took her time clearing the table. While she was loading the dishwasher, he came back down the stairs. She waited to see if he would come into the kitchen. Instead, she heard him cross the foyer and leave through the laundry room entry. A minute or so later, an engine fired up in the garage. The garage door opened. And then closed.

He was going to his lover. She didn't think he knew that she knew. Men were so transparent. The condo uptown, the business trips to the Caribbean, the States. She almost balked when she came across that first jewellery invoice; it did seem extravagant. But when she worked it out it was a small price, really.

She had known, almost from the start. So, she didn't have to perform for him. His needs were met. Hers were met other ways, ways she controlled. It was better this way. Mature and calm.

She moved to the CD player and took out Handel from the shelves above. *Water Music.* From Tafelmusik. Some baroque pomp, some strings, some sense of legacy. That is what she needed. That and a drink. She opened another bottle of wine, and finished off more than half of it just sitting in the great room, breathing in the notes. Occasionally she wondered about Beth, if she was coming home soon, but mostly she just sat there, listening to Handel. After Handel, Mozart. By the time she made her way upstairs, everything had a nice gauzy layer on. She ran a bath. Filled the deep tub with warm water and scented oils, lit some candles and soaked her whole body. It was so strange. Drunk. She knew she was absolutely drunk. And yet, she felt so alive. Absolutely conscious of everything. But still all wrapped in a soft, filmy gauze.

She towelled herself dry, listening to the sound of the water rushing through the narrow drain. Deliberately, she bent over the candles and blew them out, one by one. She chose a satin nightgown, blue with white ribbons. She delighted in the way the material slipped over her shoulders and fell against her skin. She traced her fingertips up and down her bare arms, over her chest. There were wrinkles at her elbows, dry patches, pockets of fat. Her breasts, tired and sagging. How different she was. Once. *Her arms ... her shoulders ... her back ... his breath, hot on her face.*

She could make love to herself. She closed her eyes and the room spun. She opened them again. Maybe not.

She fell onto her bed and drifted. The room moved first in a spin, and then in undulations. An earthquake. She should open her eyes. She dreamt.

His hands, so strong, pressing her. She raises her hips, responds to his touch. He reaches up, up under her dress. She opens her legs, feels his fingertips. Such sweet treasure, ja. Mäuschen. Liebste. *Beautiful.* Ja. *She is. She is beautiful ...*

Sheila opened her eyes to the dark. Kenneth. Kenneth was on top of her, breathing, pushing against her, sliding himself inside her. And she was pushing back, her hips lifting in a swift rhythm of response. It had been so long since her thighs had gripped his hips. So long since he wanted her. Since she wanted him. In the back of her mind, she wondered if she had ever wanted him. With each insistent thrust, each gasp from his straining mouth, she wondered if it was really him. She closed her eyes. She heard Chopin. Tasted tea and biscuits. Fingertips. She felt her climax rise up, rise up and meet his. It had been so long. She almost cried out his name.

Sigmund. My darling Sigmund.

CHAPTER TWENTY

WHEN SHE WOKE IN THE morning, she was alone in her bed. She stayed very still and waited to sort out the blur in her head. There had been a dream – she remembered a dream or a nightmare – someone touching her. She rolled over and the vague shadows vanished; she couldn't remember what the dream was about, only that someone kissed her. She touched herself, sniffed at her fingers, inhaled sex. After several long minutes she got up and went to take a shower.

She drove into work with Vaughan Williams playing; it seemed a good morning for it. Blue sky to hold the high sweet notes. Warm spring sunshine that would be too warm by noon. But the music was too sweet. Almost cloying. She flipped to Jann Arden. It was an Arden kind of day: lyrics you could think about. Or not. And her great sense of musicality. Arden must have had classical training at some point. *Learn from the great composers, Sheila.*

She almost missed her turnoff and had to change lanes in an unpopular sort of way. She ignored the finger from the guy in the van and merged into the line of cars travelling on the exit lane.

Great composers. As if that was all there was. She had developed her ear with someone devoted to a narrow range of music. *The great composers, Sheila. They are all dead. No one creates the rich complexity of these masters today.* She remembered asking why there were no women composers. Sigmund had looked at her in the oddest way. He never did answer. And she never questioned him on that again. And as if it all had to be the 'masters'. *Good Mother* came on. Would he like Jann Arden? Would he ever sit still for Billie Holiday? Annie Lennox? Oscar Peterson? The Barenaked Ladies?

Thank God for high school music teachers. Like Mr. Bernstein. Mr. B.

After that whole 'finding herself out west trip', she came back home. Well, actually to Willowdale, near the Scarborough border. Close enough to feel not so adrift; far enough away that they called it something else. But she was a Scarborough girl after all, and her 'mixed-used' zoning just didn't fit the 'strictly residential' mould.

It must have been God or the fates or karma that placed both her and Mr. B at the Mac's Milk that Saturday afternoon. She was asking the girl behind the counter for an application, and the bitch was looking at her like she was scum. Of course, the long stringy hair, bare feet and unmistakable odour of cigarettes and Mary Jane might have been scum inspiration.

A hand had touched her shoulder. "Sheila Barnes?"

That same nice face and laughing eyes. Same gentle voice. *That's okay, Sheila. This time, just slow down your fingering and tighten up your lips a bit on the mouthpiece.*

Unlike the bitch behind the counter, he didn't seem to notice she needed a bath.

She spent that night with him and his wife in their North York apartment. Mrs. B gave her some clothes. She had a shower. Ate. Slept in their second bedroom. She stayed awake in that clean comfortable bed for a long time, waiting. But nobody came in and asked her to do anything. When she finally fell asleep, it was the best sleep she'd had in a long time.

By the end of the week, he'd found a group home for her.

It was crazy but she finished school. Actually graduated with honours. Got a full scholarship for university. Studied music with a minor in business. Had affairs with two of her profs. Was asked by one to go west with him when he was offered a new post. Declined. Moved in with the other prof. Had her second abortion. Graduated.

The car driving in front of hers stopped for the yellow light and Sheila hit her brakes hard. She glanced at herself in the rearview mirror. She looked like hell. Like sleep wasn't possible. She decided to cancel Sigmund for that afternoon. What was she doing it for, anyway? She'd written the letter, extolling his virtues and incredible impact on her, and confirming his tidy and responsible habits. He had a high-profile lawyer. There was no point in her staying involved. The more she thought about it, the more she realized she was just indulging a little fantasy, trying to recapture a half-remembered idea of someone. Enough already.

She called Robin into her office almost as soon as she arrived at work. "I need you to call Mr. Maier and cancel my meeting with him this afternoon."

"When do you want to rebook?"

"Never." She caught his expression and continued. "But don't tell him that. Just figure out some sort of delay, you know, something about the merger coming up. Tell him I have to travel to Europe."

Robin shook his head, and let out three distinct tsk sounds.

"Well, I do have to meet with the Quebec group next month. He doesn't have to know it's next month, does he?"

Robin shrugged. "Guess not. Okay, I'll take care of it. Speaking of the Quebec group, they wanted another look at the stats for the move into the southeastern States."

Sheila frowned. "Do you think they're getting nervous again? Not sure we'd be a hit in Nashville?"

"Not really. More likely they think they can jig the numbers and ask for a larger share purchase."

"Let's put a stop to that. You call the banks on this one, Robin. I'll follow up with that poutine myself. If Costair thinks I'm going to blink and give him a larger piece of la tarte, he is in for a wake-up call, eh?"

Robin blew her a kiss. "Oh, I adore you when you're nasty."

She grinned. "Only when I have to be."

He paused at the door. "You're sure about that other thing?"

"Other thing?"

"Mr. Maier."

She nodded. "Oh yeah. That's for sure. Cancel."

It was nearly 9:30 p.m. when she arrived at Sigmund Maier's apartment. Somehow he'd sweet-talked the usually unmoveable Robin and ended up speaking directly with Sheila. "You are so busy, Sheila. I know this. But I think it is important, you understand? I promise, this will be the last time. Just this once."

And so she found herself, as before, in his dining nook. This time Sheila was seated, just to his left. The file sat unopened to her left, a pad of lined paper before her. Otherwise, the table was bare. She looked at the pad of paper. This wasn't a business meeting. Why did she have it? Nonetheless, she gripped her pen and wrote the date in the upper right-hand corner. Focus, Sheila. Just focus and get this done with and then get out. Like any other unpleasant but necessary meeting.

"Tell me again how you came to the camps."

He nodded. "As I told you, we were sent to help with certain mechanical problems."

"Why did they pick you?"

"I was good. I had been apprenticed as machinist since I was fifteen, and I had some electrical skill as well. Pipefitting. Many skills, yes? The foundry I trained in was quite large. The works extensive." He smiled slightly. "It was so different then. They were not strict about double shifts and overtime. You could learn other trades."

You follow me like a puppy, Maier! Here – at least be useful and hold this.

He shrugged. "I had good reports. They made me part of the team."

"The team?"

"We were not official, we were to observe – make suggestions. We had to be careful of ah, egos, you understand?"

"Apparently you made good suggestions."

"Yes, just so."

She opened the file. "Is that your picture? There, with the clipboard?"

"Yes." He barely glanced at the picture before him. "As I told you yesterday."

Sheila put a hand to her throat. She looked away. Saw the baby in her mother's arms. Small baby fist in her tiny mouth. Satin ribbon under her chin, holding the lace bonnet in place.

"Remember, Sheila, to refuse was dangerous. For me and the others."

"You made recommendations that increased the rate of, of exterminations? 27%?"

"We averaged 21%, but my supervisor recorded the best results."

She cocked an eyebrow. "How nice."

"I was part of a team. They expected results. And after, it was more humane."

She swallowed again. "Humane?"

"Yes. Before, the saturation was less efficient, the gas is heavier than the air. The granules were released in a far too haphazard way. Before, it took too long for some to die – in agony, Sheila. I equalized the distribution; increased the outlets. They were going to die; it was a matter of how long."

"I see." She wrote "27% was 21%" on her pad. Beside it she wrote "protect resistance". She wrote "more humane" and then scratched it over.

"Coffee?"

She shook her head. "The resistance. Can you tell me who was with you? Maybe Douglass can track some of them down."

"The foundry was destroyed in the raids. Anyone from my cell either died in the foundry or in the streets of Dresden. Or, between the two." His blue eyes narrowed, became vague. "Before 1945, before 13 and 14 February ... There were already few of them left ..." He looked down at his hands. "They say the asphalt ran like rivers. The air was sucked away by the heat it was so hot, and the stonework of the Frauenkirche melted, dissolved. The Semper, a shell. The foundry in Freiberg where I worked ..." He sighed and shook his head.

"You managed to survive?"

"I was ... detained elsewhere. Soon after, I was a prisoner of war."

"You joined the army?"

"Yes. In 1944, they were already starting to take skilled workers. By spring of 1945 it was an army of old men and children."

A soft thumping noise travelled across the ceiling overhead. Sigmund Maier looked up and smiled tightly. "Mrs. Staworski and her walker. I am afraid these apartments are not very sound-proof. Shoddy materials and poor work habits."

Sheila kept her mind on the file's contents on the table. She removed a piece of paper from the file. "And this recommendation. Are you the Sigmund Maier it refers to?"

He took the paper from her. His back was to the balcony door. She could see some of the text reflected behind him. Handing the paper back, he shook his head.

"No. It was someone else."

"Did you know another Sigmund Maier in the resistance?"

"No. We did not learn anyone's names. Only code names you needed to know. To accomplish the task."

"What task?"

"Whatever task was assigned."

"By who?"

"By whom. Grammar, Fräulein."

She slapped her pencil down on the pad. "What! What did you say?"

He rose slowly and moved to the kitchen. "Would you like a coffee?"

She kept silent and he returned, steam rising from his mug. He sat. Sighed. Sighed once more. Reached out to touch the back of her hand, but she withdrew it to her lap immediately.

"Sheila, I am sorry, but you question me like a policeman." He picked up his coffee. The mug trembled as he held it to his lips. "Please. That was a long time ago. I am an old man now. It takes time to remember, to think."

She rubbed the back of her neck. "This is insane. Why should I give a care what you remember?"

He managed a half-smile. "Mr. Douglass – my lawyer – his questions are much softer."

"You don't need me. This is what he's supposed to be doing." Turning slightly, she lifted the briefcase onto her lap and slipped the file and papers inside.

Sigmund Maier took another sip, his shaking hand threatening to spill the hot liquid. "Yes. Just so." Papers tucked inside her briefcase, Sheila rose from her chair. He put down his mug. "Perhaps, I need to tell you."

"Tell me?"

"Yes." His eyes tried to capture hers, to draw her back. "This could be an old man's wish. Nothing more, Sheila." Lowering his eyes, he struggled to rise also. "I want to tell you how it was for me at that time, because ... because you were good to me and I was always ... fond of you."

She sat back down but continued to clutch the briefcase. The old bugger. Fond of her. "What is it you want from me?"

He stopped his attempts at standing. "I am not certain. But I think, Sheila, I think that it is important that you listen."

She said nothing, and he removed his glasses and rubbed his eyes. "I had gone to Berlin. There was a shipment from the foundry and I accompanied it."

"By yourself?"

"*Ja.* Yes."

"When was this?"

"12th February, 1945."

"So this is when you were detained?"

He shrugged. "The fates were kinder to me than the others."

"Your co-workers?"

"*Nein, nein.* I should have been with the others at the train station."

"Do you mean the leaders? Of the resistance?"

He nodded. "Yes, I was supposed arrive first, to look the station over. If it looked bad, I was to walk to the corner and wait. They would see I was there, and keep going."

Once more, Mrs. Staworski thumped across the ceiling. Automatically, Sheila looked up.

"I was sent by truck and then by train to Berlin, with a shipment of tools. I had also a small package for my contacts. I was to observe at the station and then, if it was not good, go to the corner and read a newspaper. If it was safe, I was to wait by the station sign. No newspaper. Simple enough." He rested his head against his raised right hand, his elbow taking the weight. "Everything was normal. Quiet. I was early, so I went to find cigarettes. I thought it would be easy to find them, black market goods were everywhere if you looked. It was all normal." He took his head from his hand. "I had never been to Berlin before. I was lost. When I came back, there were cars and Gestapo and soldiers everywhere. I saw them take the three. One of them looked over at me, and then I was taken too."

"And the package?"

"Package?"

"The one you had for them, the leaders?"

"Oh, that. I had placed it under a trashcan at the corner. I suppose they never found it, or I would not be here today." Mrs. Staworski crossed overhead once more, the dining room fixture trembling as she passed. "I was held and questioned for some time, a day perhaps, I am not sure how long. Then, someone decided I was not part of it. They released me. I kept saying I knew nothing and I had the right papers for the foundry shipment and finally, someone just said, 'You can go,' and I left. I made my way back; the works were gone. Smoke covered the whole valley below Freiberg, it was all smoke and ash."

Every building on Pragerstrasse, Goethestrasse, Burgerweiss Strasse – black rubble, the Frauenkirche gone, the Semper, cobbled streets now puddled, reformed. Burned-out walls hold nothing inside. Nothing left of the apartment building, the fine staircase, the ceramic floors – Russians everywhere ...

He held a hand over his eyes. "Dresden was gone."

"Did you return to Berlin to meet up with other resistance friends?"

He took his hand from his eyes and shook his head in disbelief. "Have you not listened, Fräulein? They were gone, everything, everyone – gone. I had no other contacts." He placed his hands flat on the table. "I joined the army."

"You decided to fight for Hitler? A resistance fighter in the army of the Third Reich?"

He slammed a fist on the table. "For Germany, Sheila, for Germany! The fatherland was being destroyed! Boys with pitch-forks, Sheila. Boys and girls and old men, teenagers. Of course I joined." He took a deep breath. "Our unit was sent to Italy with Kesselring, but it was late. We had little training. We became lost." He glanced out the windows. "We surrendered to the Americans."

"Shh!"

"Maier, can you see anything?"

He peers over the straw. The sun crests the hills behind the farm and is warm on his back. Through binoculars he sees an armoured division snaking along a distant hillside. It is several kilometres away. He tries to calculate how much time they have. They are farther behind the lines than he realized.

A jeep drives into sight from the bushes along the road in front. He has not heard its approach. Wheeling into the compact farmyard, the vehicle holds a driver in front and one passenger. An officer. He has this colonel in his sights, the crosshairs overlaying a broad, confident face. The sound of more vehicles drifts over the bushes and the radio crackles in the rear of the jeep.

He eases back to the others crouched behind the haystack. "There are more coming; tanks, soldiers. We kill these two and then what?"

Fritz licks his lower lip, the faint fair hairs of his foolish little moustache barely visible in the shadows. Erik and Hermann keep their arms encircling their bent legs and stare at the ground. A sudden gust of wind lifts some loose dirt next to his boot, mixing with the steam of his breath. "One's an officer. It is better to surrender."

He drained his coffee. "When we got to the camp, the prisoner of war camp, it was all green. Grass everywhere. In two days, not one blade remained."

"The prisoners trampled it?"

He smiled slightly and shrugged. "No. We were hungry. Coffee?"

She nodded. He returned with her mug. "Just one sugar, *ja?*"

"Thanks." Sheila took the coffee and waited for him to continue.

"It was not so terrible there. In time, we had regular rations. And we could make things to receive extras – cigarettes, chocolate, paper."

"Things?"

He held his hands close together, pantomiming. "Small wooden boxes, little footstools from scrap wood, whistles. The soldiers liked them."

"Is that where you got that box with your initials?"

His eyes narrowed and he shook his head. "How did you know about that?"

"I used to clean your room. Remember?"

"Ah, yes, just so. I had forgotten." He rubbed the back of his neck. "No. The box was my mother's."

"Did she give it to you after the war?"

"No. She died before. When I was fifteen."

"I'm sorry." She glanced down at her hands. "How did you manage to keep it? I mean, how did it not ..."

"I carried it with me."

She tried to imagine how that could be possible. How he could keep it safe even as a POW.

He rubbed his hands together. "So, after I left the camp, I found work on a farm – on the western side. Planting, harvest. I worked for ... ah, I cannot remember the man's name. He kept pigs and he looked like one. Ha! His name was ... Spiering. Albrecht Spiering. I was to clean out the sties. Then I was repairing the equipment." He smiled. "Now, that was a challenge. I had to be creative, you know. For a long time, no parts, no tools, oil was like gold ..."

"Is that why you immigrated?"

"No. No. Europe was all death." He ran his hand over his face. "Old churches and cemeteries. Even work on a farm was like death, the stench hung on everything. You could not go anywhere without someone, something, to remind you of war. I could not go home – Dresden was gone; the Russians were like the Gestapo."

"Why Canada?"

He smiled. "I could be a farmer in a place where there was no stench."

Sheila tilted her head. "Canada?"

"Of course. Your wars were all in other lands."

"Well, the war of 1812 ..."

He laughed. "And you defeat the great United States of America with so few casualties. Even your 1837 rebellion was civilized. No, this country is as close to peace as I could find. I did not know all of this when I chose Canada, but the pictures were of great forests, prairies, empty space, land without people. I thought a land without people would be a good place to live. I was correct."

She shrugged. "Okay. Where did you go when you got here?"

"I worked for a short time on a farm, near Kitchener. Did you know it used to be called Berlin?"

Sheila nodded.

"After a few months, I got work as a machinist in a small factory. The owner died in 1956 and I moved to Toronto. I thought, such a large city will have work for me."

The phone rang. Sheila looked at her watch: 10:45 – late for phone calls. Sigmund rose and walked to the kitchen, picking up the phone on the third ring. He listened for a moment. Even from the kitchen, she could hear the caller's fury.

He hung up, then returned to the dining room and sat back heavily into his chair. He sighed. "I will get a new number."

The phone rang again but he remained seated. After the third ring, Sheila rose to answer and he lifted his hand.

"*Nein!* Sheila, do not answer." He coughed, looked down at the table. "I will get a new number."

"Have you told your lawyer?"

"Yes, and he has all the documents, my records, everything."

"No. Have you told your lawyer about the phone calls? They can trace them, you know."

Sigmund shrugged. "It is of no importance." The ringing stopped.

"Look, Mr. Maier, there's a lot of strange people out there. This country is not quiet any longer – if it ever was. I think you should consider moving someplace temporarily. At least, contact your lawyer and tell him about the calls. Have you received many?"

The phone started again. This time Sheila rose and rushed to answer. She said nothing. A voice started into a screaming tirade of filth; she could barely make out any of the words and held the phone away from her ear. She put the receiver down on the counter and raced back to the dining room to pick up her purse. As she hurried back to the phone, she rummaged around inside her bag and extracted a small brass whistle on a key ring. The caller was still at it. Placing the whistle between her lips, she blew a long, shrill blast directly into the telephone mouthpiece. The sound echoed in the kitchen as the connection was severed.

She walked back into the dining room and sat down. "Well, maybe he'll have a headache for a while." Sigmund looked stunned and she smiled. "I'll leave you the whistle."

He started to rise from the table, then sat back down abruptly. "You know, Sheila, that letter of commendation for 'Sigmund Maier'? Did you notice something odd here?"

She shrugged and shook her head. "What do you mean?"

"Can you imagine that the Gestapo was in the habit of writing down the names of their agents?"

She thought about it. It didn't make a lot of sense.

"*Ja*. I do not think so. That letter was a lie, to discredit someone – make them a traitor. Make me a traitor to my compatriots. Something they did to build a case all those years ago in Berlin – before they let me go." He smiled, and shrugged. "It is ironic. Unless there was another Sigmund Maier, that letter could be Hitler's revenge fifty years later."

Not knowing what to say, she gathered her notes and files, and placed them into the briefcase. "It's late. I'm tired and I'm sure you could use some peace. How much time do you have before your court appearance?"

"I am told that this is a hearing. As soon as my lawyer has the date, I will let you know. I think it will be soon." He reached across the table and put his hand to her cheek. "You must leave so soon?"

His skin was old. Dry. She did not pull away, and he moved his hand to touch her hair. He smiled. "Still lovely, Sheila. Still beautiful."

She stood up. "Don't do that. I'd rather you just didn't do that. Okay?"

He dropped his hands into his lap. "Yes. Foolish old man. We old men do foolish things. I am sorry."

She waited for just a moment. It had occurred to her to tell him that she was sorry too. But for what? She had no idea where that came from. So she gathered her things and left.

As she drove home, she thought about the resistance and his part in all of that. Surely, someone was still around who had known him then. Maybe not an actual member of the resistance, but they must have had families, others who might have known. She hoped Douglass was doing all that he could to track somebody down.

A high-profile lawyer billed high-profile fees. How was this man with no pension, no visible means, paying those fees? She turned on the CD player. Must be pro bono. Waiving fees for an old man.

CHAPTER TWENTY-ONE

IN THE PAPER THREE DAYS later, there was an in-depth article about suspected Nazi war criminals in Canada. The story offered details of unsuccessful prosecutions, new investigations and a change in tactics, including Sigmund Maier's upcoming immigration hearing. Right on the front page, there was a photo of him entering his apartment building: *full story, see A3*. Kris Douglass was quoted: "It is evident that certain persons have an agenda here, a need for scapegoats. They will go to any length to concoct stories about my client. Our evidence will uncover that conspiracy." Sheila scanned the details; most of the rest was about earlier attempts to prosecute "war criminals". Douglass was quoted again later on in the article. "Not only was Mr. Maier not a war criminal, but he was also a heroic member of the German Underground. He will not be part of some bureaucrat's need to produce results just to satisfy special interests."

The lawyer for Immigration declined to make any statements.

She called Sigmund Maier right away. "Have you seen this morning's paper?"

"Yes."

"What evidence is your lawyer talking about?"

He cleared his throat. "Mr. Douglass has my statement of my resistance activities. My record of military service. My records in Canada."

"Nothing more than what you gave me? What you told me?"

"Yes."

"Mr. Maier. He's going to need more than that. What about the pictures, the letter that Mr. Szabo has?"

"I was at the camps because to refuse meant exposing others. I had no choice. And the letter is about someone else, some other Sigmund Maier." He cleared his throat again. "Sheila, Mr. Douglass believes that my evidence is sufficient. They have no true witnesses – two old and senile men – a few pictures and a doubtful piece of correspondence. I have nothing to hide."

"When is the hearing?"

"Next week, the 20th."

She bit her lower lip. "And just when were you going to tell me?"

"I left a message for you at work, yesterday. Your, ah, male assistant said he'd give it to you."

Robin must have forgotten in the madness of pulling together the banks' support to head off the manoeuvring by Costair and the Quebec investors.

"Okay. Okay then. I'll call you next week."

She hung up the phone, returning to the article in the paper. Douglass sounded too confident; he'd said too much to the press. She was no lawyer, but she knew that much. Sigmund Maier would still need someone to speak on his behalf – someone who knew him in the resistance. And if that idiot lawyer wasn't going to find someone to speak, well then, she figured she'd better at least try. What was it Sigmund had said to her when he was researching where to find her? The Internet: such a useful tool. She shrugged. Yup. Sure could be.

Finding the right bulletin boards on the 'Net was simple enough. Robin had shown her how when Kim Lee first developed the online retail system. While she didn't trust cyberspace, she got past her nervousness and posted her notice. One English version on three different sites, and thanks to online translation services, she also had a German version:

RE: Sigmund Maier/German Underground – WWII.

Urgently seeking information about German underground resistance fighters, circa 1940 – 1945. Of interest, any knowledge of a Sigmund Gunther Maier, born February 1915 Dresden Germany.

Reply in confidence: S. Martin, Ontario.

Twenty-three replies by the end of the week. Most contained useless information; they were either not about her Sigmund, or they were spam. Or hate mail.

Dear filthy Nazi loving piece of sh—
One nice thing about the delete button was how fast it worked. There was one message, however, that was promising.

I knew a Sigmund Maier in Europe, 1942.
I met him in Poland.

It was signed "Anton Pottel" followed by a telephone number; the number was 416 – Toronto. She picked up the receiver, hit the first couple of numbers then hung it back up and pulled out the phone book. She found a B. & K. Pottel and the number was a match; the address was in Willowdale. She ran searches on the Internet. There were no matches to Pottel in any neo-Nazi, Nazi-hunting, fascist or anti-fascist sites. Still, she hesitated, remembering her trip downtown to meet Ernest Szabo – what she learned that she didn't know before.

Szabo was in a public place. With others around. It was safe enough in public places, she supposed. She called Mr. Pottel's number just after noon. A child answered on the third ring.

"Jusaminute. Grampa!" Sheila winced as the receiver was dropped and rattled against a wall. She heard the approach of soft footsteps on uncarpeted floors.

"Hello, yes." His voice was rich, musical. She envisioned a handsome, older gentleman, grey-haired and tall. "This is Anton Pottel."

"Mr. Pottel, my name is Sheila Martin. You answered my posting about Sigmund Maier. He's an old friend, and I'm trying to help him. He's been accused—"

Before she could say anything more, she was cut off. "Yes, yes, I know. It was in the paper. My son showed it to me. Listen, I knew him for a short time back then, but he – he had an effect on me." He paused, and then, "Sigmund Maier saved my life."

"How?" She could barely contain her excitement. "What did he do?"

"We should meet somewhere."

"Shall I come there, to your home?"

"No." His answer was curt then he regained his pleasant manner. "I am sorry, but this is not something I discuss often. And never around the children."

"There's a coffee shop close to my office in North York. Is that anywhere close to you?"

"I live with my son and his family in Willowdale."

"Great then. Can we meet there tomorrow afternoon?"

"Not tomorrow. The next day."

"Sunday?"

Yes. That will be fine."

"Three o'clock? It's on the southwest corner of York Mills and Leslie."

"Yes, yes. Three o'clock."

She hung up the phone and then sat back in her chair. How would she know how real this guy was? She knew she was a bit sketchy on the whole WW II thing, most of her knowledge gleaned from a few documentaries that she didn't fall asleep watching, or from movies and such. She was probably one of the only two people on the planet that didn't haul themselves in to see *Schindler's List*, one more depressing movie about a depressing time. It was all so long ago.

The next day, she stopped by the library on her way back from her lunchtime hair appointment. Every single computer had somebody at it. What were all these people doing here? She checked the time on her watch. More than half of her day was gone, and now Anton Pottel and all of his stuff would cut into her afternoon. She had no time for this. Sigmund had no time for this. But she still felt stupid, like she wasn't getting the whole picture. Strange, all the things she studied, she just didn't do much history. She knew Robin could get her all the info she needed but something held her back from asking him. She admitted to herself that she didn't want anyone to know how much she didn't know about this. Besides, if she knew more she could ask Sigmund intelligent questions. And if she were called as a character witness, she would be knowledgeable.

She walked over to the helpdesk. The librarian behind it peered up at her from behind huge glasses. All librarians look the same: glasses, short hair and a small constant frown. Another job she would not have been suited to: too many interruptions with stupid questions.

"I want books on the Second World War," she told the librarian. "For research," she added, as if that made it better.

The woman frowned. "Well, that is a rather large topic. Is there a specific area of interest we could focus on?"

"Concentration camps, I guess. Something on Nazis. You know. What they did there."

"Is this for research – a paper perhaps?"

"No. I'm just interested."

The librarian pursed her lips and turned to her computer. "Still a bit wide-ranging, but let's see what I can do."

Armed with a list of several titles, she walked along the aisles and aisles of books. She took all the books suggested, and found a few more in the process. Her arms were full when she arrived at the checkout desk.

There was a teenaged boy behind the desk; Catholic school type – white shirt, tie, grey pants. He eyed her selection, raised a brow and then shook his head. "Only four books per subject, Ma'am."

"I'm doing research."

He shrugged. "It's still four per subject."

She sighed, and picked four. "There. These ones."

He pointed at the bottom one in the leftover stack. "You can take that one too. It's not the same subject."

She slid it out from the bottom. *Justice Delayed: Nazi War Criminals in Canada.*

Sheila traced a finger over the hourglass illustration on the cover. "Okay." She added it to the four she was taking out.

She drove back to work. Robin was out on lunch, so she was able to bring the books in, close her office door, and actually get some reading done.

CHAPTER TWENTY-TWO

ANTON POTTEL WAS NOT THE dapper European she had imagined. He was tall but with hunched-in shoulders and a balding head as round as his thick-lensed glasses. He walked into the coffee shop with a slight limp and made straight for her table. He looked like he was trying to smile at her. There was a small gap between his two front teeth.

"So, about Sigmund Maier, Mrs. Martin?"

She hadn't even introduced herself. "How did you know who I ...?

He shrugged. "Elimination." Pottel manoeuvred himself into the plastic booth. He gestured around the room; all other occupied tables were busy with conversation or laughter. He smiled and, this time, it seemed genuine. "And, you seemed the most anxious."

"Fair enough. Would you like a coffee?"

He nodded and Sheila signalled the server for another coffee.

"Mr. Pottel, I can't thank you enough for coming."

"My son – it was his idea. He found your note on the Internet. He has this thought about obligations. That I am ..." he looked away for a moment, then finished, "obligated."

She allowed herself a brief pause then put the newspaper picture on the table, face up. "All right. Mr. Pottel, is this the same man you knew in 1942?"

He barely glanced down and then looked hard into her eyes. "Yes."

"You're sure?"

He waved his fingers in her direction. "Of course I am sure." The server arrived with his coffee, and Sheila was spared making a response.

After adding four teaspoons of sugar, he ignored the cream and sipped and slurped at the hot liquid. She ran her tongue over her lips and started. "You mentioned on the phone that he saved your life." He continued to sip noisily, his large brown eyes watching her from behind the cup. "Mr. Pottel? I need this information. It's very important."

He set down his cup. "Why do you care, Mrs. Martin?"

She didn't know what to say, and it was a peculiar feeling. "I'm just trying to help him. Be a friend, I guess. I knew him years ago, as a child. He was very ... kind to me." She shrugged. "I guess I am – uh – obligated also."

He peered at her closely, unblinking. "He is fortunate to have such a friend. Fortunate." He sat back against the booth seat. "Now, as I said, Maier saved my life."

"What do you mean? Where?"

"At the camp. He took me with him and saved my life."

This was just what she wanted to hear, something much better-sounding than 27% improvements in executions. "Go on."

"They asked our ages and some younger women and men were told to line up to one side. My mother, brother and sisters, they went to the left with the others. My mother called to me to come with her but I pretended not to hear. I was thirteen, almost fourteen. I was tall for my age. I said I was sixteen and they kept me." He coughed gently. "That was how I got there and lived. I was put to work – carried bodies to the pits. Put lime on them. More bodies. More lime. All day. Every day – weeks, months, I don't know. I was tired, tired and sick, and one day, I dropped my end of the cart and some bodies fell off. I was trying to lift them back on and one of the guards was hitting me with his gun. Like this."

He held an invisible rifle, butt down, pounding through the air toward the ground.

"Then he stopped and after a moment I looked up. I thought I should see the guard who would shoot me, but he was looking over at this other man instead. A tall man." One eyebrow lifted slightly, and then he continued. "I remember thinking to myself, this is a clean man. In all that stink and filth, this was a clean, clean man. This man held the guard's arm with one hand and the rifle with his other, and his face was very close to the guard's. *I can use this boy* he said. After a moment, the guard licked his lips and laughed. I think he was embarrassed but I am not sure."

Pottel rubbed his face. "I went with the man. I thought he was going to use me, you know," the eyebrow again, "have sex with me, but he just had me carry his equipment to the truck. And then he said to the guards there, he said the same thing, *I can use this boy.* And they let him put me in the back of the truck with all the equipment and boxes and we left. He had a driver and me, and we left like that. Just like that."

His voice held amazement and for a moment he remained silent, his face still. "Later, we stopped at a farmhouse for some food and he got for me pants and a jacket – a wool jacket. And boots. I don't know what he told the farmer. The boots were too big but I did not mind. The shoes I had were too small – my toes were coming out the ends.

"I put on the boots, but I still did not know what he wanted from me." He looked down. His cheeks pinked and he pressed his lips together. He looked back up, looked at her with his dark eyes and started again. "I did not know what he wanted. I still thought, you know, because they did that all the time, to boys and girls. It made no difference. But while the driver was getting water for the radiator, he told me that I should go." Pottel shook his head slowly. "'Go?' I said. 'Where?' 'I do not care, Jew, just go.' I was ready to run into the field but still, I touched his arm and I asked him 'Why?'"

Sheila sat very still.

Pottel shook his head. "He pulled back his arm and for a long time, this man, he said nothing. I will never forget his eyes, they were so angry, so cold. He just said, 'For the old man' and then he laughed like he had a mouth full of ashes. Again he told me to go, and he was no longer laughing. So, I ran to the woods behind the fields and I made my way through there, hiding, running, hiding again until it was over." His voice cracked as he finished; he took off his glasses and wiped his eyes. Clearing his throat, he spoke again. "In the pocket of the jacket, I found a piece of bread and some cheese."

Sheila closed her eyes. *They did that all the time, to boys and girls. It made no difference.* She opened her eyes. "When was this?"

He shrugged. "Winter, 1942, maybe '43."

Sheila waited but there was no more. Her throat was dry but there was nothing left in her coffee cup. She attempted a swallow. "How did you know that it was him, that it was Sigmund Maier?"

He shrugged, his mouth turned down, both eyebrows raised. "That is what they called him at the gates. The officers called him Maier and the driver called him Sigmund. He still looks the same. Older, much older, but the same."

Sheila sat back. She picked up her empty cup, held it to her lips, pulled it back and looked inside. Still empty. She put it down and went over what he'd just said. This man's story placed Mr. Maier at one of the camps, which was not good because he said he'd only been at that first one. But it confirmed that he helped someone escape. And that showed he had compassion – it could support his resistance claims. "Would you be willing to testify to this? To speak for him?"

Pottel smiled but his tone was cold. "I suppose I owe him something."

Sheila frowned. She didn't understand why he'd bother going through all this telling his story just to start sounding like a prick. "Well yes. Maybe you do."

He leaned forward, grabbing the edge of the small table. "Then again, maybe it would have been better for me if he'd left me there. There, in the camp. Every night, every single night, I hear my mother call my name. The burden of gratitude carries as much weight as survival, Mrs. Martin. Together, they are like stones in my pillow." He shook his head in disgust and struggled to stand. "Just have them contact me. I will say my piece and be done with it."

Sheila tried to appear understanding but she was still confused about his attitude. She hoped it didn't show. "I – I'd like to thank you for coming forward, Mr. Pottel. It would help if people could see Mr. Maier in a different light." She rose and offered her hand.

He laughed: a short abortive grunt. "These days everyone can be seen in a different light, Mrs. Martin." He took her hand, his grip insistent. "You do remember why he was there, though, don't you?" She tried to pull back; he wasn't letting go. "When you meet people and talk with them, you do remember that much I hope. Even Hitler can be seen in a different light. Someday, perhaps schoolchildren will be reading about a kinder, gentler Adolf. All you need is a different light."

Releasing her hand, he left the restaurant.

Sheila stayed in the coffee shop, breathing away the trembling in her hands with slow, measured inhalations. She watched him get into his car and pull away from the parking lot before she got up and headed for the door.

* * *

Sigmund Maier sat in Douglass' waiting room. He disliked sitting there, sunk deep into a large leather couch, surrounded by some effeminate decorator's idea of Old Europe. Furniture: heavy oak, stained dark. Lighting: an approximation of 18th-century lamps and nearly useless at casting any illumination. At his feet, thick carpets over ceramic tile in a faux stone finish. They had no understanding of the depth that centuries of layer upon layer of history, of art, of design bring to a culture. No. This place can never come close to capturing his Europe. His Germany. He thought of the marble staircase, the arched entranceway in the old apartment off Pragerstrasse. Of the last time he saw it, just after his mother's death. Of his return to Dresden from Berlin in the winter of 1945. He could almost smell it.

Dresden beyond desolation. Jammed with others into the back of the farmer's cart, his legs dangling off the open end, the smoke and dust rising from the uneven ground. The smell of burnt dust, burnt air, burnt brick, fabric, flesh. Adjusting the bandana around his mouth. Rubble piled at the sides of the road.

In moments, the cart would stop and he and the others would clamber out to move more rubble, shovel up blackened corpses, uncover bloated hunks of maggoty parts and clear out more space for armoured vehicles to move forward. Russian soldiers everywhere; knots of people clustered around open fires, lean-tos rigged up from blankets, old coats. He was keeping his arm inside his jacket, in the sling. Slack-jawed and automatic, his frozen breath clouding his head, his face masked and expression dull like an imbecile. He knew he had to appear like the rest of these shells so no one would notice him.

In the cover of darkness, he would make his way from this crematorium. He would find whatever army was left and he would fight for Germany. It was, he knew, a useless gesture. He had no chance of making it through the Russians. He kept his eyes down on the road; it would be, at best, a gesture.

In the waiting room, Sigmund did not hear Douglass' secretary call his name. She finally had to get up from her desk, walk across the room and touch his shoulder to get his attention. When he turned to look up at her, she took a quick step back, drew in her breath and held it. She was afraid he would hit her.

* * *

Sheila called Douglass' office the minute she got into work on Monday morning. She waved an advancing Robin away, closed her door, and held tight to the phone until the lawyer finally came on the line. "Yesterday I spoke with a man who knew Sigmund Maier at the camps. His name is Anton Pottel and he says that his life was saved by Sigmund. That he helped him escape. Gave him clothes and food."

Silence on the line.

She frowned. "I have his number. You'll need to call him. Get him to come in and sign something, have somebody transcribe his story and all, and have him sign it."

He cleared his throat. He spoke slowly. Deliberately. "How did this Pottel contact you?"

"I posted some notices on bulletin boards. Electronic ones. And he answered me there. He's terrific. Well, he's not all that happy about what happened to him, but his story is wonderful. How Sigmund got him out of the camps. How he saved him."

"You posted notices on the Internet?"

"Yes." And then, because she didn't like his tone, she added, "Somebody had to be doing something besides pulling out dry-as-dust documents that say almost nothing."

"Are you a lawyer, Ms. Martin? A private investigator, perhaps?"

Now she really didn't like his tone. "No. I am not. So what? I have pulled together helpful information. Mr. Pottel is willing to speak on his behalf. To tell others. I mean, he's still pretty upset about what happened to him – and rightly so – but he does recognize Sigmund's picture as the man who put him in the truck and drove out of the camp to freedom. He can confirm his name from what the others called him. He's a perfect witness – not exactly glowing about Sigmund, but he'll acknowledge what you need—"

"Just write this all down and send it to me, Ms. Martin."

"Send it to you? You need to get Mr. Pottel in right away, get his signed testimony. He's an old man. Anything can happen. The hearing is soon, right? You can't sit around waiting. I'll e-mail it—"

He cut her off again. "I agree that your Mr. Pottel is an old man. And he is mistaken, Ms. Martin. The person he thinks is Sigmund Maier could not be our Sigmund Maier."

"What do you mean?"

"Sigmund Maier was not at any concentration camp."

"Sigmund told you about his duty to the camp, about what he had to do to protect the resistance. He told me, and he told me that he told you."

Douglass continued. "Our Sigmund Maier was just a worker in the German war effort, Ms. Martin. He joined the resistance movement, but played no large part in any undertaking."

"There was a trip to Berlin to deliver a package. He was arrested."

"He spent all of the war years at his foundry job in Freiberg. All of them."

"But Pottel recognized—"

"Until his foundry was bombed and he joined the army and was shipped to northern Italy. Where he was captured and held as a prisoner of war. A soldier." Douglass paused.

"You've got to be kidding. What about the pictures? The gas chamber efficiency reports?"

"Reports that refer to an S. Maier, technician. Siegfried perhaps. Maybe Stefan. Some S. Maier. Perhaps even Susanne. Pictures of some young technician in overalls who vaguely resembles an old man today. There are no witnesses who actually place him there. None."

It was not official, Sheila. We had to protect certain egos.

Her throat felt dry. Tight. "You're not going to talk to Pottel, are you." It was not a question.

Douglass continued as if she had not spoken. "Sigmund Maier was repatriated in 1946. He worked as a farm labourer, then as a machinist and then emigrated to Canada in 1950, Ms. Martin. He was a quiet and hard-working man, as you have attested, and he was kind to a disadvantaged child. And because of that, you have created a wonderfully successful life and business, Ms. Martin. All the advantages. And your business is a leader, Ms. Martin. A leading enterprise that employs many people. And, as I understand, soon across Canada. Perhaps even the US. No doubt this will take much of your time and your attention."

"You're just going to let me send you this. You're not going to look at it, not even do anything."

"I understand your wish to help, Ms. Martin. Mr. Maier is grateful for your kindness. But you must leave all this to me, his lawyer. In your enthusiasm, you move into areas for which you have no legal training. Forgive me, but I will have to ask you to let this all alone now."

"Let it all alone."

"Yes." And then he added, "Please."

Sheila shook her head, holding her tongue.

"And Ms. Martin?" He didn't wait for her response. "Mr. Maier thanks you."

"He thanks me?"

"Yes. He is in my office right now, and he thanks you for your interest, for your concern. It is unfortunate that Mr. Pottel is mistaken, but he is mistaken. And there has been a great deal of confusion about Mr. Maier's identity. We don't need to further cloud the issue."

"Let me talk to him."

"Ms. Martin?"

"Put Sigmund on the line. Let me talk to him."

There was a few seconds' silence. Then, "Sheila. Mr. Douglass thinks—"

"Listen to me. That man does too much thinking. Anton Pottel is willing to come in and speak on your behalf. Why are you letting that – that lawyer tell you what to think, what to say?"

"Mr. Douglass is a good lawyer. He has worked hard on my behalf."

She heard his tone. Practised. Careful. She gripped the phone and lowered her voice, enunciating each word clearly. "Just tell me something, Mr. Maier."

He said nothing.

"Just tell me you were not at that concentration camp – that it wasn't your picture. That you lied to me about 21% increases in exterminations. That there really was no arrest in Berlin. That Anton Pottel is just a confused old man who can't keep his information straight. That all you have told me ... is ... a ... lie. All of it."

Listening to his breathing, the rasp of his deep exhalation being released into the mouthpiece, she waited. He remained silent. She stared at the phone display and counted. Two seconds. Five seconds. Twelve seconds. Twenty-two seconds.

Nothing.

She hung up the phone. For the longest time, she just sat there looking out her office window. Billie Holiday was crooning softly from her office speakers. Something about the summer. She used to know this song, but now it was just words and music.

It was still spring outside.

Spring and sunny. She sat up and took a deep breath.

First, she called Ardith's office and cancelled her appointment for the afternoon. "And while you're at it, Maria, cancel the rest of all my appointments."

Ardith's secretary paused before she responded. "All of them? For how long?"

"For from now on, Maria. Just tell Ardith I've decided it's time to move on."

"But—"

Sheila hung up. She nabbed her purse, slipped on her trench coat and reached in the pocket for her keys. Robin met her in the woodwind section. He put his hand on her arm to slow her down.

"Hey, Sheila. Where are you going? We're supposed to have a working lunch here. Go over the trip itinerary."

She turned. "A walk, Robin. I need some air and I'm heading over to the park to clear my head." She pulled her arm away. "Hope that meets with your approval. Actually, I don't give a shit if it does." And then because she knew that was a nasty, hurtful thing to say, she added, "Well, I will give a shit, Robin, eventually, but not right now. Not now."

Carson River Park was a narrow greenbelt that meandered south through the same industrial section of North York in which Musicians' Clearinghouse was located. Sheila always thought that 'river' was too grand a term for something little more than a creek, but it was spring and the water was high and running fast. Right now, it was a river.

Sheila had forgotten that she used to like coming here. It was rare that she had the time anymore, but in the past there had been sporadic health kicks when she and Robin left behind their neighbourhood of warehouses and light industry and walked the park trail at lunch. For a short while she'd even tried jogging, but putting on the gear, stretching and all that stuff, took up too much time. Plus, she sweated like a pig afterwards, and that hardly went with her image.

So, she opted for climate control and showers at the club. And visits to Carson River Park just faded away.

She entered at the top end, between Buttery Biscuits on the west and TorBest Graphics on the east. As she followed the asphalt path the bordering scrub trees and bushes on either side gradually rose upwards and eventually became an impressive wooded ravine. The buildings overlooking the narrow meadow and edging trees morphed from warehouses to small retailers and then apartments and townhouses. Soon enough, large private homes peeked through the trees masking the lip of the ravine. She had no idea how far she travelled; the park just seemed to go on and on, and she listened to the sound of her footfalls on the path and the rush of water just to her right. She passed other people here and there, but didn't really see them.

When she realized that she was short of breath and her legs were aching, she plopped down onto a bench just beyond a bend in the river. Likely a farmer's field or meadow at one time, the surrounding area was now respectably trimmed with plantings of trees and hardy bushes. A large cluster of lilacs nearby scented the light breeze. She didn't think she'd ever come this far before – never gone this deep into the park.

It was a lovely afternoon. She could have closed her eyes, allowed the sun to warm her. Breathe. She decided to just people-watch instead.

There were more people to watch here than where she first started out. Occasional benches and picnic tables held park visitors who, like Sheila, were taking advantage of the warm spring afternoon. A couple of mothers monitored their children at play; an older couple nodded as they strolled by. At the far side of the meadow, a group of teenagers were bunched together on an arched wooden bridge. Their laughter travelled across the grass, carrying their confidence, their cackling youth. They should be at school, she thought.

She supposed she should be at work. It didn't seem to matter; Robin would hold everything together, deal with any of the problems. If there were any problems. She wondered how he would have handled Mr. Kris Douglass, LLB. What Robin might have said to Sigmund Maier as he denied everything. Now, that was a problem, wasn't it? Or was it? She didn't want to tell him. Didn't want to have Robin give her that look, and know that she was supposed to do something with the information she had gathered. Be reminded about *the right thing*. He always stayed on top.

He asked her just last week what was going on with Maier. He'd held the paper out with Sigmund's picture and waved it at her. "I guess you've already seen this."

She shrugged. "Yeah, I did."

"And so?"

"And so, what, Robin? This is expected, I guess. People are out to make an issue over him, so it hits the paper."

That look again. "Sheila. Have you given any thought at all to what this might do to the business? Your business. The expansion."

"Oh, it's a little blip. A juicy sound bite."

"Do you think Costair will consider it a sound bite? He's all about image."

She crossed her arms. "Robin. What was the name of that guy who killed his wife last summer? You know, it was on the news everywhere, his picture all over the papers, how he'd tracked her down, shot her in the street. There were all those articles about predator ex-husbands. Wife abuse. You know." She dropped her arms to her side. "What was his name, Robin?"

He was silent, just staring at her.

"Like I said. An article or two and it'll all be forgotten." She shrugged. "And the irony here is that when we prove he wasn't who they say he is, when all that gets sorted out, there won't be anything more than two inches of column on Page 18. If it gets a mention at all."

"Sheila. Do you have the vaguest idea what they did to us back then? What being homosexual meant to the Nazis?"

"Oh, Robin. Let's not go there. I understand they did some nasty things to people."

His eyes widened.

She continued. "Terrible. Nasty terrible things to gays. To anyone 'different', right?" She stood up and walked around from behind her desk. "But are you telling me that you think Sigmund Maier was part of all that?"

There was the sound of a transport passing by on the road outside. Music drifted up from the retail area below; she heard the bustle of people moving through the store, murmurs, things being shifted, doors closing. The sounds of her enterprise, and she really liked hearing them. But the room in which she and Robin stood, that room was absolutely still.

He had looked at her with such an intense expression. Back then, she knew how wrong Robin was. Sigmund Maier got himself trussed up in a complicated mess, but the man he was – the man she knew – he was not capable of atrocities. She told Robin how he was just a kid when it all started. Just a kid on his own, and when he matured, he realized it wasn't for him.

Sheila sat up on the park bench. *He was not capable of atrocities.* She said that to Robin five days ago. Looked at him with level eyes and said just that: *The man I knew was not capable of committing atrocities, Robin. I know that absolutely.*

Nothing had changed. She had to believe that.

As she struggled with the tension of her guts, her shortness of breath, Sheila continued to stare at the kids on the bridge. Observed them cross over, a bunch of hyper teens, making those large, flung-arm whirls and dashes of kinetic energy, the shoulder-hits of camaraderie, the heads-back and crow calls of those who know they are watched.

Of course, she wasn't really watching. Wasn't really observing. They were mere movement to her eyes, something to be processed later. Instead, she was repeating a mantra to herself: *He was not capable of doing that. Not.*

The teens' rough laughter drifted downwind to her, punctuated by the guffaws of boys trying to outdo each other. Their faces, had she actually been processing, were more defined now, taking on as much individuality as they would allow. If she were listening, Sheila would have heard the profanities – stock-in-trade of those who owned the language. Or, at least, figured they did.

She caught the whiff of tobacco.

And now she saw them. No longer idle images, they strutted along the path, heading straight for her. She realized she was staring, and looked down at her hands in her lap.

It made no difference. Girls or boys. They did it all the time.

She wondered how these ones would have fared in the camps. Puffed-up. Self-aware. How long would they have survived? She glanced up to get a quick look at the parade, to better imagine their fates.

There were seven of them, six of them boys. At first, she didn't realize one was a girl. Their clothes were as uniform as their lingo: dark bomber-style jackets – some leather, some nylon; jeans of varying shades; solid, sensible black army boots, threaded with white or red laces; cropped or even shaved heads; no hats, though two had sweatshirt hoods on their heads. The girl's several earrings traced the outline of each ear, and she alone wore army fatigue pants. The earrings and her eye makeup distinguished her from the others.

"What are you lookin' at?" The boy closest to Sheila had stopped, the others following suit. Sheila turned slightly and looked at the river.

"She thinks you're fucking hot, Gary." The girl's voice was contemptuous and harsh. The others laughed.

"Bitch!" His voice cut across the narrow strip of grass separating Sheila's bench from the path. She heard him clear his throat and spit. A gob of yellowed mucous landed on the bench next to her. They continued to laugh as they passed by and cut across the grass.

She closed her eyes: before her, the baby's flushed cheeks, the whites of her half-closed eyes, the pleats of the starched bonnet. Sheila cast about in her mind, searching for any other image, something else to think about, focus on. Then the baby opened her eyes wide and spat.

Sheila stood straight up, and tried to breathe. She walked to the riverbank and looked down. The water was slower here, deeper. She watched tiny fish undulating, holding steady their position against the current, barely visible against the pea-green tinge of their surroundings. The shapes of submerged rocks caught the afternoon sun. They were the colour of the gob of spit that had glistened on the bench behind her. "Stupid. Stupid kid."

Something approached her from behind, moving fast over the grass. She spun around as a large multi-coloured ball rolled to a stop at her feet.

"Hey Lady!" Two little boys – twins, maybe five or six years old – stood several feet away by the path and waiting, their hands resting uncertainly on their hips. "Lady? Can you give us our ball?"

Sheila stared at them for a moment, thinking of that Nazi Mengele and his twins, then scooped up the plastic ball into her hands and walked quickly to where the little boys stood. She could see their mother heading over, a chubby baby perched on her hip.

"Here you go, Fellas." Her voice was deliberately light, cheerful as she rolled the ball toward them, though inside her head she heard a ringing sound, faint but constant.

The boys scampered back to their mother.

Sheila strode back down the path, upriver, back to where she had first entered this park. With each step she quickened her pace. By the time she reached the street and the familiar outline of her store was visible, she was flat out running, shallow breaths of air burning her lungs, her feet raw inside leather shoes. She didn't stop until she reached the Clearinghouse parking lot, where she collapsed her whole body against the hood of her car.

When Robin came out and found her she was sitting on the curb next to her car, sweating and exhausted. One look at her and he was clucking like a mother hen. He took her keys, ushered her into the passenger side and slipped into the driver's side.

Sheila didn't want to go home, and she started to tell him that, that she would be just fine in a minute or so.

"Who said anything about home?" he snorted. "I'm taking you to Hector. If ever somebody needed time with Hector, it is you, Boss. We'll get you to the club, and I'll grab a cab back to the office. We'll get you massaged, showered and changed into something, um, less ripe, okay?"

God! She must stink – all that sweating.

"We'll stop at the cleaner's on the way, and pick up the stuff you dropped off last week. There ought to be something you can change into."

Sheila leaned back against the headrest and closed her eyes. She wasn't going to argue. She was going to have a massage. Get cleaned up. Change. And then she would think. Think about what she had to do.

By the time she got back into her car at the club, she was thinking again. And completely focused.

She had to let Sigmund know how Douglass was screwing up his whole case. At his age, she reasoned, he didn't understand what he was doing, and somebody had to watch out for him. Maybe he didn't mean to look like he was lying. She realized she should have gone over to Douglass' office, picked Sigmund up and taken him somewhere to talk this out. Make him see that Anton Pottel's story was a good thing. It didn't make sense to pretend he hadn't been at the camps. If she had found Pottel, maybe there were others who might have come forward. Douglass didn't know this side of Sigmund Maier like she did. That lawyer could say all he wanted about the witnesses being old and muddled, Sigmund stood a better chance with Pottel speaking up for him.

She picked up the phone three times and punched in Sigmund's number. Before she allowed it even to ring, each time she hit the END button. She had to be ready, ready to say things just right. Help him see what he was doing to himself.

The fourth time, she took a deep breath and kept herself from hanging up. She had to get him to listen to her. If he didn't, Douglass would take him down along with his other clients. Frankly, she didn't give a damn about the rest of the lot. But Sigmund had a chance if he let his whole story come out. She waited for the rings, only the phone didn't ring; it just made a single click noise and then: *The number you have dialled is not in service. Please check the number and try again.*

She held the phone a few inches from her face, and peered at the number in the tiny screen. She fumbled through her purse for her glasses to be sure.

It was his number. Her chest constricted, and then she remembered the phone calls he was getting. She'd told him to let his lawyer know about the calls. Douglass, genius lawyer that he was, probably told him to get his number changed. Probably unlisted. That's why the recording didn't give her another number to call. He'd had his number changed.

She shook her head. Silly old fool. Why didn't he just call her to give her the new number? Too easy. Too much like common sense. She knew Kenneth would have given her the number. Kenneth would have written it down on a piece of paper. And Kenneth would have emailed the new number to her just to be safe. Sigmund? No – just change the damn number and let Sheila figure it out.

You were always a good girl, yes?

The whole way driving over to his apartment, she kept thinking that this time he had to listen. This time, he had to get a new lawyer, someone less like a booster boy for the Aryan Race Society and more like a lawyer who kept his mind on the case and his mouth shut with the media. She glanced up into the rear-view mirror. Maybe a lawyer who would keep her mind on the case and her mouth shut. She lowered the window and yelled as she drove, "Yeah. Her mind, you crazy Nazis, her mind on the case. I'll get Sigmund to hire a raving feminist and make you all nuts in the courtroom." She laughed out loud. Sheila had no real idea why, but she liked laughing out loud. She liked it a lot.

She rang the buzzer for apartment 703 at least five times. Even if he were in the bathroom, surely he would have answered her by now. She tried the superintendent. No answer there either. She tried calling on her cellular phone. Once again: *The number you have dialled is not in service. Please check the number ...*

Of all the times for him to do this. Of course, the harassing phone calls were unpleasant, but he could have shared his unlisted number with her. He could have let her know.

She turned back to the buttons, found 703 once more and pressed, long and hard.

No answer.

She cupped her hands around the glass door and peered in. The elevator door opened and a beer-bellied man with a toolbox stepped out. Sheila pounded on the door, and he waddled over to let her in.

"I'm trying to reach Mr. Maier, Sigmund Maier in apartment 703, and he is not answering."

"Look, Lady. I keep telling you people, he's not here. He doesn't live here anymore." There was ice around her heart; had to be, for it to feel like this. Sheila inhaled deeply and then nodded.

"Oh, I understand – the picture in the paper. Look, I'm not a reporter. And I'm not one of those problem people, either. I'm a friend of Sigmund's." She smiled brightly. "I guess he's been getting so much flak that he's cut himself off, you know." She went to move past him and he stepped in front of her.

"You're a friend of Maier's?" The faint odour of garlic and poor dental hygiene wafted out with his words.

"Yes. Now if you'll just let me—"

"Well then maybe you can tell me where the SOB has gone."

"Gone?"

"Yeah. Pulled a skippy. Seven months left on the sublet. The Willises will be really ticked off."

"Willises?" There was a problem with her hearing. Or he was speaking with his mouth full of marbles or something. What was he saying? What was he saying?

"Mildred and Ted Willis. It was their place he leased, furniture and all. They'll have to find somebody else for seven months and that's tough enough without them being out of the country."

She blinked several times. "He's gone?" She blinked again. "Skipped out?"

He nodded.

"Oh."

The super squinted and leaned in, his unpleasant breath reaching her full force. "You don't know where he is, then?"

She shook her head.

He nodded, started to turn away. "If you find him, let him know that he's forfeited his last month's. And he can forget the security deposit, too."

"Yeah. Sure. I'll tell him." How could she speak when she had no air in her lungs?

As he started to cross the lobby, he called out over his shoulder. "And if you know anyone who wants an apartment for a few months, pass the word, eh?"

But at this point Sheila was already out of the building and running to the parking lot.

CHAPTER TWENTY-THREE

SHEILA PARKED IN HER GARAGE, pressed the automatic door button then sat in the quiet dark of her car for a long time. It seemed that she was sitting in this spot a lot lately. She risked a glance in the mirror. No tears. Not much of anything on her face. She nodded. Good. If she didn't think about it, if she just cleared her mind, did Ardith's breathing thing, and just didn't think about it, well, maybe she could see about getting out of the car. Getting out and going through the door, past the laundry and maybe into the kitchen. She really wanted some tea.

She opened the car door, and made her way inside.

The house was dark. But Sheila could hear voices coming from the kitchen and great room area. The radio was on back there, but no one was listening. She turned it off and heard the floor creak upstairs. Oh yeah, the sound people make when they are trying not to be heard. How familiar.

For a moment, she wondered if maybe it was someone who broke in. Beth's book bag was on the sofa across from the fireplace. Sheila turned and walked silently into the foyer. Beth's jacket was in a heap just inside the front door; her shoes lying where she had apparently kicked them off, still laced.

There was more noise coming from upstairs – Beth on her bed. Oh Christ. If she was up there with that Colin boy ... Sheila glanced down again. Only one pair of shoes. Maybe he was in such a goddamned hurry he didn't bother to take off his shoes. She raced up the stairs and marched to Beth's door.

Sheila didn't knock. She just flung open the door, prepared to confront the pair of them.

Beth was alone. She raised her head from the pillows and scowled at her mother. No, it was not a scowl. Sheila remembered

Beth looking like this after a nightmare years ago, so miserable, so frightened. Her eyes were red and swollen. Something was wrong – maybe she and the boy had broken up. Maybe the little shit hit her.

"Beth, I heard a noise – what's wrong with you? Are you sick – in pain?"

Sheila picked her way across the islands of dropped clothing and teen garbage and stood at the edge of her daughter's bed. As she lowered herself onto the mattress, Beth moved as far from her as possible and buried her head back into her pillows. Sheila tensed; any second, her daughter would start screaming at her to get out of her room.

Instead, she raised her head once more, took a look at her mother and started to wail.

Sheila would have preferred being yelled at. She cast about in her mind for something to say. "Beth, what is it? What's wrong?"

Her daughter could hardly choke out a few words – Sheila heard "Colin". She heard "baby" and she heard "abortion".

Ah. This was the "no, I didn't – not yet" of the other day. Jesus Christ, now what? Sheila wanted to slap her daughter's silly face, knock something resembling sense into the little idiot. And she wanted to be her mother. That came to Sheila as something of a surprise and she tried it on for a while, in her head. She was the girl's mother – had been all her life. But this feeling, this actually wanting to mother, it was so long distant that it was alien. Another surprise: it felt okay. She moved her hand forward, to touch Beth's back, to pat it. Before she reached her daughter, she pulled her hand back into her lap. Clearly, that would have been too much, too soon. She remembered how she'd held her the other night, almost like a mother then. But right after, Beth had taken off. Clearly Sheila had moved too soon then. She wouldn't make that mistake this time.

Instead, Sheila waited until the sobbing died down enough that she figured Beth would hear her. She kept her voice calm. Level. "Beth. I know how you feel right now."

"What do you know about how I feel?" She spat out the words in Sheila's general direction then wiped her eyes on the edge of her duvet.

Sheila took a moment to answer. "Oh, I know. I know absolutely how you feel right now."

Beth's expression changed; she angled herself up, leaned on an elbow and folded her legs underneath herself. Good. Sheila sighed and continued, "I had an abortion. In fact, I had two."

"Two? Holy shit."

"Yeah. Holy shit."

Beth was now sitting straight up. "When? What happened to you?"

Sheila swallowed. Cast her mind back to a spring day in 1977. "The last one was in university. I thought I was in love with one of my professors. He didn't want a baby – not yet, he said, we'll have time for babies later on – and I believed him." She shrugged. "Knowing him, the thing would have had two heads or something anyway."

Beth's mouth hung open. "You're kidding."

"What – about the abortion or the two heads?"

"Jesus, Mother. About the abortion, I guess."

"No. That was true." She looked down at her hand, examined her ring finger. "It was for the best. I had one year left for my degree, and he was already screwing another girl in first year." She smiled. "Of course, I didn't find that out until later, but it helped knowing."

They were silent together for a moment. And then Beth spoke again. "And the other one?"

Sheila rubbed her knee and glanced around the room. She hadn't realized how terrible Beth's room was looking; it had been so long since she'd been allowed in here and had a good look. Maybe after, she could suggest some paint – perhaps replace the carpet, the drapes. She glanced back at Beth, who was staring at her. Sheila shrugged. "I can't remember."

"You can't? You've got to be kidding."

"You're right – it sounds strange, doesn't it? Because I do remember some things, Beth. I remember exactly that horrible awful feeling in my guts that something was going on with my body, you know? That I was changing. And I remember, absolutely remember the panic when the test came back at the doctor's office and it was positive. I can still hear the doctor's voice. Not one ounce of sympathy, not one thread of concern as she was leaving the room. That woman reeked of disgust: 'Do you even know who the father is?' she said. The door of the exam room was open, and the waiting room down the hall was full of patients and I was sure they all heard her question. I remember thinking that if I were older she wouldn't dare say that, she wouldn't dare. And then I said it to her, I said in a loud clear voice, 'If I was older, you wouldn't dare ask me that question with the door open.' And she went all red. And then she left." Sheila swallowed. "I guess she was angry, you know. So many kids were having babies back then."

"But that didn't give her a right to do that, Mom, to say that to you."

"No, Beth, it didn't. But things were different."

"What did you do?"

"Found another doctor, I guess." She closed her eyes. "Yeah, I found a nice guy. He didn't need to call my mother and ask her permission. He just looked me in the eyes and said, 'If you are old enough to get pregnant, you're old enough to make this decision.'" She opened her eyes. "So. Have you decided?"

Beth glanced down at her hand and then back up at her mother. "I think so."

"Want to tell me? I mean, you don't have to. I can just—"

"Mom, I don't think I can go through with it. Having it, I mean."

Sheila wanted desperately to know if she meant the abortion or the baby. She was terrified of either answer. Beth continued before she could ask her to clarify.

"I mean, Colin's okay and all. He wants to do the right thing, he says. But I don't want to be moving in with some guy. And how could I ever be a mother?"

Sheila nodded, working hard at offering nothing more than an encouraging look.

"So I called Dr. Frazier. She and I, we talked about adoption – private adoption. I was thinking that's what I would do, but I'm not sure."

"What about school next year?"

"If I time this right, I could have it around the change in semesters." She bit her lower lip. "I can work something out for exams if it ends up a problem. I won't miss that much time, a week at the most."

Again they sat together in silence. Sheila wondered if she should push for an abortion. She decided to suggest that Beth reconsider, and she opened her mouth to say just that. Only she said something else. "You could keep the baby. I could help you out. Your father and I, we could help you out so you could keep the baby."

Beth was looking at her as if she were insane. "Keep it?"

Sheila leaned forward. "Yes. Why not? It's not like other people don't do that."

"Get serious. Why would I want a baby? Why would you want me to keep it?" She started to scowl. "Oh yeah, I get it. What a great way to control my life, eh? Beth, you can't go out tonight, you have to take care of your baby. Beth, have you fed the baby? Beth, you should take the baby for a walk."

Sheila shook her head. "No, Beth, no. That's not what I'm saying."

"What are you saying then, Mother? Why else would you want me to have this baby and keep it?" She turned away. "I'll have an abortion first."

"You're right. It was a crazy thought. I'm sorry."

"Damn straight. Jesus."

There was nothing left to say and Sheila moved to get up. She stopped. "Have you told your father?"

Beth shook her head.

"Do you want me to do it?"

Her daughter looked so relieved. "Yeah. I – I don't know what to say to him. He'll be disappointed, but he won't say that, you know. He'll just be upset inside." She picked at the duvet. "He always holds onto stuff, you know? It eats at him and he holds it inside."

"He does?"

Beth waved a hand. "Of course he does." She frowned. "But then, you'd have to pay attention to him to know that. You'd have to notice him."

Sheila opted to leave that challenge unanswered. She couldn't imagine telling this kid about the years of a marriage, about compromise and making do to achieve success. "Look, Beth, I'm not going there with you. Your father and I have worked out our lives together. It may not be your ideal, but it works for us."

Beth shook her head. "Yeah. Sure it does. What a partnership – you two are something else."

Sheila kept silent. She stood up and walked to the door. Before she left, she turned around to face her daughter. "Beth. I am sorry. I want to help, but you will have to tell me what you need from me."

"Just tell Dad."

"Okay. I'll tell him. Tonight." She was through the door when Beth called her back. "What now?"

"Nothing."

Sheila sighed. "Obviously it was something. You called me."

Beth narrowed her eyes. "Yeah. It was. I wanted to ask you something."

She waited.

"I wanted to ask you who was the father – that first time?"

They looked at each other for a moment before Sheila spoke. "I can't remember."

"You really can't remember?"

She shrugged. There was something – something she thought of before it vanished from her mind. "He was just a big dumb kid. I met him at a party. A football player; all muscle between his ears." Before Beth could say another thing, she left and made her way to her bedroom.

She had to plan how to tell Kenneth.

He arrived home before nine. He carried his gym bag as he walked through the hall from the laundry room. Sheila met him in the foyer.

"Did you go to the gym tonight?"

"Yeah."

"Are you hungry?"

"No. I grabbed some Chinese." He took a couple of steps and then turned around. "Why? Did you eat?"

She shook her head. "No. Not yet. I'm not too hungry." She wet her lips. "We need to talk. About Beth."

"Now what? Is she okay? Is something wrong?"

"Yeah. She's okay. But something's wrong." Sheila gestured toward the kitchen. "Let's go sit where we can talk."

He dropped his bag in the front hall and followed her into the kitchen. "What is it, Sheila? What's wrong with Beth?"

She took a deep breath. "She's pregnant, Ken."

He paled. "God. You've got to be kidding."

"Wish I was."

"Jesus Christ! What a stupid thing to do."

"Yeah."

Kenneth ran his hand over his head and rubbed at the back of his neck. "Jesus. Unprotected sex – with all the stuff around. And pregnant. Jesus. Has she seen a doctor?"

Sheila nodded. "She wants to have the baby."

"My God. At sixteen?" Sheila followed him as he strode past the breakfast bar and into the great room. He nearly threw himself down on the couch then looked up at her. "She wants to be a mother?"

"No. She wants to have it and give it up for adoption."

As if someone had pricked him, Kenneth expelled all the air within and he fell back against the cushions. He sat there, hands limp on his thighs, head lowered, empty-looking. After a moment, he sat up. "She can't. She'll have to have an abortion."

"She doesn't want to."

"She doesn't want to? So what? You tell her, Sheila. You tell her she has to have one. This pregnancy can screw up her life." He was clearly angry, frustrated.

"Ken, you need to calm do—"

"I don't need to calm down. My God! Twenty years from now, she'll have someone knocking on her door, seeking 'closure' or some such crap. She'll have her life together. Her goddamn past will arrive and blow it all apart."

"She's not going to—"

"You tell her, Sheila! You tell her she can't do this. She's just a kid. You can't let your own daughter fuck up her life like this. You know what this can do to her. You know." He was nearly screaming now, his face flushed and spittle flying from his mouth. And he was crying; Sheila could see the tears running down his cheeks, his eyes now pleading at her. "You know what this will do. For Christ's sake, you're her mother. Make her!"

"Daddy! Stop it!" At the sound of Beth's voice, they turned to watch their daughter stride through the room to stand across from where they both sat.

Kenneth looked at her, his face still contorted, one hand wiping furiously at the tears on his face. He shook his head. "Jesus. How did this happen?" He held up a palm. "No, I don't want to know. I don't want to hear anything other than you telling me that you are going to take care of this mess, Beth. Your mother and I have talked and—"

"You've talked alright. I could hear you from my bedroom, your talking." She lifted her chin. "But you are both forgetting that this is my life, not yours." She was now close to yelling as she continued. "And if I want to have this baby – if I choose to have this baby, then I'll goddamned well have it."

As Beth stood, arms crossed and legs firm on the ground, Sheila heard another voice. A fifteen-year-old voice. Hers. And that doctor. What was his name? Lysander. No – it was Lyzinder, Dr. Ephram Lyzinder. She had to take the subway to get to his office, but he was so nice. Somebody gave her his name. Somebody … it was the school nurse. That was it. She'd been throwing up in the girl's bathroom, and Julia Newton brought the school nurse, Mrs. Something-or-other.

That lady figured out the problem pretty fast.

She asked Julia to leave, then hunkered down and patted Sheila's back. "Have you seen a doctor, Sheila?"

Sheila wanted to tell her how she'd seen the family doctor, but she wasn't going back there to be embarrassed. She wanted to tell the nice nurse how mean and miserable her own doctor had been; instead, she kept her eyes on the tiled floor and shook her head. "It's just the flu."

"Mostly a morning flu?"

Sheila held still then nodded.

The nurse didn't say anything for a moment, after which she pulled a small pad of paper out of her pocket. She wrote down Dr. Lyzinder's name and number, and handed it to her. "If it turns out to be more complicated than the flu, this doctor has helped other girls. Girls in trouble."

Sheila took the note. She did not look at the school nurse.

"Listen, Honey. It is nothing to be ashamed of. It's happened to a lot of young girls."

Sheila wiped her nose with the back of her hand. "Okay."

The nurse started to rise, then lowered herself to sit down again next to Sheila. "Can't tell your family?"

"No."

"What about the boy? What does he say?"

Sheila looked over at the woman. She felt the tears in her eyes. "He's gone. He disappeared before I could tell him."

The nurse patted her hand. "Oh. I see. Well, call Dr. Lyzinder. He's a great listener."

Dr. Lyzinder turned out to be a fabulous listener. When he kept asking about the baby's father, Sheila told him all about the boy who she met at a party. A boy from out of town. A football player, tall and not too smart, but he was sweet. And he drove her home in his car, but first they stopped at the Bluffs and he'd been so nice, kissing her and all.

Dr. Lyzinder nodded then asked as he continued his pelvic examination. "Does he have a name, this boy?"

Sitting in the great room of her Thornill home, next to her husband who was crying and yelling about their daughter mere moments ago, and looking up at the red face of their daughter

Beth who'd just finished yelling and screaming at them, Sheila remembered the name she had given to Dr. Lyzinder thirty years ago.

"Sigmund," she said. "His name is Sigmund, but he's gone."

Beth and Kenneth turned and stared at her. Beth spoke first. "What? What did you say?"

Sheila realized she had spoken out loud. Why did she say that? "I – I just was saying ..." As her voice trailed off, she struggled to make sense out of what she had just said.

Kenneth leaned forward. "What does Sigmund Maier have to do with this? Honest-to-God, you are obsessed, Sheila. Obsessed!"

She looked from her husband to her daughter and back again. "I don't know. I don't know why." She put her hand to her head. "Oh, sweet Christ, I have no idea why I said that. I was remembering back, to when I was Beth's age, to when I – I ..."

Beth's mouth dropped open. "Omigod. He was the father, wasn't he? The father – that first time. Your first abortion."

Sheila was cold. Like the whole room had been dropped through the ice of a frozen river, and she had no time to take a breath. No time to inhale before the water closed over the top of her head, the top of the room, maybe the top of the house. There had been a late spring freeze, and the dam burst and the river had swept them all along. She had no arms, no legs, and her lungs would not work beneath the surface. She was drowning.

Then, because she wanted to breathe again, because she wanted to be warm again, Sheila nodded. "Yes," she said. And then she said it again, "Yes."

CHAPTER TWENTY-FOUR

IN THE THREE DAYS AFTER Beth's announcement, Sheila and Kenneth said little to one another. When they spoke, they talked of necessary things – the house, the business, groceries – and their very occasional small talk was confined to headlines in the paper. They nearly tiptoed when they walked.

Beth, too, travelled through the house in a soft and quiet manner, coming home after school each day. There were few phone calls, none of them from Colin.

Sheila went into the office every day, but kept her door closed. She was waiting, but for what, she couldn't even say. Robin cornered her the day after everything fell apart. One look at her face that morning was all it took to trigger his questions. "What's up, Sheila? What's wrong?"

She didn't even look at him, just kept her eyes on her desk. "Oh, nothing much. Ken and I have reached a whole new level of disgust in our relationship, and Beth's pregnant. And Sigmund Maier is gone. No forwarding address. But that's it. Nothing much."

Robin was silent for so long that she almost glanced up.

"Oh. Nothing much. My God, nothing much. Yeah." He stepped around her desk and placed a hand on her shoulder.

She touched his hand with her fingers. "I just need some time. Time to sort all this shit out."

"Look, Sheila, Beth's a smart kid."

"Yes, so brilliant that she neglected to protect herself."

"Now just shut up for a minute. I said she was a smart kid. The smartest kids still make mistakes. She – and you and Kenneth – will get beyond this and it will work out. It's tough right now, that's all, but life hands us shit. That's nothing new. As to you and Kenneth and your marriage, well, that too will work itself out."

She sighed. "Yeah. Not much longer before it works itself right out the door." She looked up at him. "Either him or me – out the door."

Robin frowned at her. "Did you ever stop to figure out why neither of you has taken that step? All these years, and still married?"

"Habit?"

He shook his head. "I guess that's what most people might think."

"You think something different, I suppose?"

He shrugged.

"C'mon Robin. Clearly you have something on your mind. What is it?"

"I guess I don't think it's habit, Sheila."

"Then what?"

He shrugged again.

She put her head into her hands. Beth, Ken, Sigmund Maier. Way too much to even think about. She was so tired.

After a moment, Robin spoke again. "Why don't you go away for a few days? Someplace quiet."

She shook her head. "We're a couple of weeks away from finalizing the deal – maybe even a couple of days. I can't be taking off with personal crap. Hardly a confidence-builder for the investors."

"You can find others. Screw the investors."

Sheila looked up into that familiar face and smiled. "Did you have one in mind?"

Robin smiled back. "Well, the young one at the Sherbrooke meeting had a real nice ass."

She laughed out loud. It felt good. "I think he was frightened of you."

"Did you? I just figured he was fighting the attraction." Robin sobered. "Why don't you just take off, you know? Even for a day or so. I can cover here – you know I can."

In the silence of him waiting for her answer, she could hear the sounds of full-throated commerce in the store. It was a busy day downstairs. "I know you can too, Robin. You are amazing. But I need to stay here, to keep working, and let all that stuff filter through while I figure out what I am going to do."

"Okay, Kiddo. You know where to find me."

And with that, he left her alone.

It wasn't until the second day that she truly thought about working. She powered up her computer and started out by checking her email. She didn't realize it was almost noon until her meeting reminder popped up – 1:00 with Ardith. Sheila sighed. She'd forgotten to delete those standing appointments off her calendar.

Just as she finished expunging the appointments, her phone rang. She didn't recognize the name on her display:

Hennessy Fillmor— There was not enough room for the whole thing to show. When Robin didn't pick it up on the second ring, she realized he was at lunch. Wondering if it was a new player in the Costair affair, she picked up the line.

"Ms. Martin? This is Sonya Elgin. I'm a paralegal with Hennessy, Fillmore, Kavenaugh – Peter Fitzsimmons is one of our associates and he would like to arrange an appointment with you to discuss an estate matter."

"He would? What estate?"

There was a long pause. "Well, it's complicated – a matter of mutual interest – and Mr. Fitzsimmons would prefer to—"

"What estate, Sonya? I'm not aware of any estate."

"It relates to a Sigmund Maier."

Sheila felt her throat constrict. "His estate? He's dead? Sigmund is dead?"

"Oh no. I don't know. I mean, I – I – look, Mr. Fitzsimmons just needs to speak with you. He'd like to see you in person if he could."

The barest thread of excitement moved in her chest. Mutual interest. He was in hiding but had not left her after all. This time, he'd made provisions, and this Fitzsimmons was being very, very careful. Sigmund had given him her phone number. "Of course. Of course I can come in – this afternoon, in fact."

"Well, Mr. Fitzsimmons is not available until 3:00—"

"That's fine. I'll wait." Sheila hung up without even saying goodbye. Or getting an address.

As it turned out, Hennessy, Fillmore and Kavenaugh had their offices in Ardith's building. They were several levels higher, and a good deal more expensively furnished – lots of textured wallpaper and rich, dark woods. Even the floors were finished hardwood. Sheila found it unsettling; a suite of offices without broadloom. And a central staircase between floors. Like somebody's house in an office building. She sat in the waiting area and watched legal types and their lackeys dash between the 15th and 16th floors, arms filled with papers, files. All looking sharp, busy. Professional. And she wondered why she was fixating on central staircases and office types. She gave her head a shake just as the pert young thing behind the desk called her name.

"Ms. Martin? Mr. Fitzsimmons will be out in a minute." All offered with a fresh young smile.

Peter Fitzsimmons was also young, but with that stodgy quality of a man without much imagination. The size and relatively spare qualities of his office confirmed his status in the firm. Nonetheless, he was impeccably turned out and not too hard on the eyes: dark hair, dark eyes and an acceptable handshake.

"Thank you so much for coming in, Ms. Martin."

"I'm not sure how I can help you."

"Well, Ms. Martin, I am an executor for an estate. And I am advised that you know Sigmund Maier. That you've met with him a few times recently."

She took a deep breath before answering, trying to catch his tone. "What is this about, Mr. Fitzsimmons?" She inhaled again and held herself very still.

"We were hoping you could help us contact Mr. Maier. Do you know how I can reach him?"

She let out all the breath she had been holding. He doesn't know either. She worked to get her breathing slowed down. "Have you, uh, tried his lawyer? Douglass?"

He glanced at the file on his desk; a hint of a frown passed over his face but was quickly gone. "I did. He was unable to help – other than to give me your number. He said that you were a close friend to Mr. Maier and may know where he is."

She nodded. "Sure, I bet he did." Right now, what she wanted more than anything was Mozart. Just about anything by Mozart always brought her focus. She smiled at the round-faced lawyer. "Sigmund Maier moved and left no forwarding address. His phone is disconnected. He hasn't called me since – I haven't spoken to him in a couple of days." She looked down at her hands. There was a burning in her throat and it was hard to swallow. "And somehow I doubt I'll be speaking to him again."

Fitzsimmons cleared his throat. "Ah then; that is unfortunate. We had noted and followed up on the article in the paper, but his lawyer Douglass was unable to assist us. When, uh, he said that you and Mr. Maier were close, well, I hoped perhaps you might know where to find him."

She shook her head. "I did. But no longer." She was certain this room was getting smaller. "You could have told me all this on the phone. What was the point in having me come in?"

He glanced down at his desk. "It is always my preference to speak directly with people. And frankly," he looked up at her, "I wasn't at all certain that your line was safe – that you would tell me anything over the phone."

After a moment she nodded.

"You know, it's astonishing, Ms. Martin. This firm has been searching for Sigmund Maier since the mid-seventies, and to think that he's been in Toronto all this time."

Sheila wondered how hard they had looked; Sigmund was probably listed in the current telephone book. She decided to err on the side of politeness. "May I ask why you've been searching for him?"

Fitzsimmons paused for a moment before answering. "Forgive me, but may I first ask about your interest in Sigmund Maier?"

She focused on the lawyer's pleasant young face. The man gave nothing away by his expression but she sensed he was a decent person. Not long enough in the profession, she supposed.

"He used to live in our basement apartment – when I was a child. He, uh, he was kind to me – took an interest, basically, and introduced me to music, the arts, and so on. He – he was required to appear at an immigration hearing and he asked for my help."

"I see."

She waited. When he offered nothing else, she pressed him. "And your firm's interest, Mr. Fitzsimmons? Why were you looking for him?"

"It was at the behest of his paternal aunt, Florence Morrison."

Sheila did not hide her shock. "His aunt? He has an Aunt Florence?"

He smiled and shook his head. "Had, Ms. Martin, had. She died nearly twenty-five years ago, but she stipulated through her will that a trust fund be set aside with the express purpose of locating her nephew, Sigmund Gunther Maier." He paused again, watching Sheila closely. "She left her entire estate to him. It is a sizeable estate."

"How did Mrs. Morrison know to look for him in Canada?" Sheila envisioned an old European apartment house, an elderly widow addressing letters abroad from a cosy room in the lower flat. Maybe even in England. Maybe she married one of the Allies after the war, and moved to England.

She watched as he frowned, rubbed his chin and then tilted his head. "Miss Morrison was in Canada, here, in Toronto. She was born and died here."

Sheila could not make sense of his words. "But then, she would be Canadian – how is Sigmund Maier her nephew? His parents were German. I know this. I have copies of his birth certificate, all his papers. He told me of his life in Germany, in Dresden."

Fitzsimmons sat back in his chair and folded his arms over his chest. "His mother was German but Mr. Maier's birth father was not the person named on his birth certificate. According to Miss Morrison, Sigmund Maier's father was actually Stanley Morrison, her brother."

"Are you serious? Sigmund's father was a Canadian?"

"It would seem so. He'd been a student of the Royal Mining Academy in Freiberg just prior to the First World War. He met

Sigmund's mother, Hilda Mann, on a trip into Dresden." He half-smiled and shrugged. "They fell in love and secretly married. He came home to Toronto to arrange to bring her here, but the war broke out. Sadly, he was killed overseas at Ypres in 1915." He coughed gently into his cupped hand. "I don't know who the person is who is named as Sigmund's father, but Miss Morrison was quite clear that Sigmund's father was her brother. Her research bears out her theory."

"My God." Sheila opened and closed her mouth several times. She probably looked like a fish. She felt like a fish. A great flapping scaly fish chewing on a massive and ugly hook.

He shuffled some of the papers on his desk, pulling out an old sepia-toned photograph. "This is his picture – Stanley Morrison in his uniform."

She took it from him. Pasted onto thick grey cardboard, the brown image did not mask the lightness of the man's eyes, the high forehead, the upright stance. There was a resemblance. She peered more closely. More than a resemblance.

"Ms. Martin?"

She continued to stare at the photograph. The eyes. The same eyes.

"Ms. Martin?"

"Oh, I'm sorry, Mr. Fitzsimmons. This is, ah, unexpected. I'm just a little surprised." She looked back at the picture. "This might have had some bearing on his immigration case, don't you think? I mean they wanted to deport him but if his father was Canadian—"

"As I said, I called Douglass immediately." He paused, casting his glance around while he thought for a moment. "He was not convinced we had the same person. He was, um, unhelpful."

Sheila met his gaze. "Yes. Douglass has interesting ideas about evidence and disclosure and such." She paused. "I plan to contact the Law Society about his approach to law. I am in the process of drafting a formal complaint. This is just one more example of his unhelpfulness."

Fitzsimmons nodded "I see. My specialty is estate law." He shrugged apologetically. "Despite perceptions, the practice of law can be somewhat subjective – for some even more so than for others."

She shifted suddenly in the chair. "Do you think that his father being Canadian could help him with the Immigration Department?"

He was pensive, then shook his head. "As I said, immigration law is not within my field of practice. I don't think we have anyone here who has done a lot of work in that area." He began to gather the papers. "But I assume Douglass is in possession of this information."

"Why? Sigmund doesn't know about this." He looked uncomfortable, so she filled him in. "Mr. Fitzsimmons, Mr. Maier believes his parents are Helmut and Hilda Maier. He has no idea that he is, uh, at all Canadian."

"I see." He avoided her eyes.

"What do you mean, 'I see'? Sigmund Maier has provided me with all of his background, his records. Don't you think if he knew this information, that he would tell me?"

He shrugged, a pained expression on his face.

"What? What is it?"

"I wouldn't normally tell you this, Ms. Martin. But if Mr. Maier contacts you, well, it may be helpful for you to know this. According to Miss Morrison's records, she met with him nearly thirty-three years ago and gave him these details." He flipped open the file, rifling through a number of handwritten papers until he stopped and ran a finger along a page. "Here. She went to see him at 63 Lilac Valley Crescent in July of 1968."

For a moment, Sheila had a vision of a blue flowered hat and a smiling, round face ... *Mr. Sigmound Mayer.* The air left her lungs. That was just before ...

"She told Mr. Maier about her brother and what she did to find his son – Sigmund Maier. She writes here that she is afraid that she has upset him. The subsequent notes confirm that he left his job and moved quite suddenly – out West, it seems, but there was no further information, no forwarding address. She paid his outstanding rent of four months, and kept the cancelled cheque. Three hundred and twenty dollars."

Well, isn't this nice ... her mother's voice from long ago was so clear to Sheila that she wondered if young Mr. Fitzsimmons might have heard it too.

He just looked up, smiling. "Florence Morrison was a remarkable woman, Ms. Martin. She was tenacious in uncovering Sigmund's path."

"Too bad she hadn't worked for you in tracking him down here." As the words came out, she nearly winced. It was definitely her out-loud voice.

He didn't seem to notice and just closed the file and stood up. "Yes, I suppose. So, if you speak with him, you'll let him know of our interest in him, Ms. Martin? Let him know to contact us? About his inheritance."

She shook his hand. Hers was soaked in sweat. "Of course. I'll give him your message."

Sheila turned away and placed her fingers on the doorknob, hesitating. "Mr. Fitzsimmons," she began, "did you say a balance of outstanding rent?"

He tilted his head slightly and nodded. "Three hundred and twenty dollars, I believe." Sifting back through his notes, he placed his index finger on a page. "Yes, three hundred and twenty dollars, right here."

Sheila nearly laughed out loud. Four months outstanding rent. Her mother must have noticed Florence Morrison's Cadillac when she came back looking for Sigmund.

She almost stopped the elevator at Ardith's floor. Almost pressed that button and stepped off. Instead, she made her way through the lobby and into the parking lot.

It was, after all, time to go home.

Beth was waiting for her when she came in. "Can we talk?"

Sheila followed her daughter into the great room beyond the kitchen. As she settled onto the sofa, she looked around at the familiar walls, the furniture. "I love this room."

Beth shrugged. "Well, I guess I know what you mean. I do a lot of thinking here."

Sheila nodded. "I'm going to try that more often myself."

"What?"

"Thinking." Sheila shifted so she was facing Beth on the couch. She watched her daughter's profile, watched her search for her words.

"Mom, about this baby thing and all. I've been thinking. I've decided to get an abortion."

Sheila just listened.

"I mean, I could have the baby, but just giving it up for adoption – how do I know that it will go to a good home, you know? That the mother will be a good one? ... It's not like an abortion is a bad thing." She looked at her mother and frowned. "Aren't you going to say anything?"

Sheila shrugged in response. "Is this you talking, or are you saying what you think your father and I want to hear?"

"No. I really thought about it. And I think Dad is right. I think this could get a lot more complicated, and I have no idea where I'm going and what I'm going to be doing. An abortion is the best way."

Sheila leaned forward and patted her daughter's knee. "Beth, I can't tell what to do on this thing. I'd like to – Lord knows I'd like to tell you what to do about everything. But I don't think that's my job here."

Beth moved herself away from her mother on the sofa. "Great. Just like I figured. What is the point of even trying to talk with you?"

"Look. You're going to have to trust me on this. There comes a time in everyone's life when they have to pull up the bootstraps and go forward. This, Beth, this is your time." She spread her hands out in front of her. It was, she recognized, a gesture of surrender and it felt pretty good. "I don't know how to advise you. I don't know because I don't really know what's important to you. I have no clue about your dreams, or if you even have any dreams. For me to offer guidance, well, that would be pretty much a shot or two in the dark."

To her credit, Beth stayed put. She seemed to be listening.

"So you'll have to figure out how much your father actually knows you, in order to weigh his advice. But mostly, you have to figure out what it is you want for yourself. Now, and in the future. I think you've always been pretty much together about what you want for yourself. That's a good thing, Beth. You've been working through what you need to do about this. And I think when you make your decision – I mean, when you finally decide once and for all – well, it will be a good decision, and probably the right one."

She looked hard into her daughter's eyes. She couldn't read what was going on inside but she knew Beth was listening. At least the part about her knowing nothing of her daughter's hopes and dreams – that much Sheila knew to be true. And really – who ever had the luxury of knowing their choices were right? Who could say taking the road less travelled or flipping a coin resulted in the best possible choice?

But that was okay, because just breathing in and out was a kind of choice. Just like the risk of putting one foot in front of the other and going forward. Sheila understood that she had spent most of her adult life choosing to take risks, but risks that were calculated and mapped out so carefully that she'd been certain they were the right ones. Now, in this wonderful great room of her beautiful home, sitting on the comfortable sofa next to her daughter, she was no longer sure they had been the right choices at all.

CODA

a capella

CHAPTER TWENTY-FIVE

THERE WAS RAIN SPLATTERED ON the bus windows and it streaked the lights of the villages and towns that they passed along the highway. Sigmund Maier sat close to the rear; it was late in the evening and the other passengers were mostly quiet. All he could smell was the garlic from the nervous little woman in the seat next to him, and the musty odour of damp that filled the rest of the bus. It reminded him that his joints hurt and his shoes felt too small. He did not try to adjust his position, and kept his motions small and quiet.

He coughed into his fist then turned to look out into the dark through the streaks. A bus is a good way to travel, he thought. People on a bus are anonymous, the seats narrow and high so that you cannot see forward or behind without standing. And if you are in the rear and one of the last ones to leave, most of the others have moved on as you step down. No eye contact with the driver. No glances over to your seatmate. It is a good way to travel.

It was, he remembered, a good way to travel through life. Paul Stenson told him the same thing many years earlier at the plant when he came in to resign.

* * *

"What the hell are you quitting for, Maier?"

Sigmund stood in Stenson's office and shrugged. What could he say to this man should anyone ask after him? The plant manager spoke again before he could say a word.

"You are the best man I've had here, Maier, and I'm not letting you go. Is it money? I'll give you a raise. Whatever they are offering you – I'll match it." Stenson pushed a finger against the bridge of his glasses, then brought his hand down and nearly slapped his paper-strewn desk. "No, I'll go better than that – 50 cents an hour more than their best offer."

Sigmund shook his head. "I am going to go west, Mr. Stenson. There is oil in Alberta. My skills could be of use there."

"You? Out west? We can barely get you to take your two weeks' vacation, and you are moving to Alberta?"

"Yes, I wish to see the west. Travel, you understand." What he wished was that he had never come in to tell this man. He should have just left the city. But he wanted to control what Stenson said after he left – it was foolish of him. He must be getting old – he had not thought this through, and the situation was now becoming complicated.

"You? With all those cowboys?" Stenson had an odd look on his face. He seemed to be weighing some question.

Sigmund smiled. "I need a change. You understand. I will send you my address for my final cheque."

The other man narrowed his eyes and leaned in across his desk. "Maier. You trying to run away – or what?"

The tight feeling in his gut got tighter. He had to think of something. Why did he believe he needed to come in and quit? Stenson had always been a good manager, a fair man. He surprised himself when he suddenly realized he had come in to resign to this person out of respect.

Stenson crossed his arms over his chest. "I think it's a woman."

Sigmund looked at Stenson and then at the door leading back to the plant floor. He felt a trace of sweat bead up on his upper lip.

Stenson nodded, satisfied. "It is. It's woman trouble and you need to get out of town." A half-smile moved up one side of his face. "She's after you, right? Is she in trouble? Is that it?"

Sigmund nodded, mute. Perhaps he could use Stenson's misinterpretation. He would let the man's imagination play out a bit.

"Look. Do you need to give her money, you know, to fix things with her? Get her to, er, take care of things, or something?"

"No, no. Nothing like that, you understand. No. It is a woman who thinks I am someone I am not. She is obsessed, following me. I cannot make her go away, so I must leave."

"Maier. You're not letting some woman chase you off."

"It is, ah, difficult Mr. Stenson. She will call here, looking for me." He glanced down at his hands, and then back up. "She may even send others to look for me. To call, asking for me. She is eccentric, yes? And with money, I think, yes. And I am not who she says I am but she will not listen."

Stenson was quiet and still.

Sigmund realized his manager did not believe what he had just been told. Sigmund also realized that Stenson was thinking about what he would do with the information.

After a moment, he took a deep breath and spoke. "Maier. I don't know what is up between you and this woman—"

Sigmund started to protest but Stenson cut him off.

"No, now let me finish. I don't know and I don't want to know. What I do know is that you have never missed a day of work. And you have never been late. And you know every gear, every switch, every oil line, every gauge, every press – every piece of equipment out there. My God, I think you are the plant. I couldn't replace you with ten men." He let go of a short blast of air between his teeth. "Look. I need you. You need to disappear. Fair enough. Let's try this out. You take off for four or five weeks. I'll call it a leave or something. I'll give you three weeks' pay, and you go for a couple of weeks without pay. I'll tell everyone that you've quit. Everyone except for Agnes in Payroll. Agnes and I go way back, and if I tell her something, she does it. She'll keep you on the books, but if anyone calls looking for you, they'll get Agnes confirming that you quit today. And as far as we know, you headed out west, no forwarding address."

Sigmund considered the man's offer. It was generous, more than he should expect. But it was a way out. Florence Morrison and her private detectives would try to trace him in Alberta. And he would not be there.

"One other thing, Maier. We bring you back on nights. You would work with a different group for a few months, and then

I switch you to days." He smiled. "Until then, you are anonymous. Sometimes it's good to be anonymous." His smile widened. "Yeah."

Nights. It had been a long time since he had to work nights. But it would help him avoid his old co-workers for a while, avoid their questions. By the time he came back on his regular shift, Florence Morrison and her private detectives would have given up. And he would have worked out how to handle the questions. And as for the night shift, perhaps he should remain there. Fewer people to ask questions, fewer people to see that he was back. If he was careful leaving in the morning, he could avoid all the others on the day shift by leaving through the fire exit next to the kitchen. Stenson would give him a key. Yes. This would be best, and Stenson would help him.

* * *

The strange woman next to him was nudging his arm. "Here," she said, holding out a package of wrapped lozenges.

He squinted in the faint light to see what she held and then shook his head. "No. No thank you."

"Here," she insisted. "That's a real bad cough you got there, Fella. This will help."

He took one to keep her quiet, being careful to avoid the woman's eyes, attempting a small smile to appear appreciative. He put the menthol tablet into his mouth and then immediately put his head back against the seat and closed his eyes. If he feigned sleep, she would leave him alone. After a few minutes, he shifted his head to face the window. Now he could open his eyes, watch the lights travel past. And not think about being on this bus, with the garlic woman and the ache that moved from his joints to his chest. He coughed again, the glass fogging and further blurring his view of the dark.

It was all so strange to him; for the first time in his life, Sigmund felt his age both in his body and in his mind. He knew he was too old to be travelling like this, but he had no choice. Douglass would have been furious when he received his note, but that man was a fool, so simple to control. Even so, it was now of no matter. He had given instructions to his new lawyer, and it would be fixed now. Sheila also, she will perhaps understand, and if not, no matter again. She was strong, yes, and had always been strong. He smiled thinking of how far she had travelled. She left behind that miserable family and became a person of importance. Someone with influence. Power. The power of knowledge always gave control.

He heard her voice over the phone. "Just tell me something … That all that you have told me was a lie. All of it." Cold, she had sounded so cold.

He pulled at his jacket, trying to raise the lapels. There was no heat on this bus; his feet were like ice and throbbing from being in shoes too small. Like that boy at the camps. His toes coming out of his shoes – what was left of them – he was pathetic. They were all pathetic. But the boy, in all that filth and stink, he reminded him of Grimmel, the gap in the front of his teeth. And of a small boy so long ago, receiving the insults, the verbal blows of the Old Man, again and again. Pigshit. His Grandfather Pigshit.

He helped that boy with teeth like Grimmel's. And he helped Sheila. But he should have written to her. She was so young, and young girls they become confused. She made her way well enough, but perhaps if he had written to her it might have gone easier at first. Yes. That was what he would do, he would write to her, explain that young girls have infatuations. She is confused. She must be a good girl, bide her time with her miserable family, finish school, and she will see. All things will be fine, if she keeps control. Keeps with her music. Her music. Her voice holds the music. Ah. Such a sweet treasure.

He felt the bus shudder and turn. Somewhere, far off, there were voices calling out inside the bus. Something for the driver to do. To stop. Stop. Stop, Driver, stop. Good. Yes. Stop so he could leave this bus. There was no air for him to breathe, but it was fine. He could breathe the skin of his lovely Sheila. Such soft, tender skin. He felt himself shift down, down and away from inside the bus, drift and slip through the glass of the window, floating outside to move toward the music of her voice.

* * *

Sheila's phone rang in the middle of the night. She opened her eyes, fastened them on the digital readout of the clock – 1:12 a.m. – and reached for the receiver.

"This is Soldiers' Memorial Hospital in Orillia. We are trying to locate the family of Sigmund Maier."

"What's wrong?" she whispered.

"Are you a relative?"

"No. I – I'm a friend. She added, "A close friend."

"Do you know where we can find a member of Mr. Maier's family?"

"He doesn't have anyone. What's wrong?"

"We're supposed to speak with a family member, Ma'am."

Sheila shook her head. Is this woman dense, or what? "Look, he has no family." She glanced over at Kenneth's back. He was still asleep. He'd moved back in from the guest room just two days earlier. Didn't say anything. Just started sleeping there again. She hadn't said anything, either.

She sat up and eased out of bed. "Hold on a minute." She walked with the phone into the dressing room. She closed the door and leaned against it. "Did he ask you to call me?"

There was a pause. "No."

Sheila bit her lower lip. The dressing room seemed to shrink, get darker. "Is he dead? Is Sigmund dead?"

"No – no, he's not. He's sick, though. He had your name and phone number in his wallet. He wouldn't give us any next of kin. So that's why we're calling you."

"I'm not his next of kin, but I – I am his friend."

"I don't know, Ms. Martin. He's not too coherent, and when he came in through Emerg—"

Sheila straightened. "Not coherent? How is he now?"

"He's comfortable. All things considered. But—" Sheila heard something behind the woman's voice.

"But what?"

"If you're a friend, you should probably come to see him soon."

Sheila swallowed. There was that faint ringing sound in her ears, in her head. She put a hand out and steadied herself. She spoke slowly into the phone, enunciating every word so that this woman would hear her. "Listen. Sigmund is my friend." She pressed her forehead against the door jamb. "A dear, dear friend. He doesn't have anyone else. Please. What is wrong with him?"

"I can say this much. He is a very sick man. Considering his age, it is remarkable that he is, well, he's in the latter stages of congestive heart failure, Ms. Martin. Do you understand?"

Sheila nodded, wordless.

"You need to come soon."

She concentrated on her driving for the ride up Highway 400. She had loaded jazz and New World music into the CD player, thinking the tempo switches would keep her sharp, awake; that the jazz would take the chill off the air. Just past the turnoff for King City, she had to pull over and change all the CDs; she chose Jann Arden for the lyrics, but put her back almost immediately. Lyrics would make her think. She needed something lively, so she chose the Mozart concertos. She was surprised when the opening notes of Tchaikovsky's Francesca Da Rimini filled the car. It was not like her to mix up the cases, but lately, mix-ups seemed to be the norm. She let it go.

It was not until she recognized the sound of the whirlwind that she remembered what he had told her about this one. Dante's two lovers, their souls forever caught in a storm, and she who answers Dante's questions about love, about that one moment when desire overcame sense, smothered logic.

Sheila reached for the controls and switched off the CD.

Because of the hour, few people were on the road with her. As she continued up the highway Sheila knew that, later, she probably wouldn't remember what she had passed or how long it had taken to reach the hospital. Still, at one point, she did think that if she missed her exit and went too far north she would remember seeing Webers food stand. Everybody knew Webers – the gateway to cottage country. Knew on sight the special overpass installed to keep people from crossing the four-lane highway. Imagine: wanting a hamburger bad enough to risk the front grill of a Mack truck. Some people would do anything if they wanted something badly enough.

She wondered if this was her Webers; was she driving more than a hundred kilometres in the middle of the night for the truth?

The hospital room reeked of urine, menthol and antiseptic. The walls were a ghastly shade of peach, and fluorescent lighting added a peculiar tone of blue-grey to everything. Sheila hated hospitals, and she hated this one worst of all.

The first bed was empty, its covers flat and perfect, the pillow a white sterile mound. He was in the other bed, the one closest to the window. Frail. Frail and small. Tubes snaked around his body, draining this, adding that. The low hiss of oxygen grew louder as she neared his bed. His eyes were closed. A green plastic mask covered his nose and mouth.

Sheila lifted a chair from the end of the other bed and placed it almost soundlessly next to him. She tucked her purse against a chair leg, draped her coat over the back, and sat down to watch him sleep.

Sometime later, his eyes opened. He blinked once, twice, and then moved his head in her direction. He squinted, tried to focus, raised a thin arm and touched her upper arm with the back of his hand.

"Whaaahh?"

She could barely hear him through the mask. "It's me. It's Sheila."

Fingers now grabbed at her jacket sleeve. "Uhnh." He licked his lips, and then gestured to the bedside table. She reached for the glass of water, lifted aside the edge of his oxygen mask and held the bent straw to his lips. It took a few seconds, but his mouth closed over the straw and he drank a bit.

She put the glass back on the table then leaned forward to adjust his oxygen mask. He waved her hand away and pulled the mask down around his neck. He ran his tongue over his lower lip and whispered, "*Danke.*"

"Do you want something?" She started to rise. "Should I call a nurse?"

"*Nein.*" He waved her back down. "Sit."

His voice had gained in strength, but his lips were a strange, dark colour and the rest of him was so pale. Age spots sat in stark relief against his sagging white skin.

"Would you like your glasses?" She opened the bedside drawer and found them.

He moved his head in something resembling a nod.

Sheila slipped the arms over his ears and adjusted the bridge to sit just above where the oxygen mask would go. She smiled and he lifted the corners of his mouth in return. She sat back in the chair and for a few moments, the only sound was the hiss of air.

He cleared his throat. "Sheila?"

She nodded.

"I have to – to tell you …"

"Sshhh. You should be resting."

"*Ja*, but I – I try to …" He wiped at his mouth.

"It's okay. Do you want a drink?"

"*Nein*." He waved a hand and started again. "Years ago, you understand. When you and I, we were – yes, when I, I touched you—"

his hands moving everywhere … his finger tracing a slow, tingling line …

"I did not mean, I should not have, I should not—"

"—not have left me. You shouldn't have. I looked for you. All the time." A hot coal fired up in her gut, and the words just tumbled from her mouth. "In stores, on the subway, the buses, on the streets. I even read the want ads, looking for where they were hiring tool and die makers, and then I'd go to those places – the ones I could get to by bus – and I'd go there, hang around, you know, and look for you there. The ones I couldn't get to, I'd phone and pretend to be your – your – wife, you know, looking for you." She took a deep breath. "If only I'd been smart enough, I would have gone where you used to work. You were still there, you were, you were still working there and I didn't know. I didn't—" She slapped her forehead. "Stupid me. Stupid Sheila. Stupid. Stupid. Stupid." Something was blurring her eyes. She was going to say more, she was going stand up, tell him he was a nasty son of a bitch, a baby-killer, a piece of shit who got her pregnant and then left and who was gonna rot in goddamned prison.

Instead, she lowered her head onto the side of his bed and wept. "Stupid, stupid, stupid." She repeated the words, punctuating each with a tight fist beating her thigh.

She felt his hand on the top of her head, patting, trying to stroke her hair. She raised her face from the mattress. He was turned toward her, his eyes bewildered and sad, his mouth moving. "I am – I am sorry, *Mäuschen*."

"Why did you leave? Why?"

"Many things, Sheila, many."

"Why didn't you take me? I would have gone with you."

"My fifty years and you – a young girl? *Nein*."

She shook her head. "You're wrong. We would have figured it out. We could have done it." She swallowed. "I loved you, Sigmund. Like I never loved anyone."

He took in a sharp breath, and then coughed, a wheezing exhalation. "You, you were so young, yes? Young girls, they—"

"Like I never loved anyone. No one since."

He shook his head slowly. He was breathing through his mouth.

"Sigmund. What if we had somehow worked it out, if you and I had run away together?"

He continued to shake his head.

"Imagine this. First, you move away – not too far, so we can still see each other."

His eyes widened.

"We wait until I'm sixteen. We go away, maybe to the west end of the city, maybe to another city."

He closed his eyes. "Foolish dreams."

She sat next to him, taking in the set of his mouth, his lips tight and turned down at the corners. The room was once more silent except for the oxygen hiss.

Then he moved his lips and whispered, "Montreal?"

"Yes. Montreal. You speak French, right?"

He nodded, his eyes still closed.

"Yes, Montreal then. We find a small apartment."

He raised an eyebrow. "In Montreal?"

"Yes."

Silence again for several seconds. And then, "A flat, yes? Over a shop in the Altstadt – the old city."

She smiled. "Yes. A flat."

He nodded again.

"Every day, you go to work and I study. I work on my high school French, I read books and practise my music. I take care of the apartment, and I have supper ready every night. We speak in French while we eat the main course, German while we eat dessert, and you correct my grammar, my pronunciation. Every evening, you listen to me play the clarinet, and you correct my fingering, my tone. You are impossible to please."

The trace of smile played on his mouth.

"We have terrible fights. I call you a stubborn old man and you call me a foolish little girl." She stood up, and lowered herself onto the edge of the bed. She took his right hand into hers and held it. "And every night, we make up. I try to ignore you, I am so angry, but you rub my shoulders, you kiss the back of my neck, you call me your *Mäuschen* and we make love for hours and hours. Every night."

His lips shifted into a lopsided grin. "Every night?"

"Yes. Every night."

He almost chuckled. "Just so. Every night. And on Sundays, we go to the concert halls, yes?"

"Yes, and drink tea at the cafés."

He lost the smile and opened his eyes, looking hard at her. "And when they think you are my, my daughter—"

"I kiss you full and hard on the mouth, a long deep kiss that shuts them right up." She raised his hand to her lips, and kissed each finger at the knuckle. Then she placed his palm above her left breast. "And every night, I go to sleep listening to the sound of your beating heart."

He swallowed. "Every night?"

"Every single night."

His eyes were fierce, the vagueness gone, and there was colour in his cheeks. He turned his palm from her breast and gripped her hand, and drawing it to his lips, he kissed her palm again and again. He stopped but did not release her.

She reached with her other hand and stroked his cheek.

He coughed, a thick phlegmy sound that she felt through the mattress beneath her. His eyes still fierce but now angry, he released her hand and pushed the other one away from his face. "Foolish. You speak like a child. Simple stories for simple minds." He turned away, wheezing and struggling to find the oxygen mask with one hand, the other swatting at her. Sheila avoided his hand and lifted the mask back into place, adjusting the elastic straps. She raised the head of his bed, and sat back in the chair.

He stared at her for a few moments, his distant eyes cool, appraising her face, her hair, her shoulders and back to her eyes. Then, he lowered his eyelids.

She remained there. Nurses came and went, checking this, adjusting that. Sigmund slept through it all, his breathing ragged, his chest struggling to rise and fall. Once, one of the nurses asked her if she wanted something, a cold drink perhaps. She nodded, grateful.

The woman whispered as she handed her a juice. "Are you his daughter?"

Sheila shook her head. "No." Then she added, "He's my lover."

The woman hardly missed a beat. "Oh. It's good that you can be here." She was almost out the door when she turned around and came back. "Does he, uh, have any family?"

Sheila realized this was asked for many reasons, not the least of which was concern about a jealous wife arriving. She glanced over at Sigmund, then back to the nurse and answered, "No. Just me."

The nurse nodded. "Well then, like I said, it's good that you're here."

Sheila turned to look back at Sigmund. "Yes. It is. Just so."

As the sun began to rise and the first thin lines of light came in through the spaces of the mini-blinds, he stopped breathing. There was no struggle. No gasps. Just a long, tired exhalation and his eyelids opened, the blue eyes now blind.

She did not cry or call out. She just waited for the nurse to start her morning rounds.

Later, when Sheila finally came out of the room, Kenneth was waiting in the hall. She just looked at him standing there, coat slung over one arm, the other arm behind him, between his back and the hospital wall. Completely out of context.

Her lips were dry. She could barely speak. "You? Why are you here?"

He shrugged then gestured with a head movement. "Maier."

"How did you know?"

"I heard you on the phone." He lifted his chin. His face was drawn, the lines pronounced in the dreadful hospital lights.

"I'm sorry."

"Me too."

Kenneth was here. She could not get her head around that fact. Maier had just died and Kenneth was here.

"Is he gone?"

She nodded.

"The nurses at the station said he was pretty close."

She nodded again.

He straightened and offered his arm. "Let's go, Sheila. I'll take you home."

Kenneth was taking her home. She took a step and then stopped. "Oh, my car is here. I'll have to follow you."

He shook his head. "Robin came up with me. He left with your car about an hour ago."

"He did?"

"Yes." Kenneth held out his arm again. "Let's go."

She walked a few steps beside him, and then slowed to turn back. "I don't know if I should go yet. I don't know if the arrangements—"

"They're taken care of. I asked the nurses. He'd arranged things a couple of days ago when they admitted him." He held his arm against the open elevator door. "Neat and tidy, I guess."

She stepped inside the elevator, nodding. "Yes. He was always a tidy man. Always."

They did not speak again until she was sliding into the passenger's seat. She looked up at him as he held open the door and waited for her to buckle in. "You are, Kenneth, a good person. I – just now … it has come to me just now …" She was so tired. Her train of thought drifted away, leaving almost no trail for her to follow.

She slept most of the way home.

CHAPTER TWENTY-SIX

THERE WAS NO FUNERAL, NO memorial service. He had told the nurses at the hospital that he wanted to be cremated. Sheila arranged to have his ashes sent back to Germany, to Dresden. Robin gave her the number for the same funeral home they'd used when Sheila's mother passed away, and it was taken care of.

Sheila figured she should be grieving, but instead, she felt this curious sensation of something like relief. It was probably something that Ardith could categorize for her, if she chose to go back. She didn't.

Kenneth moved once more into the guest bedroom two days after they came home from the hospital. He even looked sad when he told Sheila he would be looking for his own place. "I wanted to wait for Beth to finish her school year. Keep things normal if I can." He shook his head. "Normal. Whatever that is."

Beth had been to the clinic and was taking a couple of days before heading back to classes. Sheila knew it was all so much more than he had bargained for all those years ago – Beth's pregnancy was just the icing on his melting cake. Just as she knew her own attitude was part of the reason he'd looked outside their marriage, and that she was most of the reason he was moving out now. It wasn't his fault that she was never truly there.

She did regret that there was no heart-to-heart with her daughter when Beth came back from the clinic. But Sheila didn't really expect one – and it would get worse when Beth discovered Kenneth was leaving. The girl adored her dad, and in all likelihood would move with him.

One good thing over the days following Sigmund's death was that the deal with Costair was finalized and press releases went out about the Montreal and Quebec stores opening in September.

Robin even showed up in her office with a small bottle of champagne which he duly popped open to the music of *Les Misérables* as they shared a glass on the eve of the announcement.

"Well, Boss, I have to say it's been a roller coaster of a ride, but you managed to pull it off."

She raised her glass in his direction. "I'm pleased you're happy."

He cocked an eyebrow. "And you?"

Looking into her glass, she watched the bubbles break the surface. "Let's just say I'm relieved."

"Relieved? You've taken the first step to coast-to-coast coverage and you're 'relieved'?"

She put down her glass and shrugged. "Well, sure I'm relieved. After all, if the deal hadn't gone through, how could I rationalize your new position?" She grinned. "Mr. Regional Vice-President Responsible for the Eastern Division of MC Enterprises."

She wished she'd had a video camera. It was the first time she could recall him being speechless. He just shook his head.

"Oh, and did you realize that Montreal is merely an hour and a half or so from Ottawa? In case you had a reason to visit Ottawa, or something." Because he still looked so stunned, she continued. "Look, Robin. I don't want to give you up here, but let's face facts. You are brilliant. You are completely bilingual. And you are absolutely loyal. I can't think of a more capable person to have in that spot than you. In return, I've agreed to put up with a Costair appointment for Ontario." She wrinkled her nose. "And find a new assistant. As if anyone could ever—"

She didn't get to finish because at this point, Robin tossed his champagne glass over his shoulder and grabbed her into a bear hug. "I guess," she ventured, "this means you accept."

A few days later she received a call from Peter Fitzsimmons. "You and I need to meet, Ms. Martin. Can you come into the office?"

"What is this all about? I called your office and told your paralegal about Sigmund Maier's death. There's nothing left to discuss."

"Well, actually, there is. I'd rather explain it all to you in person. It's complicated. Can you come in later today?"

"The last time we did this, you thought my phone was tapped. Surely you don't—"

"Oh no. Nothing like that. But I may need your signature."

Once more, she sat in the man's too-small office. His desk was clear except for two file folders. One she recognized as the old folder full of Florence Morrison's papers. On top of it was a more slim and newer folder.

Fitzsimmons smiled. "Mr. Maier called me the day after you came to visit. I guess Douglass told him about my call after all. We chatted for some time. I explained to him about his inheritance, and he came in to meet with me. He was going away, so he came in that evening."

Sheila said nothing. She could have asked if he encouraged Sigmund to call her, or if he'd advised Sigmund to contact the authorities with the information about his Canadian father. But to what end? Who really needed to know anything about Sigmund Maier now? She realized Fitzsimmons was talking and she hadn't heard a thing. "I beg your pardon."

"I said he left his entire estate to you. There's over $875,000 in cash, GICs, and various investment plans. And there is the property – a cottage in Muskoka and a small apartment complex in Gravenhurst, plus several other holdings. It's all valued in excess of $7.5 million."

Sheila blinked. "He left this to me? How? When?"

"It was Florence Morrison. It was her estate, and she left it to him. He, in turn, wrote a will and named you as his sole beneficiary. Unless there are children or a widow somewhere, this all now belongs to you."

She shook her head. "I – I don't want his estate. I don't need it, and I don't want it."

Fitzsimmons opened the file folder. "That's what he said you would say."

"He did?"

"Yes. So he left this note for me to give to you, Ms. Martin."

She took the envelope from him. She recognized his handwriting on the front. *Sheila* was all that was written there. Surprisingly, her hand did not shake as she slipped the nail of one finger under the glued flap and ripped it open.

It is my hope that you understand.
You will perhaps not want this.
I leave you these things because I
could not know what to do with
them. You will, Fräulein.

S

Sheila refolded the letter and slipped it back into the envelope. She stared at it in her hands for a moment before looking up at Fitzsimmons. "Well," she said. And then because she could think of nothing more to say, she repeated, "Well."

He shrugged. "It is a lot to take in, Ms. Martin. You don't have to decide what to do with all this right now."

She shrugged right back. "You're right there, Mr. Fitzsimmons. It is a lot." She stood up. "I don't want his money. I don't want anything except to be able to travel back thirty years or so." She heard the irony in her voice. "But I guess, short of that, I better find some use for all this."

She sighed. "Before I leave, Mr. Fitzsimmons, I wonder if I could ask you to look into something for me."

"Yes, of course."

"I'll need to know how to go about setting up a foundation."

"A foundation?"

"Yes. I'm not yet clear on it all, but something to provide support to young people studying music. A grant or bursary or something."

"It sounds like a worthwhile endeavour."

"Yes. I hope so." She nodded as she stepped out of his office. "I surely hope so. I'll be in touch tomorrow."

Sheila did not go far into the hall before she turned around and re-entered Fitzsimmons' office. "Excuse me, but I have to ask one more thing."

"About the foundation?"

"No. About Sigmund Maier." She remained in the doorway, gathering her thoughts. "Do you ... do you think he was a Nazi? Would they have deported him after all?"

He sat back in his chair, his hand raised, palms out. "I've told you, Ms. Martin, my field is estate law."

"I know that, but I'm not asking your legal opinion here. I'm asking you as a person, as someone who met the man, spoke with him – you spoke at some length – I'm asking you person-to-person. Could he be that man?"

"You want a tidy answer, Ms. Martin." He was about to say something else, then stopped. "May I call you Sheila?"

"Yes, sure."

"Fine then, Sheila. And please call me Peter."

She nodded.

"Well, person-to-person, as you say. According to what is known, there are pictures, documents, and eyewitness testimony. Evidence that is impossible to ignore. Even testimony intended to support him seems to undermine any claim of innocence. But there's also evidence that he worked with the resistance – such as it was. Nonetheless, the law deals in proofs – facts – and the weight of those proofs is what tips the balance, so to speak. The Crown must bear the burden of proof, the obligation to prove its case. As a lawyer, I would say proof beyond reasonable doubt has probably not been achieved in this case."

She took a deep breath.

"But as a person, I would say he was sympathetic to the Third Reich."

She released the air from her lungs.

"But also as a person, I would say there is no simple answer, only conjecture. And I can suggest he probably never allowed himself to think about what he did. I think he saw it as something he had to do because of circumstances. I suspect even his work in the German resistance was because of circumstances. And I think perhaps ..." He looked away.

"Perhaps what?"

He shrugged and looked back at her. "Perhaps that what he tried to do for you, all those years ago, he was also trying to somehow reclaim something of himself." He narrowed his eyes. "You want a simple, straightforward answer, Sheila. But there isn't one."

In the parking lot, she sat in her car and just listened to the sound of her own breathing. There was no music; for once, she did not reach for a CD to adjust her mood. There was no music for this.

She did not go directly home. Instead she drove across town to Bathurst Street and headed north. With the sunroof open, the air that slipped inside was warm and fresh as she made her way past all the delis, medical offices, bagel shops, and apartment buildings that lined the street. She turned into the rear lot of the Bathurst Street Jewish Community Centre and parked her car.

She had come this far once before, when she was reading those library books. Even stepped inside the building. She couldn't really remember why she left back then without going all the way up to the museum. But nothing slowed her as she headed upstairs this time.

The Holocaust museum was open. A very few people were inside; in the dim light they were more like silhouettes. She hesitated for the barest of moments, and then stepped through the entry hall and into the main room. The hush was almost palpable and her feet were slow to respond as she passed the photographs and poster boards, the glass display cases of Zyklon B cylinders, the travel documents stamped with *JUDEN* and the Star of David, the concentration camp clothing, the tiny shoes without any laces. At the far side of the museum, light spilled out from an entrance to another room. She made her way back there and stood at the door, but did not go in. Unlike the dimness out in the museum this small room was brightly lit. Small light-coloured tiles lined the walls, some inscribed with names in English but most etched in Hebrew. She didn't understand the writing, but she understood the meaning. More names; family relationships probably, or maybe dates. She wished she could read them, understand the words. Before she turned around to leave, she had to resist reaching out and touching one to feel the cool ceramic, to trace the script.

She strode out of the museum and made her way outside. There was a bench next to a walkway, and she sat down and glanced around, waiting for her brain to kick in.

The buildings at the Centre were all modern in that concrete and pillar sort of way that she didn't care for, but the setting around them was really rather lovely. The buildings faced a busy street, but behind them a ravine with a rise of trees made a stunning vista. In this place, on this sunny afternoon, she would sit and think. And without any music other than the whistles and chirps of the birds in the trees behind her, and the whiz of traffic echoing up from the street beyond the buildings. She closed her eyes and thought.

Sometime later, someone sat at the other end of the bench and Sheila opened her eyes and glanced over. A dark-haired young woman smiled at her. "It's a gorgeous day."

Sheila nodded. She tried to smile back. "I – I think I need something."

The woman leaned forward, concerned. "You've been out here a long time. Are you waiting for someone?"

"No. I was inside before. In the museum."

"Of course. I see. You needed the sunshine."

Sheila nodded. "Yes." Then she shook her head. "No, that's not it." She took a moment to gather her thoughts. "Do you work here?" Before the woman could respond, she continued, "I need to arrange for a plaque in that room in the museum. The one with all the names." She looked down for a moment. "At least, I think they're names."

"For family?"

"No. Not at all. I'm not even Jewish."

The young woman nodded, encouraging.

Sheila shifted on the bench, turning more fully toward her companion before continuing. "It's for a little girl, a baby actually.

I don't know her name. I don't really know anything about her – she might even be a he and not a she at all. They dressed baby boys and girls alike back then, didn't they?" She blinked to clear the blur in her eyes. "I just know she was a lovely little baby, and she died a terrible death. Horrible. And I wanted to make a memorial to her. So she would be remembered. I thought, well, I thought it could be here." She swallowed. "Is that – is that okay for me to do? I mean, not being Jewish, not even knowing who she was, is that okay?"

The young woman leaned forward and placed her hand on Sheila's arm. "This baby. She was Jewish?"

Sheila nodded. "Absolutely."

"How did you see her?"

Sheila could not begin to imagine how someone so young could sound so grounded, so reassuring. At that age, she'd been a complete cynic. She took a deep breath. "She was killed, gassed, and I saw her pictures, first alive in her mother's arms, sucking her little fist – and I saw her after. Still in her bonnet, so beautiful. A perfect baby, lovely long lashes. Perfect. I didn't understand, really, I didn't take it all in and get it, you know, until recently. Somebody I know, somebody I loved, he did that. Killed that baby." She looked down at her hands. "I loved him. I still do, in a way." She looked back at the young woman. "Is that terrible? That must be terrible. And for me to tell you this, I must sound like a crazy person."

The woman sat very still and said nothing for a long moment. Then she shrugged. "Love makes all of us crazy." Now she looked down at her hands. "The man you loved, is he still alive?"

"No."

They sat in silence for a few moments. And then the girl continued. "Was he sorry?"

Somewhere overhead, the distant drone of a plane rose and then fell away. Sheila looked across the parking lot into the forest of light green leaves covering the ravine rising behind the building. "I'd like to think so. I would like to believe that I loved a man who had regrets." She turned back to the young woman and shook her head. "But I'll never know."

262 | RUTH E. WALKER

"Ah. That is harsh."

Sheila nodded.

They sat together for a minute longer, neither of them speaking. Then the young woman rose. "Well, I think you'd better come in and speak to somebody inside. Make the arrangements. I'll take you in, okay?"

Sheila stood. She nodded. "Yes," she said.

And as she followed the young woman back into the building, Sheila felt the strangest combination. Her chest was filled with a kind of lightness – giddy almost – and yet her blood throbbed heavily inside her hands and feet. Placing one scuffed shoe in front of the other, she knew each step was leaving a trail, and she imagined her shadows dancing on the walls of the building.

It had been such a long time that she had held herself steady, certain and deliberate. And she wasn't at all sure that she liked letting herself go like this. But she thought that it might still be a good thing. Yes. Good to feel something, to hear the sound of clarity in the timbre of her own voice.

"Yes," she said again. "Just so."

WITH MY THANKS

MY FRIENDS – OH, SO many – who kept the candles burning through the darkest of times. Especially: Linda Jones, my beloved friend for over four decades; Gwynn Scheltema, my dear Zimbabwean sister and Writescape partner; Ingrid Ruthig, crazy Aquarian and damn fine poet. My amazing and constant cheerleaders: Dorothea Helms, a.k.a. The Writing Fairy, and Sue Reynolds, and a chorus of encouragement that includes Carole Enahoro, Kathy Himbeault, Carin Makuz, and Theresa Dekker.

To the faculty at Trent University: opening my eyes and mind made all the difference – and in particular, Rachelle Lerner, my first mentor.

Special thanks to the home of my writer's heart, The Writers' Community of Durham Region, for their encouragement. Thanks to Durham Write On, my first writers' workshop. And my deepest gratitude to my tireless colleagues, past and present, at Critical Ms and in particular: Kimberly Gerson, Nora Landry, Gavy Mansfield, Heather O'Connor, Jason Pyper, Jocelyn Stone, Bill Swan, and Erin Thomas – you made me want to make it even better.

My gratitude to Rabindranath Maharaj for his generous encouragement in the early days, John Metcalf for restoring my faith in the manuscript, and Adrian Michael Kelly for nudging John in my direction. My thanks also to Shelley Macbeth of Blue Heron Books in Uxbridge who always believed this would happen and Roy C. Dicks for his expert help with opera details and translation. Thanks to Julie McNeill for a wonderful cover and gorgeous layout and design. Thank you George Down, my patient and perceptive editor, for keeping me steady and true, and thank you so much Maureen Whyte, my publisher, for loving my story enough to publish it.

Finally, and ever and always, my devoted family – my dearest Auntie June, my wonderfully enthusiastic children, their partners, and, most especially, my darling Cameron, who is the reason that any of it has meaning.

Ruth E. Walker's award-winning fiction and poetry have appeared in Canadian publications such as *Geist* and *Prairie Fire*, in the US in the *Utne Reader Online* and *Literary Mama*, and in the UK in *Chapman* and *Rain Dog*. She is a founding editor (1999-2007) for the Canadian journal *LICHEN Arts & Letters Preview*. *Living Underground* is her first novel.